SOHO TEEN

Dear Reader,

When Robin Epstein first told me that *HEAR* was inspired by actual ESP research conducted on undergraduates at her alma mater, I thought: *Nobody has written about this before? It's crazy. It's genius.* Robin is not only the trailblazer; she is unquestionably the right author for a YA novel based on real events. Because what I love about *HEAR* is the truth of it, not the reality. Its wild ride is tied to a fundamental and very human emotion, something universal. Revealing any more would spoil the plot, but Robin's ingenious fictional conceit, revealed over time, dazzled me as much as any of her clever twists.

Above all, I love how Robin's thriller is propelled by such a complex soul. Seventeen-year-old Kassandra Black is at turns confident, rebellious, fearful, skeptical, sharp (hilariously so), and bewildered. She believes that her future depends on making the best of a weird and increasingly dangerous situation. But she is also unique in the balancing act she imposes on herself: she fights to adapt, but never at the expense of either her doubts or her convictions. She fails as often as she succeeds and is stronger for it.

I hope you enjoy her wild ride as much as I did.

With gratitude,

Daniel Ehrenhaft
Editorial Director, Soho Teen

H.E.A.R.

ROBIN EPSTEIN

SOHO
TEEN

Published in the United States by Soho Teen
an imprint of
Soho Press, Inc.
853 Broadway
New York, NY 10003

Library of Congress Cataloging-in-Publication Data

TK
ISBN 978-1-61695-581-6
eISBN 978-1-61695-582-3

Interior design by Janine Agro, Soho Press, Inc.

Printed in the United States of America

10 9 8 7 6 5 4 3 2 1

dedi TK

"There is no logical way to the discovery of elemental laws.
There is only the way of intuition, which is helped by a feeling
for the order lying behind the appearance."

—ALBERT EINSTEIN

PROLOGUE

"You're cheating."

Pankaj laughs at me, flicking his hair away from his eyes. His hair is jet black, and his amber eyes broadcast the confidence of a criminal who believes himself bulletproof.

I look at the three others and wait for them to respond. Surely they know he stacked the deck; they must.

But Mara just sighs, pretty-girl-speak for "Enough, loser, you're boring me." Alex slowly turns away to face the sun, which is dropping out of view beyond Sinclair Lake. At least Dan gives what I think is a nod, but he won't meet my glance. His light blue eyes remain inexplicably focused on the building to our left, the Henley University boathouse.

"Come on, you didn't catch the way he manipulated the cards?" I ask them.

Alex stretches out on the dock, resting on his elbows. Maybe he does this on purpose to show off his biceps. Of course he does; seeing that doesn't take a mind reader. Guys like Alex know exactly how good-looking they are. He closes his eyes. "Sorry, Kass, I didn't see anything. My head's not really in the game."

"He's thinking about the action he's going to be getting at the party tonight. Aren't you, tiger?" Pankaj flings a card at Alex, making him smile.

"Should be fun," Alex says.

I shake my head. "Not if our one great hope here keeps playing this badly."

"Me?" Pankaj points to himself with one hand, sweeping his winnings out of the center of our circle with the other. "Correct me if I'm wrong, but didn't I just beat you? Why, yes, I did! In fact I *schooled* you. I think you're just jealous you're not as good as I am."

"Jealous?" I snort. But as much as I hate to admit it, I am impressed. I know how hard it is to pull off an artful sleight of hand, and to put one over on this group requires more than just skill: it takes *huevos*. Hardboiled *huevos*. "You're just lucky that no one here was paying attention. But if you start screwing with the deck tonight and someone catches you, the only action you'll see is an EMT giving you mouth to mouth."

Pankaj smirks. "For someone who thinks she knows it all, it's amazing you don't realize how dumb you sound, Kass."

I take a cue from Dan and turn away, toward the campus, toward the view of the towers and spires. Thanks to the university's prosperous alumni, Henley maintains the well-groomed look of country club awash in sunshine and green.

"Mara, back me up," I say in the silence. "You know as well as I do that those weren't the cards he was dealt."

She curls a lock of hair around her ear, thinking, and leans forward to examine Pankaj's hand. Then she takes the cards and lays them in front of her. After a moment, she replies, "These are the cards he was supposed to get."

This gets Alex's attention. "You're basing this on what?" he asks. "Regular playing cards or your special voodoo deck?"

"Tarot is not voodoo," Mara says, an edge in her voice. "And you can get a reading on someone with any deck of cards if you know how."

"Wait." Dan's eyes dart to Mara before quickly looking away again. "You just said those were the cards he was supposed to get? What does that mean?"

"Means I didn't cheat." Pankaj sounds as cocky as ever.

I shake my head. "That's not what she means."

"Kass is right," Mara concedes. "Regardless of how you got those cards, Pankaj, they suit you."

"I'm *suited* by three sevens and a pair of queens?"

Dan's eyebrows knit together. "Three is a prime number, and seven is a 'happy prime,' but when you combine them with the queens, it's forty-one. So what's the significance? What does that mean?"

"Let's just say the sevens and queens fit his path," Mara says.

For the first time all afternoon, Pankaj looks rattled. "Say what?"

"If your perception's so great, shouldn't you be able to see it?" I tease. When I give Pankaj a "gotcha" glance, there's a flash—clip in the reel of real life that shouldn't be there. Just like that, a murky vision there and gone. But something still blazes between us, and I know this means we both saw the image, that we both just shared the same disturbing glimpse of the near future.

What the hell? I ask silently.

I don't know, he answers. *But we don't tell anyone about this.*

No, we do not, I agree.

"What's going on?" Alex asks us.

"Nothing," we answer at the same time.

Mara, Alex, and Dan glance between Pankaj and me. And though they're all tuned in enough to sense we're lying, they're not on our frequency. So they don't yet know the hazy, partial vision we just shared: that three members of our group will form a powerful union, and one will die.

CHAPTER ONE

There's no announcement when we arrive. Everyone else just seems to know we've reached the final destination. I wait for a moment before I stand and watch those around me hoist their suitcases and backpacks. They all look calm and confident. Even the ones who are forced to turn around when they see the train conductor's "wrong way, asshole!" gesture. But I'm as nervous as I am excited, and I'm so excited I feel like I might throw up.

I still can't believe I'm here. I'm lucky, I know it. I always have been. Henley University's footprint is small, but its reach and reputation make it one of the most prestigious liberal arts colleges in the country, a staple on those US News and Blah-Blah-Blah lists. And though my father took advantage of the system to get me here, I'll do whatever I have to do to stay.

When I step off the train, the sticky-hot summer air assaults me. It's as if the atmosphere itself is testing me by turning up the heat.

"Kassandra?"

I turn to see a tall, elderly man striding in my direction. He's dapper in a crisp Oxford shirt rolled up to the elbows and green-and-white striped seersucker pants. Though I haven't seen him since I was little, I recognize Great-Uncle Brian right away because the family resemblance is striking; he's the much older image of my dad.

"Kassandra?"

"Kass," I say with a nod.

"Welcome to campus, Kass." He scans my face as if doing a computer analysis. "Well, you look nothing like your father."

"Thank you," I reply quickly, before realizing the potential offense. "I mean—"

But Brian laughs. "Come, let's go. I'm afraid we have quite the hike back to my office. They built the engineering quad on the other end of campus, presumably to prevent our majors from trying to escape."

Uncle Brian is the reason I'm here, and I need him to like me. He only let me into his summer workshop because my father begged him—and though Dad wouldn't tell me the specifics of how the deal was struck, he did let me know that the favor was costly. So if my great-uncle wants me to take that hike barefoot on glass, off go the shoes.

He threads his way through the people loitering on the train platform. As we trek across Henley's campus, I gawk at the buildings and their cool mash-up of designs. I didn't appreciate the architectural details when I was here as a kid, but there's a heavy dose of Gothic architecture interspersed with hypermodern stuff, which makes it all feel vaguely CGI. It's like it's a movie set version of a college, not the real thing.

"Not far now!" Brian says over his shoulder. I approach the curb where he's waiting for the light to change. "Once we get to Greaves Street, our quad is right there."

"And how much further is Greaves Street?" I ask.

"A mile or so."

"What?" I gasp.

"That's not so bad, is it?"

Maybe this *is* a test. "No, no, that's fine," I say as I try to rebalance the beast of a bag I'm carrying before it cuts off the circulation to my right arm.

Brian smiles. "Okay, green light. Let's roll."

TWENTY MINUTES LATER, MY arm feels as if it's about to fall off.

"We have arrived," Brian announces. "Welcome to our SEAS, the School of Engineering and Applied Sciences. We're big on the acronyms here at Henley."

I have no idea what Brian's specific area of study is. All I know is that he's the J. J. Dyckman Distinguished Professor of Applied Engineering. He opens the glass doors of the Merion Building, and we enter a two-story atrium. The space is open and bright: floor-to-ceiling glass partitions, white walls, oak doors.

There are a few indoor picnic tables, and he points to a fancy-looking hot-dog truck with a Henley blue and gold umbrella in the corner of the lobby. "If you're hungry, the Snack Wagon has all manner of sugary supplements as well as a large selection of healthy items. Too many healthy items if you ask me. But we're very fortunate here."

I nod, struggling to keep up.

"Most of the other buildings in the SEAS quad were designed in the nineteen seventies, by people I assume were blind," he continues dryly. "They were constructed almost entirely out of cinder blocks, giant fortresses of ugly. The Merion Building, however, was built by architects who knew something about aesthetics—it even features drywall." Brian raps on one of the walls with the knuckles of his right hand. He seems genuinely enthusiastic about the white drywall. Before I can wonder why, he adds, "You can tell how important a professor is by how much drywall he has in his office. Onwards."

His office is almost too predictable. There are papers and books piled everywhere; models of an anatomical cross section of the human head, the solar system, some sort of chemical structure. What's surprising is how sunny it is. Of course, this might have something to do with all the bright white drywall. There's a lot of it.

"Sit, sit, please!" He removes the stack of papers from the visitor's chair. Pile in hand, he walks behind his desk then promptly dumps it on the floor. "It's my own system of organization. I call it 'dis-organization.'"

I try to smile, try to feel at ease. Not so easy. Dad gave me the impression that Uncle Brian was, in essence, a brain with teeth. Someone so brilliant he couldn't relate to normal people. "Peculiar," "cold," "never been married"—those were the descriptors overheard at the family gatherings Brian didn't bother to attend. The party line is that for all his eminent genius he isn't "quite right in the head." On the other hand, by letting me come here, he's saving my ass, so I'm trying to give him the benefit of the doubt.

"Kass, close the door, will you?"

"Sure." I turn around in my chair and swing it shut. On the back of the door is a poster with four class photos attached. At the top someone has stenciled HEAR SUMMERS, and underneath each headshot, names are printed.

"What are HEAR Summers?"

"Ah yes," Brian says. "They're the Henley Engineering Anomalies Research team. Meet Mara, Alex, Dan, and Pankaj—pronounced like punkedge."

"Punk edge?"

"Run it together like one word," he corrects. "Punkedge.

They're the students you'll be spending your time with while you're here. Now look at me."

As I turn back from the door, his phone's flash snaps in my eyes.

"Not bad." He nods and hits a few buttons on the screen. The picture begins to materialize from his printer. "An action shot. Here." He hands me the printout along with a thumbtack. "Will you put that up there with the rest? I'll print another to use with your Henley ID."

I glance at the photo, and he's right; it's not terrible. My straight blond hair is frozen midswing, and my lips are slightly open, still stained with the strawberry lip gloss I dabbed on while I was on the train. But as I'm about to tack the photo to the poster, I look more closely at the pictures of the others. They are not an average group of teens. They're all gorgeous. Like, modeling agency attractive.

"Truly an extraordinary group of young people," Brian says.

"They certainly look extraordinary," I hear myself say as I attach my photo at the bottom of the bunch.

"Yes, they also happen to be good-looking; it's true. So you'll fit right in, Kass."

I turn and laugh. "Thanks, but I don't think—"

Brian holds up his hand in a "spare me" gesture. "As I was saying, your peers all have some marvelous qualities. Mara's an excellent artist. Alex speaks multiple languages. Dan is well known in the tech community for having created an alternative programming language. And Pankaj . . ." Brian pauses. "Well, he's what I'll call a character. He—"

There's a knock at the door.

"Professor Black," a voice says, "you home?"

"Yes, come in, come in."

I open the door, and one of the poster boys is in the hallway.

He's even hotter than his picture: chestnut hair, slate-grey eyes, and swimmer's shoulders.

"Hi." He extends his hand to me. "I'm Alex."

"Kass."

"Kass is our newest HEAR Summer," Brian says. "She just arrived this morning."

"Glad you made it." Alex touches my arm just below the shoulder.

"Thanks." I awkwardly lean against the wall. "I was just learning about your group . . . Are you the computer guy?"

Alex shakes his head. "No, that's Dan. My claim to fame is that I can speak a couple of languages."

"He's being modest," Brian interjects. "He speaks *five* languages. And not just your standard slacker Romance-language fare. In addition to Spanish, this young man is fluent in Arabic, Mandarin, Greek, and Hindi. He can communicate with at least one of every three people on the globe in their native tongue. He's bound for Harvard in the fall. The State Department nearly had me killed for taking him out of their intensive language program so he could join us here this summer instead."

I try not to stare at Alex, opting for his photo instead. "That's . . . amazing."

Now Alex leans against the wall, managing to appear much less awkward about it. "Languages are easy for me. So it isn't a big deal. And I'm sure people would kill for you too. I mean, just *look* at you."

I feel a bright, hot blush spreading across my cheeks. "Speaking five languages sounds like a good party trick at the very least," I say quickly.

He laughs. "Trust me, where I'm from in Texas, it's considered only slightly cooler than juggling fruit. So I'm curious, Kass: What's it like to have an uncle like Professor Black?"

I try to think of the most diplomatic way to explain it. I catch Brian's gaze but can't read his expression. "We haven't really spent much time together," I reply honestly. "I'm glad that's going to change this summer."

"We did spend *some* time together when you were a young child, right here on campus," Brian clarifies. "I have pictures somewhere around here . . ." He picks up one of the avalanche-worthy piles on his desk, looks underneath it, then shrugs, acknowledging the futility. "Well, I'll find the photos at some point. Your parents would bring you when they came back for reunions. And you were also here for one of the many summer enrichment programs my colleague Chris Figg and I used to run on campus."

Dad reminded me of that too. But I only have the vaguest memories of the camp and the ponytailed man who ran it. Mostly I remember that it wasn't very camp-like. Not much fun, no swimming or volleyball, but lots of puzzle matching memory game type stuff. What stands out most vividly, still, is one mean little boy stomping on a popsicle-stick house I'd built. My first reaction was to cry; then I punched him. I think I was "excused" from the rest of the day's activities. I don't recall going back to camp after that.

"My parents met as students at Henley," I tell Alex, mostly to fill the sudden silence. "At a Hounskull party. It's one of the Concord Clubs." I hear myself spouting the story of my parents' romance, and I feel slightly ill.

"You wouldn't think so by looking at me, but there are some very good genes in the Black family pool," Brian adds.

"Obviously." Alex smiles agreeably and gives me a wink. "So, Kass, are you staying in the dorms with the rest of us?"

I look at my uncle.

"She'll be residing with me," Brian explains. "My nephew, Kass's father, made that a condition of her stay here."

"Well that's too bad," Alex replies.

When our eyes meet, I wonder if he has a girlfriend. He must . . . though maybe they have a "what happens at Henley stays at Henley" policy?

Brian wags his finger at Alex. "We might have to watch out for this juggler." Before either of us can reply, he continues, "Kass, I know your dad hasn't told you much about what's expected of you this summer."

I nod, feeling Alex's eyes on me.

"As I mentioned, HEAR stands for Henley Engineering Anomalies Research," Brian explains. "It was established in the nineteen forties as an interdisciplinary department, comprised of engineers, physicists, neuroscientists, and psychologists." He pauses and I feel like he's waiting for me to ask a question.

"So . . . what do you study?"

For some reason, this makes Alex laugh. I can feel my face getting hot again.

"As the name suggests, we study anomalies," says my uncle, shooting a stern glance at Alex. "Phenomena that deviate from the common order."

"Let me translate," Alex says wryly. "He means they study random stuff that no one can seem to explain."

"You could do your research at my high school," I say, hoping to redeem myself.

Brian arches an eyebrow. "Really? What makes you say that?" He leans forward across his desk.

"I, um . . ." I summon my confidence. "A lot of kids pride themselves on being 'anomalies' . . . you know, bizarre and unknowable creatures. But most of them are just basic, trying to act cool. Then there are the kids who are far from normal but have no idea that's the case."

Alex laughs again. "That's every high school, isn't it?"

"Indeed." Brian nods. "And what we also find is that many young people who possess truly extraordinary minds try to hide their gifts. They're worried they'll be thought of as different, even freakish. But even average teenagers have fascinating brains from a neurological standpoint, far more interesting than the average adult brain."

I picture the lunch line in my high school cafeteria. I'm not sure I can agree with that statement. "What makes them—us—so interesting?"

"The adolescent brain is still growing and forging neural pathways, the roads on which thoughts travel. A teen brain also processes at lightning-quick speed. It tends to respond rapidly to chemical stimuli. That's part of the reason why teenagers frequently act on immediate desires and gut instincts. Previously I worked with research volunteers and our graduate-student population at Henley, but I've found them lacking. The group I've recruited here this summer is special in part because yours is the time in life when people's minds are most open and receptive to triggers. That's what I'm interested in exploring and tapping."

Tapping? I look at my uncle. "Can I ask—"

"How do I plan to do this?" He laughs. "You're picturing me sawing open the top of your skull and poking around in your brain?"

"Well I wasn't until just now," I mutter.

"She's funny, your niece," Alex says.

Again, I feel a flush. I keep my eyes focused on my great-uncle.

"I want to access your brain at the point thought processes form," Brian says, all business again, looking back and forth between Alex and me. "We'll be testing the chemical reactions that are involved in activating key neurons. We'll be trying to establish simultaneous reactions in all the group members. And we'll be running tests to see if we can establish neuronal net-working."

I have no idea what he's talking about.

"Does that make sense?" he asks.

I nod. At least I'm not lying out loud.

"Everyone in the group has already signed their releases."

Releases? To access our brains? I glance over to Alex.

"When I heard about the chance to work with Professor Black . . ." He shrugs as if he needn't bother completing the thought.

The skin between my eyes pulls together, a habit my mother tells me will lead to a set of wrinkles known as the "angry eleven."

Uncle Brian catches my reaction. "Kass, you're not having second thoughts, are you?"

"No," I lie again. But duh, yeah, of course I am. Neuronal networking? All I can picture is a mad scientist running jumper cables between jars full of brains—mine included. Still, I can't risk getting tossed out of here on day one. "No, no, of course I'm not having second thoughts. I'll sign whatever you want." I smile, trying to diffuse any tension. "So, have you guys already started this testing?"

"Individually, yes, among the other four these past two weeks. But I planned to wait for your arrival to begin the rest."

I shoot my uncle a *that's impossible* look.

It was only decided that I'd be coming here two days ago. That he "planned" for my arrival can't be right.

CHAPTER TWO

I confess I wasn't upset when I was escorted to the principal's office back in May and informed, "Because of your reckless and delinquent behavior, Kassandra, we are expelling you." Getting booted from high school during the last few weeks of senior year seemed more like a present than a punishment. Especially since I had justice on my side. I may have been breaking the law, but I was doing it for a righteous reason, and my principal knew it.

Then the news from Columbia University arrived.

The letter, henceforth known as TLTRML (The Letter That Ruined My Life), stated that my admission to the incoming freshman class had been revoked.

That was it. I couldn't petition or argue or plead. Since I'd applied and been accepted early decision, I hadn't bothered applying anywhere else. In short, I was now hugely screwed. Everything I'd worked for in high school was gone along with my prospect of an Ivy League diploma. My prospect of *any* diploma.

I didn't fall into a depression exactly. It was more of an extended panic attack. And it was in the throes of this "I have no future" meltdown that my father stepped in. After lecturing me about responsibility and the need to think about "the consequences of your actions," he promised he'd handle it. My father, a hedge-fund manager, is a guy who has a way with these things; if there's an angle to work, he finds the corner. The *Wall Street Journal* even printed a cartoon of him in a wizard's hat for his seemingly magical ability to make the stock market move in whatever direction he wanted.

So a few days later, when Dad told me he'd indeed found a solution, I naturally assumed I'd be in New York City come fall as planned.

I was wrong.

The rest of his words came out in a jumble. Apparently I was heading to his alma mater, Henley University. Dad explained that his Uncle Brian, a prize-winning professor at Henley, had a "gold card" there, which entitled him to one student admission—no questions asked—per year. If I was willing to participate in Uncle Brian's research this summer, his gold card would go to me. "I know you had your heart set on attending Columbia, but people kill to go to Henley; just remember that."

I started crying.

At least I think I did, because my normally unaffectionate father pulled me into a hug. He whispered on the top of my head, "Kassandra, everything will work out."

I started packing my bags for Henley. That was less than two days ago.

NOW, FORTY-SIX HOURS LATER, I am in my great-uncle's office, trying to figure out what the hell is going on. Alex has fallen silent. Brian has crossed his arms across his chest. I am tempted to bolt, future or no future. I find myself leaning toward my bag.

"Rest assured, your dad's on board with all of this," Brian

says. "A fair number of people object to my test subjects being minors. They find it controversial; they think I'm coercing subjects who don't have the discernment to say no."

I stiffen like an animal who knows she's trapped.

"You don't feel like I'm coercing you, do you, Kass?"

"No. I'll do whatever you need," I reply, steeling myself. I hear my dad's words: *People kill to go to Henley.* "Sounds like it's going to be a lot of fun."

"Wonderful," Brian replies. "And don't you worry; the electroshock treatment will only curl your hair temporarily."

"What?"

Alex nudges me. "I, uh, think your uncle's kidding, Kass."

Brian laughs. I start to laugh too, weakly—but then his lips press into a tight line.

"I've kept you here long enough. There are two more things I must mention in all seriousness. Texting is a distraction, and it muddles brain function."

I open my mouth to object.

"You may protest, but you know it's true," he continues. "That's why I ask that you limit the amount you text, doing it only when absolutely necessary."

Annoying. "Can I write letters?"

"I don't know," he says. "Can you?"

Really annoying. "*May* I write letters?"

"Yes," Brian answers. "To your friends. And this brings me to my second request. You'll see on the release that I ask my subjects to refrain from contacting or speaking to their parents for the first six weeks of our program."

"As if being here could get any better!" Alex exclaims.

"That won't be a problem for you, will it, Kass?"

It's less a question than a statement. Brian knows very well that my parents are leaving later today for a business trip to

China; it's why they couldn't drop me off themselves. He knows that they'll be hard to reach. Which makes me wonder again about what exactly had been "planned," and what my dad was willing to get "on board" with before leaving the country.

"Very good," Brian says, before I can respond. "Okay, so now that you've gotten the lay of the land here, let me take you home so you can drop your bag and relax. I think it's best to get a fresh jump on things tomorrow morning."

I turn to Alex. "It was really nice meeting you."

"You too," he says. "Hey, what about getting dinner with me later?"

My great-uncle is sitting less than five feet away, and I can feel him watching me. He already indicated that I should watch out for this boy; this seems like a test. So despite how much I'd like to accept, I know what I have to say. "Thanks, I would love to, but tonight I'm going to cook for my uncle to thank him for letting me come here—"

"Nonsense," Brian interrupts. "Yours is a very generous offer, Kass, but I insist you take Alex up on his invitation."

I turn to him. "You're sure you don't mind?"

He shakes his head, gathering up his belongings. "Go."

I try not to smile too widely at Alex. "Okay then."

"Great," Alex says, giving me another wink. "I'll meet you at Rosalie's on Shea Street at seven thirty."

CHAPTER THREE

Brian wants to give me a tour of the campus before he takes me home. I follow him, dutifully feigning interest by repeating, in question form, each fact he tosses out.

"Eighty-four miles of books in the Peabody Library?"

"And that's spine to spine, not cover to cover," Brian says. "The librarians will be quite pleased to tell you that our campus offers a higher number of books per student than at any other university library in the world. Over there is the art museum. Some very important collections. I'm sure you'll like it."

I'm more drawn to the students on the grass: sunbathing, reading, tossing Frisbees. I'd like to stop and rest, maybe even nap, but Brian continues to power walk across the green. I hustle to keep pace. The straps of my unwieldy suitcase have begun digging into my neck, and the bag drops as I try to swing it to my other arm.

At the sound of the thud, Brian turns around. "Forgive me! I completely forgot you're carrying all the necessities of your summer vacation. I'll bring the car around. Meet me at the front of Amory Gate. I'll pick you up."

And he's off.

A shame I don't know where the gate is. My uncle is already out of earshot. How does a man his age move so fast? I start twisting the signet ring on my right pinky, a nervous habit; I've worn it (and anxiously twisted it when needed) ever since my parents gave it to me for my thirteenth birthday. I find myself hurrying in my uncle's wake, past a building with two bronze lions perched at the sides of the stairs. From here I can see another green where a large, wrought-iron gate looms, topped by the blue-and-gold Henley shield. That has to be it.

I'm about to walk through the gate when I feel a firm shove to my right shoulder. It almost knocks me to the ground.

"What the hell?" I bark, spinning around.

"You're welcome," says a preppy-looking guy in a Henley T-shirt. "Students can't leave through gate's middle exit until they graduate. You can enter the university through the middle door, just can't leave through it. I saved your skin."

I stare at him openmouthed. Saved my skin from what, exactly? Some ridiculous campus superstition?

"Like I said, you're welcome." He stomps off, making a big point of using the exit at the far edge of the archway.

Before I can process any of this, I see my uncle's arm waving out of an old Volvo station wagon idling in front of a bus stop. Not wanting to risk another tackle, I take the side exit and dash across the street. After I throw my bag in the backseat, I open the front passenger door, and with a whoosh of air, papers cascade from the seat to the floor. I get in and slam the door shut behind me before anything can escape.

"And we're off!" Brian says. "Nothing fell out of the car, did it?" he asks after we're halfway down the block.

I look down at the massive pile at my feet, wondering if he'd really miss any of the loose pages. "I don't think so."

"Good, that's some sensitive stuff there."

I glance back at the papers, and what I see resembles the contents of a calculus book: lots of Greek letters and equations that will make me carsick if I try to focus on them. I turn to face the window and close my eyes instead.

THE FIRST THING I notice is how organized his house is.

"Nora comes through on Mondays and Fridays to clean up for me," he says, answering the question I didn't get the chance to ask. Then he adds, "I'd wind up barricading myself in here if she didn't keep the mess at bay."

I make my way over to the mantel in the living room and spot a photo I recognize among the framed pictures: my parents on their wedding day. There are several other photos, taken in an era before digital cameras. There's one of Brian with two male colleagues. They're standing in front of a wall engraved with some sort of large company seal. The man on Uncle Brian's left is skinny, wears blocky glasses, and appears mildly constipated. The man to his right stands proudly with his chest puffed out, a dark ponytail flopping over his right shoulder. The unfortunate hairstyle is "awesome" enough that I recognize it; I know I've seen this man before.

"Wait, is ponytail guy the one who ran the camp here?" I ask.

"Yes," Brian replies, "that's Chris Figg."

"Ah." I have nothing else to say about the man since I last saw him ages ago, but I think the ponytail speaks for itself.

The final photo shows Brian in a goofy Hawaiian shirt, sitting at an outdoor café in some tropical foreign locale. He looks to be in his thirties, and a woman, about the same age, sits next to him wearing a pretty peasant blouse. She has her hand on top of his, and looks as if she's holding his hand down for a reason. He's gazing at her with obvious affection, clearly enjoying the game. He looks truly happy, smitten. I'm immediately curious about the woman.

"These pictures are terrific," I remark. "I love that last one."

He waves me away from the photos. "It's . . . I was . . . That was a long, long time ago." He seems embarrassed. "Let me show you where you'll be staying. You'll be boarding in the observatory."

We head up a wide staircase.

"A bed and closet space are all I need," I tell him. Though it would be nice to have a television, wifi, air conditioning, and a minifridge.

"Then this should do the trick."

Brian opens the door. He wasn't kidding. The room actually looks like an observatory, the kind meant for astronomers. The deep blue walls are stenciled with constellations, and there's a refractor telescope perched on a tripod, its long, gleaming tube trained out the window.

"That's a pretty powerful gadget, that telescope. You can either get an excellent view of the moon or insight into our neighbors' sleeping habits. But I trust that you'll use it only for the purposes of good?"

I'm not sure what he means. Maybe this is another test. "Education only, I promise." I swing my bag off my shoulder and set it down on the enormous bed in the corner of the room. I nearly jump when the comforter rumbles and undulates. When I put my hand down on the mattress, waves ripple out.

"A water bed?" I exclaim, grinning. I've never actually seen one of these things before.

Brian nods. "They were all the rage once. I could never get used to the bobbing, though. You don't have issues with motion sickness, do you?"

I climb on board and lie down on my back. It feels like I'm

on a raft in a pool. "I think I'll be fine." I stare up at the ceiling. "Are those—"

"Afraid so." Brian flicks off the lights, and the star stickers on the ceiling glow in the dark. "I created this observatory around the same time several of my colleagues were conducting the first governmental experiments with LSD."

I struggle to sit up. "The government experimented with LSD? Why?"

He chuckles. "A lot of people asked exactly that question. Initially those in charge were convinced the drug would unlock the secrets of the universe."

"Which secrets?"

"Chaos theory for one."

We did a unit on chaos theory in physics. Feeling the need to impress the professor, I decide to show off. "Oh yeah, the uncertainty principle, right?"

"Correct." Brian seems pleased. He taps his index finger to his nose. "And if we pay attention to the uncertainty principle, what's the one thing we know we shouldn't rely on?"

I rack my brain for an answer . . . something . . . anything . . . Nothing comes.

He smiles. "Well, it's a bit of a trick question, because I was referring to those extended weather forecasts. We know weather is a complex system made up of the total behavior of all the molecules that comprise the earth's atmosphere. So if even one of those tiny particles starts dancing around in an unexpected way, it creates chaos. And chaos, as the name suggests, throws everything off, making your weatherman, Storm Fields, look as silly as his stage name sounds."

I laugh, and Uncle Brian's eyes twinkle. He clasps his hands behind his back. "The other key element of chaos theory, of course, is its paradox. *Despite* all its seeming randomness, no matter how complex a system may be, it still relies on an under-lying pattern. It still follows a certain order. And the trick—the trick!—is figuring out what that order could be."

I close my eyes for a moment, the mattress rocking gently beneath me. "So the government thought they could find the order by giving its scientists hallucinogenic drugs?"

He chuckles. "It was the early seventies. We've come a long way since then."

I open my eyes and struggle to get up from the water bed; I also struggle to imagine my great-uncle hanging out with people who took LSD. Both prove difficult.

Brian lends a hand and pulls me up. "That part just requires some practice," he says. "Now I'll leave you to do whatever it is young women need to do to get ready for the evening. My quarters are upstairs on the third floor, so while you're here, this will be your domain. I'll stay out of your area if you stay out of mine. Deal?"

"Deal," I echo, though now, of course, he's got me wondering what he's hiding above me.

"Good. One last thing: I tend to pace. It's a habit I formed when I was a young man, much like your ring twisting." He nods toward my hands; they instantly fall to my sides. "If the shuffling overhead gets too loud or wakes you up, just bang on the ceiling with a broom. I'll get the point."

I glance around for a broom. I don't see one. I force a smile. "I don't think you'll need to worry about that. I'm a champion sleeper. Fire alarms have blared, and I've slept through them."

"Well, that's very reassuring," he says dryly. "These will get you into the house." He hands me a key ring. It's anchored to two thin strips of metal. One looks like a flattened IKEA Allen wrench; the other tapers to a squiggly line with three rounded ridges on one end. If you didn't know better, you might think they were dental instruments. But since I do know better, I laugh out loud.

"I take it you know what they are?" Brian asks.

I nod. "They're redundancies."

"Clever girl. Though I prefer to think of attaching keys to a lock-picking set as an example of my wit."

"Or maybe it's an example of your craft?"

His eyes twinkle again. "Yours as well, perhaps? It seems like my nephew's been doing at least one thing right all these years. We did have our doubts."

Before I can ask what he means by that (or get a sense of how much he knows about my lock-picking past), Brian hurries out and closes the door behind him. An overwhelming—and rare—desire to speak to my parents wells up, driven entirely by the need to pump them for any and all information about this peculiar relative of ours. I look at the clock. It's not quite three o'clock. I might be able to catch them before they board their plane for China. But as I twist the ring on my pinkie, I think about Brian's request that we not communicate with our parents. My mind—that impulsive teenage mind, so ripe for research—drifts from them back to my own predicament.

What the hell *have* I gotten myself into?

CHAPTER FOUR

I get to Rosalie's early. I've been a meticulous planner my whole life. Some people might say this is to compensate for an impulsive streak that occasionally gets me in trouble. Those people might be on to something. But in practical terms it means I end up arriving early everywhere. Obsessive attention to detail requires knowing the lay of the land, so I build in the extra time to observe.

The restaurant is cute and has the three elements vital to a date spot: good atmosphere (brick walls, wooden tables scarred with graffiti), low lighting (to maintain a little mystery), and a wide selection of cheap entrées (self-explanatory.) The bar at the front is devoted to screens playing *SportsCenter* and to loud conversation.

"Kass?" says a voice behind me.

I turn around with a big smile. "Hey!"

Alex isn't alone. He's sandwiched between a guy and a girl. I briefly wonder if they just happened to come through the door at the same moment, but my smile wavers as I recognize them. I saw their pictures in Brian's office. They're two of the HEARs.

And, like Alex, they're both even better looking in person than they are in photos.

"Kass, this is Mara, and this is Dan," Alex says quickly.

Mara curls a lock of dark hair around her index finger and smiles at me with closed lips. There's something about the gesture, something about *her*, that tugs at some fuzzy memory. But there's no way I know her. I would remember someone that pretty.

Dan gives a nod without making eye contact. His bright blue eyes focus on a point somewhere on the floor. He's shorter than Alex, maybe five ten to Alex's six feet, but he's powerfully built. There's something contradictory about him; that muscular frame doesn't match the faraway gaze, the pale skin, the rumpled dark hair. He also seems to be milking the "I'm an enigma" vibe by avoiding my smile.

"Hi," I say. I don't want to be rude. On the other hand, I assumed this was a date, so I *kind of* want them to go away.

"When Alex told us you'd arrived, we couldn't let the day go by without meeting you," Mara explains. She gives me one of those brutally unsubtle once-overs, making me certain that she now knows everything about me, down to the size of my underwear.

She's a petite/small.

"You know," she adds, moving closer to me, "we hadn't heard you were coming before today. It's almost like you weren't supposed to be here. But if Professor Black selected you, I'm sure you're qualified. He wouldn't lower his standards to include his grandniece."

My eyes narrow. Is she trying to piss me off or get a rise out of me?

Before I can respond, Alex laughs and steps between us. "Of course he wouldn't." He gives me a wink.

"Well, let's sit. I am starving," Mara says. She pats her flat and tanned tummy, exposed by the tiny kid's T-shirt she wears. Though it's too small, the T suits her perfectly, and I notice it's printed with the words CAMP DODONA. Like the contours of her face, the words are also oddly familiar, floating at the edge of my mind. Why do I know that camp name, that logo? The *A* in Dodona is drawn to look like the Eye of Providence, the eyeball at the top of the pyramid on the dollar bill.

Alex looks over to me. *Sorry*, he mouths.

This makes me feel only somewhat better about the fact that Mara has just looped her arm in his.

"Have any of you guys eaten here before?" I ask, resigning myself to an evening of surprises that may be unpleasant.

"Yeah," Dan replies in a monotone. From what I can gather, he is determined not to look at me, or anyone else for that matter. "Four," he says to the hostess. He starts walking to an empty four-top before she's had a chance to pick up the menus.

"Just sit anywhere," the hostess mutters sarcastically. She follows Dan and puts the menus down with a roll of her eyes.

"So, what's good here?" I ask as we sit.

"I had the spaghetti with marinara sauce," Dan says, already staring at the menu. "I'm going to get it again."

"Spaghetti and red sauce? That's so boring!" Mara reaches for the breadbasket and grabs the best looking piece of focaccia. She doesn't eat the bread; she just starts shredding it as she peers at the menu. "I think we should order the melanzana to start and then split the pizza rustico."

"I'm getting the spaghetti and marinara sauce," Dan repeats.

I'm equally unmoved by Mara's suggestion, mostly because I'm starting to wish I was back on my water bed. "I don't want pizza either."

"Well, I'm always in the mood for pizza," Alex says.

"Great, then just you and I will share." Mara pats Alex's hand and looks back at me. "We must have been an old married couple in another lifetime. Alex and I have only been here for two weeks, but it feels like we've known each other forever."

A list of comebacks shuffles through my brain. But I decide to play nice. "So, there's one more HEAR, right?"

"Pankaj, pronounced punk-edge." Dan repeats Brian's pronunciation lesson.

"Right."

"It's an Indian name," says Alex, answering the question I wanted to ask. "It's from two Sanskrit words that mean 'mud born.'"

"Poor Pankaj," I mumble.

"Ah, but it signifies the lotus," he counters, "the flower that rises from the mud. So it suggests beauty in the face of adversity."

"He blew us off," Dan states, and for the first time, he fixes his blue eyes on me. His stare is intense. I blink. "Pankaj blew us off."

"He didn't blow us off; he had other plans," Mara corrects.

Dan shrugs and turns back to his menu. "We were all at the dorm. When she told him we were going to dinner, he said he was busy."

"He said he'd catch up with us later," Mara insists.

"Classic blow off," Dan replies in the same dull voice.

"So, Mara, what brings you here?" I ask. I'd like to understand the tension at the table as much as I'd like to reduce it. When she cocks an eyebrow at me, I clarify: "I mean, to work in my uncle's lab."

"Well, I'm going to be a freshman here in the fall, and the sooner I could get out of Oklahoma the better. But I've been coming to Henley forever. Sometimes I wonder if I was born in the lab."

"It would explain your good looks," Alex says. I can't tell if he's flirting or if this is part of the rapport they've already established. When she blows a kiss back at him, I have another disorienting flash of déjà vu. That T-shirt she's wearing . . .

Then it hits me. "Camp Dodona?" I point to Mara's chest. "Wasn't that the name of the summer program here?"

She focuses her attention back on me. "Yeah, I was a camper from age four to eight."

"I'd forgotten that's what it was called." I say the words out loud, though I wish I hadn't. The longer I stare back at her, the more I start to remember: we were in the same group, the one run by the ponytail guy. I don't remember much, but I am almost certain that I didn't like her then either. It's coming back now, faintly: she was a brat, one of those presumptuous little girls who needed everything to go her way, who believed the sun rose and set on her command.

"You weren't there, were you?" she suddenly demands.

I'm about to lie. The lie feels easier. But Alex was present when Brian mentioned it earlier, so I can't deny it. "Briefly," I say.

She doesn't press me any further. Maybe she knew I disliked her. Maybe she disliked me too.

It isn't until the food comes and Dan is tucking into his spaghetti that he finally starts speaking again. "Now that Kass is here I hope we start getting into the hard-core ESP experiments. All the ESP-lite crap that we've been doing for the past two weeks has been a total waste of time."

I laugh. So that's it: Dan just needed some food to regain his sense of humor. *Boys and their stomachs*, I think. It's sort of reassuring to know that even at a college like Henley, the male species is the same. "That's so funny," I tell him.

"What is?" He twirls the pasta between his fork and spoon. "What's funny?"

"ESP . . . That's what you said, right?"

"Yeah," Dan confirms. "ESP: Extrasensory Perception. Mind reading. Psychic capability. Telekinesis."

"No, no, no. I know what it means. But . . ." I look over to Alex for support.

He doesn't smile back. In fact, he looks surprised. "Kass, you know what HEAR stands for," he says.

"Sure, Henley Engineering Anomalies Research."

"Right . . ." He seems confused that *I'm* confused. "And you know what anomalies are, yeah?"

I'm guessing he's trying to draw the obvious answer out of me, so I repeat exactly what Uncle Brian said earlier. "Anomalies are phenomena that deviate from the expected order. And they do brain mapping, study the way neurons fire . . ." It takes me a beat to process the words that just came out of my mouth.

In life there are certain connections you don't make, certain things you just don't expect: Your first really bad haircut. Your best friend turning against you. Projectile vomit. Learning your uncle runs an ESP lab. It takes another second before I think, *No way.* I can see this for what it is—a practical joke. Seems a little mean that they'd prank me on my first day, but if this is an initiation, some smarty-pants version of a hazing ritual, I can handle it. "You're saying you're all here because, rather than going to some other type of nerd camp at a prestigious university, you decided to spend your summer testing out your 'ESP skills' in this lab?"

No one answers. I've got to give it to them: they're all playing their parts really well. Excellent poker faces, all of them.

"Okay, so I should assume normal people know about the Henley ESP lab too?"

More silence.

"Obviously I've asked the wrong group that question."

"Wow," says Mara.

"Come on, she didn't mean anything by that," Alex says, springing to my defense.

Mara opens her mouth, but our waitress approaches, and everyone instinctively quiets down.

"How is everything?" she asks with a sidelong glance at Dan. "Do you guys need anything else for now?"

Sometimes I have a little problem with self-censorship. Sometimes I'm a little impulsive. It's what got me kicked out of high school, what wrought TLTRML. You'd think these experiences would have taught me a lesson, convinced me to reform my ways. You'd be wrong. "One quick question for you," I say, smiling up at her.

"Sure."

"Did you know there's an ESP lab running on the Henley campus?"

The waitress glances from side to side as if she's searching for the reality show cameras. Her own smile falters. "Well, I'm going to be a junior there in the fall, and I've never heard that before, so . . ."

Alex clears his throat. "Can I ask, what's your major?"

"English." Now she's not only smiling; she's beaming.

"That's what I would have guessed. You don't look like a woman who has spent a lot of time in the bowels of the engineering department. Your skin has too much of a glow for that. Thanks."

"No problem." As the waitress moves away, there is a little extra wiggle in her walk.

I hold out my hand: evidence presented, case closed.

"She's an *English* major, Kass," Dan mutters. "So obviously you can't expect her to know *anything* useful." It's the most emotion I've heard in his voice yet.

"Also, it's not like Henley's the only university to have an ESP lab," Alex adds. "All the best research institutions in the world have them."

I purse my lips. That can't be right.

"Henley's was modeled on the one at Stanford, the SRI," Dan confirms with a nod. "It was established just after World War Two. There was one at Princeton too, which the dean of their school of engineering set up in the nineteen seventies. Duke, UVA, University of Edinburgh, University of Adelaide—they all have them."

I don't know what to say to this except: "Still not buying it."

"You've heard of that thing called Google, right?" Mara says, all snark. "It's all there. Check it."

You better believe I'm going to check it, chica.

"You don't need to," Dan says. "I can quote the website. The HEAR lab was established to, quote, 'pursue rigorous scientific study of the interaction of human consciousness with physical devices, systems, and processes common to contemporary engineering practice,' unquote."

"These labs were a big deal in the Cold War, too," Alex adds. "When the US government discovered the Soviets were spending a lot of money on 'psychotronic' research, they started investing heavily in it to keep up. It was like a psychic Space Race."

My eyes flash to Mara and Dan, then back to Alex. I'm baffled by these three, yes; but mostly I'm fed up. "ESP. Mind reading. Telepathy. I'm sorry, but this whole thing just seems like a joke to me." I almost feel like I should be looking around for the hidden cameras our waitress couldn't find. "So what's my favorite color?"

"Blue," Mara and Dan say together.

I point to my blue shirt. "Clever." I refuse to acknowledge that they also happen to be right.

"It's not about guessing favorite colors," Mara says. "That's stupid and reductionist. It's about having insight into things that occur at times and places that are otherwise inaccessible to you. It's about harnessing the power of the brain and nurturing the sixth sense."

At this point, I figure I have nothing to lose by playing along. "Uh-huh. And you all think you have brains that can be 'harnessed'?"

"Maybe a little demonstration will help?" Alex reaches across the table and takes my hand. His skin is soft, but his grip is tight.

"Excuse me?" I say. But I don't pull away.

"You'd be impressed if I could tell you what you're thinking right now, wouldn't you?"

"Uh, yeah," I say, feeling a prickle of heat run through me. "Go for it."

He stares at me, straight in the eyes, unblinking, as if he's trying to hypnotize me. "You're thinking," he says. "You're thinking . . ." He pauses. "You're thinking we're all freaking crazy."

I laugh, and so does he. Mara and Dan go back to their plates. But it still feels like the joke is on me; I don't know what to make of any of this. What I *do* know, however, is that if I want to fit in with this group—and my future does seem to depend on spending my summer with them—I'm going to have to make some sort of gesture or peace offering. But honestly, I'd also like to show the HEARs that I'm more than the loser niece of my great-uncle.

"So," I say, trying to sound casual, "what are you all up to after dinner?"

"Nothing," replies Dan.

"You have something in mind, Kass?" Alex asks.

I nod. "Anyone interested in going to Dunning Street with me?" To those in the know, "The Street" is the heart of campus social life; it's where all the Concord Clubs are located.

Translation: it's where all the cool kids hang out. In the forty-six hours between learning I'd be going to Henley and arriving on campus, I did my research. Like I said, detail oriented.

No one answers for a moment.

"You're just planning to walk around Dunning Street?" Mara asks.

I shake my head. "I was thinking we'd go to a party at the Hounskull Club."

"You can't just walk into a Concord Club," she scoffs. "A member has to invite you."

She's not wrong. Membership and its privileges are taken very seriously here. From what my parents told me, becoming a member of one of the clubs is pretty much a necessity. They're not just the places where you eat and party; they give you an identity for your college years and beyond. Each of the twelve clubs has its own unique personality, a brand. Century is for the blue-blooded elites, McManus is for student-government types, Parker is the land of athletes and stoners, and so on. Even all these years later, when Mom and Dad meet fellow alums, they'll ask, "Where did you take your meals?" It's the coded Henley way of asking what the person's all about and what he or she stands for.

"I can get us in," I say.

They nakedly scrutinize me.

Mara gives a half smile. "Well if Kass thinks she can get us into a party at one of the famous Henley Concord Clubs tonight, I'd be very happy watch her try."

"I don't have any other plans," says Dan. "I'm in."

"We should try to find Pankaj," Alex says with an eager smile. "He's not going to want to miss this."

I smile back at him, hoping I don't wind up looking like an idiot in front of the final HEAR. It's too late for a first impression as far as the rest of them go.

CHAPTER FIVE

The Hounskull Club—a white Tudor with dark wood accents—sits just off Dunning Street at the edge of campus. The block is packed with the college kids who've hung around for the summer, and they're carousing, laughing, and drinking beer out of their Henley Nalgenes.

When we left the restaurant, Dan said he had an idea where he might find Pankaj, and before any of us could stop him, he set off at a jog. "See you in front of Hounskull in ten," he called back to us.

Now it's just Mara, Alex, and me. Mara looks a little nervous, which suits me just fine. She opens her mouth as we approach, and I feel like she's about to chicken out, but before she can get a word out, we hear Dan's voice.

"Hey!" he calls to us from across the street. "Found him in the library."

He hurries toward us, accompanied by a boy with a leaner build. The boy's shoulders roll forward with the movement of his legs, but there's almost no up-and-down motion. His walk is a glide, leopard-like. He pushes his longish, floppy black hair back with his right hand; in his left he carries a giant paper cup from Small World Coffee.

"Coffee, Pankaj? You're drinking coffee at night?" Alex asks.

"A rocket needs fuel, my friend."

The response makes me snort, which attracts the rocket's attention.

"Hi," I say, mortified. "I'm Kass."

"Is it true you're Black's niece?" Pankaj asks.

I nod. "Great-niece."

"Well, that remains to be seen," he says with a wry smile.

"She seems pretty great to me," Alex says, then turns to me. "Okay, Kass, we're all in your hands now. So let's see if you can work some magic here."

There's a beefy-looking bouncer standing at the front door, holding a clipboard. He's in a bright white polo shirt and jeans. He's probably twenty or twenty-one: a wrestler, or he should be.

"Hi!" I say, trying to establish eye contact. I have as much luck with him as I've been having with Dan.

"Hi," he replies flatly, not looking up from his clipboard. "IDs?"

"You know what? We don't have them." I keep smiling and he finally lifts his head. I motion for the HEARs to enter.

"Stop," he says. "Unless you can get a member to vouch for you, I can't let your group in."

Playing my next card is a desperate move, but trying to get five people in limits my options. I have to do it: "My parents are Hounskull alums," I tell him.

The bouncer grins. "Ah," he replies. "So you're a legacy. And you expect because your folks give a lot of money to this institution that you should have special privileges?"

"No, that's not what I'm saying." It is exactly what I'm saying.

The guard moves his right arm across the doorjamb.

"Tell you what. I'll let *you* in, but not your friends." He's clearly enjoying his game. "That's the best I can do for you, sweetheart."

I turn, dignity drooping. "Come on, guys. Let's get out of here."

Alex claps me on the shoulder as we trudge away from the door. "If it's any consolation, it felt like you were close there at the beginning."

Pankaj laughs. "Close only counts in horseshoes and hand grenades."

For some reason, maybe it's because he's so smug, I want to impress this kid even more than the others. "Oh, it's not over," I mutter.

I direct them to the right, out of the bouncer's sight line, and scan the building's facade. I remember this place from when Mom and Dad brought me here as a kid. I also recall that in the back there's a wraparound porch on the second floor. I slid down one of its support beams when my parents were deep in conversation with some of their old friends. (Mom was pissed, but Dad looked impressed despite himself.) If I could get down the beam at age five, I'm sure I could scale it tonight if necessary. We'll call that plan B . . .

Fortunately, I spot a side door on the ground floor. Bingo, plan A. "And we're in," I say, pointing to the pin and tumbler lock.

Dan hurries to the door. He tries twisting the knob open but it won't budge. "Denied."

"Huh. You sure it won't open?" I can't help but smile as I fish my new keys out of my pocket. I *almost* feel guilty. Usually I don't have such cool tools at my disposal, but from a certain perspective (mine), it's criminal *not* to use a lock pick that was specifically given to me as my welcome-to-Henley gift.

I slide Uncle Brian's tension wrench into the bottom of the keyhole and apply slight pressure before inserting the curly pick—"the Bogota rake"—at the top. I keep twisting until I feel I've gotten all the lock's pins into their gates. Within seconds, I own it. I swing the door open in front of me then turn back around to the others.

"And we're in," I repeat, holding my hand out so that they can walk in ahead of me. Mara gives me a stunned look as she passes through the door.

"Sometimes doorknobs can be tricky," I say.

Dan's normally emotionless face registers something like appreciation. Or at least surprise. "That was really nice work, Kass. How'd you do it?"

"Let's just say I have a way with hardware," I reply with a smile.

He doesn't return it, but Alex does. Pankaj just rolls his eyes.

We've entered through the basement behind the club's tap-room. There's a set of stairs on the other side of the hall, and directly above us we can feel the vibrations of a thumping bass and pounding feet.

"Now that seems like a pretty useful skill," Alex says to me. "It's no juggling produce, but it is a decent party trick."

I shrug. "No big deal. I do that kind of stuff all the time."

"Really?" says Pankaj with a snicker. "You *really* pick locks all the time? Why do I doubt that?"

I frown at him. Clearly I haven't made the best first impression with this HEAR either. But whatever, it's *his* problem now. I got us in. "Um, because you know nothing about me?"

He doesn't answer.

It's dark and crowded on the dance floor. There's a staircase at the far end. I decide to ignore him and take charge, leading the group up two flights of stairs, to a room with a pool table and a big bay window at the back. To our luck and surprise, it's deserted.

"Let's play," Alex challenges Pankaj, who nods.

Mara, Dan, and I sit on the maroon leather window bench. Pankaj sets the balls on the table while Alex grabs two pool sticks from the wall rack. He hands one to Pankaj.

"You break," Pankaj says.

Alex chalks his stick, his eyes on me until he lines up with the cue ball. The break sends balls flying around the table.

"Okay, Kass," Pankaj says, scoping out his first shot. "So enlighten us. What's your deal? Why are you here?"

His accusatory tone once again puts me on the defensive. My instinct is to say little and reveal less. But if I'm going to make it through this summer program, if I am going to earn that gold card, I remind myself that I need to fit in. Or at least get along with these people. Getting them through that locked door was easy; talking about myself is much harder. I take a deep breath and make the decision to tell the truth.

"Right. So really, it all started a year ago. There was this girl in my class who was having a really rough time of it."

"Was her name Kass?" Pankaj asks dryly.

I scowl. "Do you want me to tell this story? Because I really don't have to."

His eyes remain on the pool table. He lines up for a shot and sinks a solid. "Sorry, sorry. Proceed."

"So the girl's home situation was a mess. And this clique of girls—one in particular—started making her life hell at school too. They tortured her, called her names, never let her eat in peace in the cafeteria, and followed her into the bathroom to taunt her. Typical bullying crap, and she couldn't defend herself. Once I noticed it, it started driving me crazy. So I decided to make it stop. I suggested to the clique's 'queen' that if she didn't knock it off there would be consequences."

Alex takes his shot, sinking the purple striped ball. "I'm guessing you didn't just sit this girl down and say that to her?"

I shake my head. "I gave her the message by removing her birth-control pills from her locker. And I left a note saying she was on notice. If she didn't stop screwing with other people, her life would become uncomfortable in the way she most feared. The bullying stopped that day."

"You broke into her locker," Mara says, with what might be a hint of admiration.

"Yeah, that wasn't tough. School lockers are a joke. But don't worry. I returned the pills. To her boyfriend's locker."

Pankaj keeps staring at me. "So that was it? That's all you did?"

I can't help but smile as I avert my eyes. "No."

Alex misses his shot. He shakes his head then leans against his stick. "So, what else did you do, you little scamp?"

"There was a guy at my school who put up this 'slut shaming' site. It was totally disgusting. A freshman girl tried to kill herself after her picture was posted." I find myself twisting my ring as I tell these strangers the story, wondering what they'll think. But this is who I am, and this is what I do, and if they don't like it, we don't have to be friends. "You'd think that a suicide attempt might be enough to trouble this douchebag's conscience. But he got off on it. He even wrote this pervy manifesto saying . . . Never mind, I won't waste my breath repeating his nonsense. Anyway, I decided to do something to teach him a lesson in humanity."

Alex and Pankaj straighten. I now have the entire group's attention.

"Once I figured out who the guy was, I snuck into his house and swapped out the hard drive from his laptop. I left him with virtually zero functionality or memory. My only regret is that I didn't hijack the laptop's camera to film his reaction, because I programmed a message to pop up about a minute after the computer booted."

"What'd it say?" This is from Dan. His eyes are glued to mine.

"That unless the site disappeared, the police would receive his drive, and he'd be arrested and charged with child pornography. I might have additionally suggested he research how such sex offenders are treated by other inmates in prison. The results are pretty chilling. The site went down that day."

"I would have taken the hard drive to the police anyway," Mara says. "Or at least mailed it anonymously to make him pay for his crimes."

I nodded. "I thought about that. But if the police had the pictures, they'd look at them first, and *then* they'd call the girls in with their parents. That would have added two extra layers of humiliation. It would have given that asshole a kind of victory."

Her eyes linger on mine for an instant. "That's really smart." She nods.

"So what'd you do with the drive?" Pankaj asks. "Do you still have it?"

I shake my head. "I smashed it to pieces. I can't tell you how satisfying it was to take a hammer to that thing."

Alex turns back to the game. "So you're a vigilante super-hero, huh?"

"To whom much is given, much is expected," Dan says, still staring at me.

"Otherwise known as bored rich girl syndrome," Pankaj grumbles under his breath, chalking his stick.

My head jerks in his direction. "Excuse me?"

"Oh, come on." Pankaj waits for Alex to finish, then leans over the table. "You're going to tell me your family's not wealthy?"

My stomach knots; this is *not* about my family's money. "I mean, yeah. But both my parents work." I say this as if it excuses our affluence. The truth is my dad runs a hedge fund, and my mom has a biotech start-up. The *realer* truth is that just before the US economy went down the toilet in 2008, my dad shorted the market. He bought and dumped stock, so when everyone else lost their shirts—not to mention in many cases their jobs and homes—he made close to a hundred million dollars.

"What does it matter if her family's rich?" Dan asks Pankaj.

"Because all this 'defending the powerless' bull is being done out of a sense of liberal guilt. Out of paternalism." He glances back at me. "Excuse me, *ma*ternalism. It's about her own stuff. That's always the way it is with people 'to whom much is given.' We all know the reason Kass is here. It's because of her family connections, not because she has a talent for breaking and entering. Or for anything else, I'm guessing. Strip away that privilege, and then let's see how things go for her. Let's see what happens when there are real consequences, real jeopardy. But there never will be. Right, Kass?"

Nobody utters a word. My jaw is clenched. I'm breathing heavily.

"Dude," Alex finally says. He's glaring at Pankaj. "Harsh."

"I got arrested by the police and expelled from high school when I was trying to help someone," I hiss at him. "My admission to Columbia got revoked. How's that for consequences? My whole future now rests in my uncle's hands."

Pankaj just sighs and smiles. "You still don't get it, do you? Of course your uncle is going to come through for you. He's going to give you, his favorite niece, that one infamous gold card. The card that was going to me—before you showed up."

My mouth falls open. "What?"

"You heard me," he says, his attention back on the pool table.

"I didn't know." Although, now it makes total sense why Pankaj seemed to hate me as soon as he learned I was Brian's niece.

"There's a lot you don't know," he replies.

Dan crosses his arms over his chest and looks like he's trying to work something out. "Well, why do you deserve the card, Pankaj? What entitles you to the golden ticket into Henley? After all, you're only here because Professor Black fished you out of jail."

In unison, all heads turn in Pankaj's direction.

Well played, Dan, I think.

But Pankaj isn't ruffled in the least, or at least he's very good at hiding it. He rests his stick against the side of the table. "For the record," he says, holding his hands in front of him, a gesture of surrender, "that is not exactly true. Though for the record, yes, I do have a criminal record. But only for another six months, at which point I turn eighteen, and all my youthful indiscretions will be wiped clean."

"And your permanent record can begin," I mutter.

"You sound like my sister." His face brightens for a brief moment. "Though it's not like Nisha can talk . . . Just like us, Nisha's had her fair share of trouble with the law." He turns back to Dan. "I'm curious, Dan," he says, "do you know about my sister too? I mean, it seems a fair question considering how much you know about me. And by the way, how *do* you know about me?"

Dan is unfazed by the sharpness of Pankaj's tone, or at least he appears to be. "I did my homework. On all of you. If there was a public record, I found it." He turns his blank stare to me. "I didn't turn anything up on you, though, Kass. Then again, I didn't look that hard because I assumed you were invited because you were Professor Black's niece."

How reassuring. "So what did you do to get yourself arrested?" I ask Pankaj.

"I was in the wrong place at the wrong time."

"Spill it," Mara demands, impatient. "Come on, Kass just gave her confession."

Mara seems much less annoying to me at this point than she did at the beginning of the evening. I'm starting to wonder if we might even become friends.

"Fine," Pankaj says, lining up his next shot. "I spent a week in a hotel in New York. Now the hotel *may* have been under the mistaken impression that I was the son of one of their guests, and that error may have allowed me to stay at no cost to myself . . ."

"Why would they think that?" I ask.

"Because I *may* have slipped into his room when he was out, called the front desk, and said I needed another room for my teenage son. Then I *may* have described what I looked like and said the boy would arrive shortly to pick up his key."

"That's, like, the perfect plan," Alex says.

"I know. I still can't believe I got caught. But the man had a suspicious wife back home, and when she saw the extra charge on the credit card, she assumed he was putting up a mistress. She called hotel security to 'have the home wrecker booted,' and they found me sleeping in the bed." Pankaj examines the remaining pool balls on the table and tries to find his next shot. "It was all sort of funny. A little less amusing when they carted me off to jail."

I shake my head, not sure what to make of his story. Is it even true?

"What, Legacy?" Pankaj asks.

"I'm just wondering how you got here."

"Before deciding how they were going to charge me, they did a psych work-up."

"Did they think you were criminally insane?" I ask.

His coppery eyes glitter at me in the soft lamplight. "They didn't tell me what they were trying to diagnose," he answers, which makes Alex laugh. "It was just two straight days of psychiatric evaluation. At the end they offered me a deal. Professor Black appeared with my court-appointed lawyer and said I could come here or take my chances in juvie."

"It makes sense," Dan says. "In all the decades that Professor Black's lab has been open, this is the first time he's handpicked his test subjects."

"How do you mean?" I say.

"Normally he uses Henley students, but he reached out to all of us, made the opportunity virtually impossible to turn down, didn't he?"

Before anyone can answer Dan, we hear voices and laughter in the hallway. A moment later three Henley students walk in; I'm guessing by their comfort level—and their surprise at seeing us—that they're Hounskull members. The first through the door is a pretty brunette with porcelain skin and drink-flushed cheeks. Two large guys trail her, one with his baseball cap facing forward, the other with his turned back.

"Oh!" the girl exclaims.

Alex nearly drops his pool stick. "Um . . . hi," he stammers.

My eyes flash between him and the girl. For a second, I wonder if they know each other, but her glance skims past Alex without any sign of recognition. As he continues to stare at her with unguarded, almost childlike fascination, his veneer of confidence fades. The reaction has the bizarre double effect of endearing him to me *and* making me grateful our dinner wasn't a date after all. Had he become so blatantly infatuated with another girl while we were alone, I would have been *pissed.* And with everything else that's going on, the last thing I need is to start spinning in an angry jealousy spiral.

"Sorry!" the girl says, her British accent turning the word singsong. "Didn't think anyone was up here." The boys at her side move through the space to grab pool sticks from the wall mount, not seeming to register we're here at all. One of the guys starts pulling the billiard balls from the table's pockets and rolls them to the other, who racks them.

"Were you playing?" she asks with an apologetic smile.

As Alex continues to gape at her, his struck-dumb-by-Cupid's-arrow thing starts to become less than adorable. Mara gets up and starts moving toward the stairwell.

Dan points to the wall clock. "We have to go anyway."

Pankaj rolls his eyes. "You're really worried about violating curfew?" he says quietly.

"Yeah, I'm worried," Dan replies.

Pankaj shakes his head dismissively. "It's not like we have room check or like anyone's watching us."

"Someone's always watching," Alex says. A smile plays on his lips. "The question is if that someone is looking for anything in particular."

Before I can ask him what he means, Mara is already halfway out the door. Dan is right on her heels. Pankaj reluctantly follows, as do I, and Alex brings up the rear. But midway down the staircase, Alex hesitates.

"You know what? I'm not even a little tired," he says. "I'm going to stay and hang out here for a while."

"Don't stay too late," Dan warns.

"Thanks, Mom." Alex and Pankaj exchange a glance, as if sharing an inside joke.

Mara is also staring at Alex, and I can see she's wondering if she should offer to stay out with him. But as she's weighing her options, Alex turns and walks back up the stairs.

"Have fun," she yells after him, not sounding like she means it.

"HOW WAS YOUR EVENING?" Brian calls out as I unlock the front door. "I'm in the kitchen. Come have some ice cream."

I close the door behind me, loudly. I march in to find my great-uncle reaching into his freezer.

"You run an ESP lab?" I demand.

"Here, I got your favorite," he replies cheerily, ignoring my brusque tone. He pulls out a carton and peels the top off the bucket of Edy's Slow Churned and then tips the green mint chocolate chip in my direction. I have to hand it to him: if he's trying to distract me, it's working. Green mint chocolate chip ice cream is what heaven tastes like.

"My dad told you my favorite flavor of ice cream?"

"No," he says.

As I take the frozen tub from my uncle's hand, a chill runs through me. "Then how did you—"

"Just a guess," he interrupts. He motions to the table. "Have a seat. It's my favorite too. And to answer your question, yes, I do run an ESP lab. You know, Kass, those with closed minds are always suspicious of those at the forefront of science."

I remain standing. "I wouldn't say that I have a closed mind. I would just say a lot of the people who claim to have psychic abilities are big phonies."

"And by extension ESP can't be real because we don't have proof; is that your thought?" He takes two bowls down from the cabinet above the table and then reaches into a drawer for spoons. "But before people learned that the earth was round, what did they think? Automobiles, airplanes, the Internet— none of these things were even conceivable until one day, 'suddenly,' they were. So to think that we already know every-thing that we're going to know about how *this* works"—he sets the spoons down and taps his head—"is, if I may say, pure folly. And my job as a scientist is to explore and explain that which is not understood."

I'm worried I'll fall into a trap if I try to argue. Instead, I offer cautiously, "Do you hate it that people must think you're crazy?"

"Kassandra, I couldn't care less about that. The doubters are the ones who need to worry. I feel sorry that they are so lacking in imagination, but I have bigger concerns."

"Like what?"

He sits and scoops some ice cream into his bowl. "I believe that I'm on the cusp of a truly important discovery, an innovation that could allow anyone to access these abilities. But there are still some critical steps we need to get through. One of those is making sure my test group here can perform reliably. For that to happen, you all must first be released from the bonds of conventional thought." He looks up expectantly, waiting for me to join him at the table.

I feel the confusion settle on my face, screwing up my features, and I sit. "The bonds of conventional thought?"

He nods. "Here's an example. Picture a month on a wall calendar. Now, what comes after any given Monday?"

"Tuesday."

"And after Tuesday?"

"Wednesday."

"Yes, of course. On a calendar it's very clear that each day follows the next in a straight line going from left to right, correct? That's the 'conventional' way of thinking about time, like an arrow hurtling across a flat plane." Brian sets down his spoon and sticks his finger in the air and then makes a fist. "But what if you think of time as a sphere? So even on Monday"—he points to the back of his hand—"Wednesday already exists over here." He points to the front. "Now imagine that the sphere is transparent. If Wednesday already exists, if it's already present at the beginning of our week, we should be able to access it Monday morning. We *should* be able to see into our 'future.'"

"That's . . . Whoa."

"Damn straight," Brian says with a laugh, picking up this spoon again.

As I pick up my own spoon, I have a moment of insight, or maybe I should call it foresight. My uncle has gathered his group here this summer to send us hurtling through his spherical notions of space and time. We are his crash-test dummies. He's going to probe our heads in an attempt make these mental connections and leaps. The HEARs are his latest, greatest hope.

For him, "teenager" is just another word for "guinea pig."

CHAPTER SIX

"Eight fifty-eight A.M.," Dan says, spinning on his stool in the lab when Uncle Brian and I arrive the following morning.

The lab is spacious, even more impressive than I what I imagined, knowing what I do about Henley. Several workstations, topped with thick black slate, are scattered throughout. Along the back wall hangs a twelve-foot whiteboard scribbled with intimidating formulas and a doodle of a bulldog barking, *Let Me Atom!* The other walls are lined with built-in glass-and-wood cabinets. Their shelves are neatly arrayed with books and scientific equipment: microscopes, scales, beakers. In one corner, a mid-century modern lounge chair sits next to a stereo system. I wonder if the people who designed this place were Swedish. It sort of has the feel of an IKEA catalog come to life.

Dan is wearing exactly what he wore to dinner last night. From the redness of his eyes and the patchy stubble around his face, it looks like he pulled an all-nighter.

"Dan," Brian asks him point-blank, "were you up the whole evening?"

"Yeah."

"Unacceptable."

"But I was back in time for curfew," Dan protests.

Brian sighs. "Curfew is not my attempt to prevent you from doing things, or to keep you safe from the creatures of the night. I've established a curfew to get you to bed sooner because you need to get at least eight hours of sleep."

"Eight hours?" Dan snickers. "I haven't slept that much since I was a baby."

"Then that changes now," Brian states firmly, setting his briefcase down at his desk. "Brain function is dependent on the quantity and quality of rest you get. The brain simply doesn't work as effectively if it's tired."

Dan shakes his head. "I've done the research too, Professor. Believe me, I only need four hours of sleep."

"That's just not true. You may be functional at four hours and still sharper than your peers, but sleep makes us all more mentally agile." He flips open his briefcase, and he glances up, his face softening. "It boggles my mind that high schools start so early in the morning, forcing you out of the REM sleep you all so desperately need. It's as if those running the show are trying to keep you stupid."

Keep us stupid? Was Uncle Brian trying to be offensive, or did he just get lucky? I try to catch Dan's eyes, but he's gone back to spinning.

There's laughter in the hallway, and a moment later Alex and Mara walk in together. Mara playfully hits Alex on the arm.

"You are so bad," she says, taking a seat on one of the stools and flirtatiously crossing her legs. In that instant, last night's fleeting thoughts of possibly befriending her melt away. I can't get a read on this girl. Then again, I can't get a read on anyone here. Dan seems like he might have Asperger's syndrome; Alex is a smooth talker; Pankaj is a juvenile delinquent at best and a budding criminal at worst. That's as close as I've come to forming any insight on the HEARs, my fellow guinea pigs.

Alex offers Brian and me a smile. "Morning, everyone."

"How are you today?" Brian asks.

"Great," Mara replies.

"Me too," Alex adds. I can't help but wonder what I missed when I went back to Uncle Brian's last night. Did Alex not stay at Hounskull? Did he and Mara meet up?

Dan looks at his watch. "It's 9:01. Where's Pankaj?"

As Brian eyes a clock on the wall, Pankaj sweeps into the room.

"Speak of the devil," Brian murmurs.

"I can't tell you how many times I've heard that line as I walk through a door," he replies, raising his giant coffee cup in greeting.

"Nice one," Alex laughs.

"Pankaj Desai," Brian says, "this is Kassandra Black, my niece."

"Yes, the niece. We met last night." *The niece*, he says, as if I'm not sitting ten feet away from him. He takes a sip of his coffee, shifting his eyes to me.

"Good morning," I say, but he doesn't respond. "Looks like 'the rocket' could use some stronger fuel this morning," I hear myself add, maybe because I'm imagining myself walking over and dumping the drink over his head.

To my surprise, he lowers his cup and smiles.

In that split second, I'm jolted by a disorienting sense of familiarity. It's like that feeling of bumping into an old friend in an unexpected place, or seeing someone you know on the news. You do a double take, thinking it's not possible yet sure you saw something recognizable. But I shake it off. I must be imagining the sensation with Pankaj, caught off guard by how suddenly friendly he appears.

I turn away, toward Mara. She's taken a deck of cards out of her bag, for reasons I can only guess at, but no one else seems particularly surprised. She shuffles, pulls out six cards at random, and sets them down in a cross pattern in front of her. Then she pulls out four more cards and places them to the right of the cross in a vertical line. It seems like an odd choice to start playing some version of solitaire right now. She bends over the spread. Her lips twist in a frown.

"Whatcha got there, sister Mara?" Alex asks.

"Hmm?" She sounds like she's just been roused from sleep. "Just wanted to see something."

Alex catches me looking and cocks his thumb in Mara's direction. "Our girl here is deep into tarot cards. Does readings every day."

I have no idea what the correct response is. I glance at Uncle Brian for a cue, but he's perusing something in a folder, his face hidden.

"Oh, cool," I say, though I'm thinking something far less generous.

"Or spooky, depending on your outlook," Alex says with a chuckle.

"So, Mara, what's the outlook for today?" I ask, playing along. At least it's better than silence. "Do you see rain this afternoon?"

"Hilarious," Mara replies, unamused. In one fluid movement, she scoops up the cards on the table and pushes them deep into the deck.

Brian snaps his folder shut and clears his throat.

"Good. Now that the introductions have been made, let's get down to business, shall we? I need you to clear your minds of any distracting thoughts."

"What if there's nothing else left, Professor?" Alex jokes.

"I'm hoping for nothing left," my great-uncle answers

seriously. "I'm going to lead you through a guided meditation before we begin the experiment. So I want you to relax and turn inward. Feel free to stay in your chairs or take a seat on the ground and make yourself comfortable. Just be sure to keep your head and spine upright."

"Eyes open or closed?" Dan asks.

"Half open," Brian replies. "Gaze down the line of your nose. Start shuttering out exterior interference without shutting down entirely. Then start concentrating on nothing but the sound of your breathing."

Ugh, the focus-only-on-your-breathing business. I've never been able to do that successfully. Even in yoga class I'm always too keyed up to calm down. Whenever the instructor announces in her most soothing voice that we are to balance on our "sits bones" and "think about nothing but your breath," my brain revolts, goes into overdrive, thoughts spinning fast and furiously. I sneak a peek at the other four HEARs, perched on their lab stools, already motionless.

Needless to say, I'm a thousand times more relaxed at yoga than I am here now.

TWENTY MINUTES LATER I wonder if I've fallen asleep.

Brian brings me back to the antiseptic reality of the lab room with a quiet command: "You may open your eyes."

I blink at the others. They're all wide awake.

"Now, who's familiar with the term 'remote viewing'?" Brian asks.

An impish smile comes to Pankaj's face, but my great-uncle shakes his head. "I do not mean watching TV and using a remote control."

Pankaj rolls his eyes.

Dan raises his hand. "It is a technique used to gather

information about an unseen or unknown target." The words sound memorized.

"A target?" Mara repeats, curious. "That seems aggressive."

"It's not," Brian says. "Think of it as the bull's-eye you're trying to zone in on. I'm going to give you three prompts. They will vary—a string of letters and numbers like a license plate number, or a proper name, or an object. Write the prompt down first. Then record whatever comes to mind afterwards. Ignore no detail that comes to you. This is vital: you must record absolutely everything. If it's easier to sketch what you see, by all means feel free to draw it instead."

Nobody asks any questions. Again, I feel as if I missed some orientation or was denied some introductory package of information—something that has put me at a competitive disadvantage with the others. Then again, aside from the admissions gold card to Henley, it's not clear what I'm competing with them for.

Brian hands each of us a graph-paper notebook and colored pencils. "Write your names on the front of your books. I'll just add one more time, please be as specific as you can. But if nothing comes to mind, just write 'NA' on the page. The goal isn't to create something out of thin air or to use your imagination. What you want is for the prompt to lead you to the target, and for that target to give you feedback. Clear?"

I raise my hand.

"Yes?" Brian replies.

"Can I speak to you in the hall?" I ask, scooting off my chair.

His lips turn down, as if he's disappointed. But then he nods and follows, shutting the door behind us. I feel the others' eyes on me, even out here.

"Is there a problem, Kass?" he asks. He sounds genuinely puzzled.

"I'm just not clear on exactly what you want *me* to do."

"It's just as I explained: I want everyone to—"

"I know, I know." I shake my head. "But it's not like I think I have any extra special talent for this stuff, so I don't know how my responses are supposed to help you. Am I the control or whatever you call it?"

He sighs and pats my shoulder. "You simply need to keep your mind open. That's all I ask of you. Can you do that?"

"Really?" I press. "Just keep an open mind?"

"That's it," he says.

If that's all it takes to get the gold card from my uncle, an open mind I shall give him. "Yeah, I can definitely do that."

"Good. Let's go back inside then."

Keep my mind open. Keep an open mind.

How hard could it be?

AT THE FIRST OF Brian's prompts—"9492MD"—my brain starts spinning in concentric circles. I scrawl the numbers and letters on the page. Then I glance around the room. Alex's hand is already in motion, as is Dan's. Mara quietly taps the edge of her pencil on the table. Pankaj just sits there, his eyes half-closed.

I stare at my notebook: *9492MD.*

And then something happens.

To my utter surprise, my thoughts stop swirling. A picture begins to emerge in my mind's eye: two men in white lab coats, walking down a hallway. I can't explain it, but it doesn't feel like I'm just imagining things, or being creative for the sake of the experiment . . . It feels more like a memory. Which is weird, since I can't place it in space or time. I start jotting notes.

Bright light reflects on the shiny tile floor. The men wear green scrubs underneath their lab coats. They're talking quickly and quietly to one another as they rush through a set of doors.

I stare again at the numbers and letters, but nothing more comes. My thoughts whirl: to Mara and her tarot cards; to the mysterious pictures on Uncle Brian's mantel; to Pankaj and his eyes, hidden behind that scrim of black hair. After a few more minutes, everyone sets the pencils down. I glance back at the prompt and then reread my description. I actually think I got it.

"All finished?" Brian asks, and we murmur assent. "Good. Now how many of you saw something to do with doctors or a hospital?"

I raise my hand. I can't help but feel relieved and happy when I see Mara raise her hand too. A moment later Alex also raises his hand.

"You guys saw the gunshot victim?" Alex asks. His expression is uncharacteristically grim. He glances between Mara and me. "That old guy bleeding out as he was being rushed into the ER? That's what I saw. Came through really clearly, like the opening scene in a TV medical drama."

I shake my head. "No, mine wasn't—"

"I saw nothing so tragic," Mara says, cutting me off.

"Me, neither," I add, quickly trying to reassert myself. "Just doctors walking down a hospital hallway."

Brian nods. "Yes, that's a fairly common reaction to this prompt, since it ends with the letters 'MD.'"

"Oh." This comes out more loudly than I intended. My eyes fall back to my notebook. That momentary feeling of pride crumbles into embarrassment. Apparently my imagination is even stronger than I thought.

"That's not a value judgment, Kass," Brian soothes. "It's a trap that I want everyone to be wary of. Our brains rely on patterns to make connections and assumptions. That's how we conserve energy and get through daily life—and survive. You see something slithering on the ground ahead, its tail rattling, you don't need to get up close to investigate and make sure it's a rattlesnake. But the trick here is to try, as best you can, to empty your mind of preconceptions. To register nothing but the target's inherent feedback, aura, or pulse." He takes a breath. "Okay, your next prompt: 4NFUSQ."

After I scribble the string of numbers and letters, an image forms once again, with the same immediacy as the last. I see an airport security line, the X-ray scanner ahead of me. Several bored TSA agents chat with one another across the carry-on bag conveyor belt and pat-down area. A visibly relieved looking man collects a briefcase containing the components of an explosive device. I stiffen.

Yoga breaths. Yoga breaths . . .

I breathe in and out deeply in an attempt to shake this image free. It must be wrong. It's stupid. I must have associated "4N" with the word "foreign."

But there's something else. This set of impressions *isn't* like the last, I realize now; the final image of that briefcase that flashes at me is far more vivid, fully formed, streaking through my skull in bright detail. *Imagination,* I remind myself. I'm probably just thinking about my parents' trip to China; I'm nervous about their travel. They already feel very far away to me. Or maybe it's that all of this stuff feels so "4N" to me, and the image reflects the truth of how much I want to go home.

My breathing steadies. I stare at the notebook. *Think, Kass!* No, that's not right . . . *Free associate, Kass!*

But nothing else comes.

Brian waits another minute, then says, "Spotted tiger."

I see Henry, the stuffed bear I carried with me everywhere until I was seven years old. I loved Henry so fiercely that patches of his fur wore off, effectively making him look spotted. It's obvious why he came to mind, but Henry was no tiger. He was a teddy bear. I write *NA* under the prompt.

After another few minutes, Brian collects our notebooks and sits on the edge of his desk. "So," he says, "your impressions?"

"I mostly saw colors," Mara replies. "Very few images, more like . . . washes of pigment. Very Jungian."

I blink at her, wondering if she realizes how pretentious and full of it she sounds. Or maybe it's just that I suddenly feel ignorant. Or both.

"What do you mean by that?" Alex asks.

Mara tilts her head, as if disappointed that Alex doesn't get the reference. "You know Carl Jung, the psychiatrist-philosopher? He focused on the unconscious, dreams and symbols. He believed our senses could turn inward, and when that 'introverted sensation' happens, you don't necessarily see an image, but you get reflections and shimmers of events that are still unborn."

"I saw a few pictures," Dan says. I am grateful that he doesn't pause to reflect on Mara's psychobabble about the unconscious. "One really distinct one was a cargo plane."

"The one taking off from some rain forest or something?" Alex asks.

Dan looks surprised and nods. "Yeah. But I couldn't figure out exactly where—"

"Colombia," Alex interrupts. "From some of the other details I got, like the flag and the shoes people were wearing, it must be Colombia."

Dan stares back at him. "That's really specific. I only saw the plane and the trees surrounding the runway."

Alex shrugs and smiles. No big deal, apparently.

"What else came through clearly?" Brian asks.

"Well, the tail obviously," Alex says.

"The tail?" Mara repeats. "Like the tiger's tail?"

"No," he replies. "The first prompt."

Dan blinks. "Do you mean t-a-i-l like what's at the butt end of an animal or t-a-l-e like a bedtime story?"

"I mean tail like the person—or people—following us," Alex answers quietly.

I realize I've begun twisting my pinky ring as I stare at Alex, wondering exactly how pronounced or problematic his people-are-always-watching paranoia really is.

"You think people are actively spying on us?" Pankaj asks, a smile playing on his lips. "I mean, *aside* from the NSA?"

Alex nods, his own smile gone, his eyes serious. "Yeah, I do."

"Mm, well, this is all very interesting," Brian interjects coolly, his tone at odds with his sudden fidgeting. He takes a three by five card out of his breast pocket and scribbles something down before blowing on the ink then returning the card. "Thank you, Alex. Okay, anyone else?"

Pankaj raises his hand, but it sags. He runs his fingers through his hair. "I got something that came through really clearly, but . . ." He winces. "But it's kind of lame."

Mara smiles. "Now you have to say it."

"It was for the one you mentioned, the spotted tiger?" Pankaj has lowered his voice, like he's disappointed in himself—which is odd, seeing as he's only projected dangerous confidence till now. "I saw this old teddy bear. Its fur was worn away in circular patches. So it kind of looked spotted."

I nearly fall off my stool. I hold my breath.

"But it definitely wasn't a tiger. It was a teddy bear. Ratty and weird looking. Not the kind of teddy bear any kid would want—"

"Maybe that's what being well loved looks like," I hear myself blurt in Henry's defense.

Now everyone is staring at me. It takes a beat or two for me to calm down. Once again, Brian is furiously writing on his index card. When he looks up, our eyes meet, and he smiles.

"Well, this was a very productive first session," he says. "We'll be repeating this exercise. When it comes to remote viewing, repetition and training should have a great impact. The more often you allow your mind to go to a place of receptivity, the more you're likely to see. And regardless of how familiar or common the image, don't dismiss it. Don't dismiss *anything*. We'll filter things later. Your job is to be the medium for the message." He looks at his watch. "Okay, why don't we break and meet back here in an hour? I want you to relax for a little bit before we begin again."

"Bathroom?" I ask.

"Down the hall to the right."

I nod and head for the door.

Outside, I break into a run. I push hard on the bathroom door then lock myself in the far stall.

Rules are generally made for a reason; I get that. And generally I try to follow them. But I've been unafraid to break the bad or inconvenient rules, and so I yank my cell out of my bag and call my dad. I need to share the questions festering in my mind—share them out loud, possibly in the form of a rant. How did Dan and Alex see the same plane? Did my airport security thing have anything to do with it too? What was Alex talking about when he said someone was following us? And craziest of all, how did Pankaj see and describe Henry, my teddy bear?

After a few interminable rings, a click. "You've reached the voice mail of William Black. I'm out of the country at the moment, but kindly leave a message, and I'll return your call as soon as I'm able."

"William Black, this is your daughter, Kassandra Black. We need to have a little chat about your uncle and this place you sent me, so call me back as soon as humanly possible. Thank you and goodbye."

When I put the phone away, I wonder what he and my mother are doing in China. I can't help but think of Brian's spherical description of time. It's already tomorrow in China, so maybe they have a pretty good grasp of what happened today. At this point I'll take any insight I can get . . .

I head back to the lab. It's empty.

They've all left me behind, my uncle included.

CHAPTER SEVEN

"One with everything please," I tell the counter lady at Einstein's Bagels.

I can't help wonder what Einstein would say about being the pitchman for a college town bagel joint. Probably, *The food's not bad, relatively speaking.* Wait . . . did I just make a physics pun? Somebody shoot me.

"You're going to smell," I hear over my shoulder.

It's Dan. I try to quash the flood of relief I'm feeling: at least they're not all off somewhere together.

"I'm okay with that." I decide not to turn to acknowledge him or his rudeness, and I smile at the counter lady instead. "And give me some of that scallion cream cheese too, please."

"I am not sitting next to you when we get back," he says.

"Your loss." I pull cash out of my purse. "How much?"

But the cashier is not paying attention. She's focused on the small TV hanging from the ceiling.

I wave a five-dollar bill in front of her.

She quickly eyeballs my order. "Four dollars even," she says. "Hey, Jim, can you turn up the volume?" She takes the bill without looking at me and hands a dollar back, eyes still glued to the screen. When the volume rises, I hear a reporter saying, "We don't yet know how many dead, but we're expecting more casualties to come."

My eyes flash to the TV. A police officer is standing in front of a bank of microphones. "What happened?" I ask.

"Some asshole went on a rampage just up the road in the Bridgestone Mall," the cashier mutters.

"Oh my God." I whirl around to Dan, who's still scanning the bagel selection. "Did you hear that?" I point to the TV, wondering if his mind is flashing to the same thing as mine: Alex's response to the "MD" prompt . . .

The officer seems to forget he's on camera. He looks directly at someone in the crowd of reporters. "At this point we have only one confirmed fatality. The victim was pronounced dead at Henley Medical Center. Identification is pending. But the gunman is still on the loose, and we have every reason to believe he is still armed and extremely dangerous."

I stare at Dan.

"Plain bagel with plain cream cheese," he says.

ONCE WE'RE OUT THE door, I grab Dan's shoulder and spin him around. "You're not at all surprised or upset by the news?" I ask.

He shakes me off. "No. I mean, what are you going to do?"

I have no answer for that. I stand there, stunned, as he sits down at one of the picnic tables outside the restaurant. With stoic precision, he removes his plain bagel from the wax paper. I slide into the bench on the other side. "You aren't the tiniest bit *freaked out* that the shooting happened so close to here and the gunman escaped?"

"Not really, I guess." He shrugs.

I stare at him for a moment. "Why not?"

"People die all the time. I don't have the same reactions to things that most people do." Dan picks up his bagel and starts chewing.

This is not news to me.

"I was diagnosed autistic as a kid."

Ah. So I was on the right track in my assumptions, but I'm not sure how to respond. I swallow and look down at my own bagel. "Oh."

"I'm not anymore. If you're on the spectrum, you'll probably never be completely 'normal'—whatever that means—but you can get better. It requires intense therapy when you're young. Mom quit her job and worked with me every day to give me the best chance."

Again, I'm at a loss. "That was really amazing of her," I offer.

"Yeah. She felt guilty."

I'm midbite when Dan says this, so I have to gnaw through the rest of the chewy dough before I can speak. "Why would she feel guilty? Because she felt responsible for 'making you autistic'?" I say this sarcastically, knowing how silly it would be for someone to feel this way.

But he nods. "Also because my dad was a complete dick." Dan takes a big bite out of his bagel. "He's dead now."

His tone is so matter of fact. "Oh my God, Dan, I'm so sorry to hear that." I reach my hand out to put it on his before realizing that might weird him out, so I quickly pull back. "How did it happen?"

"Train derailment. Two years ago." His tone remains flat. "He abused my mom and used to beat me, so I'm not really torn up about it." He pulls his bagel apart and drags his index finger through the cream cheese. "She stayed with him because she didn't have the money to leave and do therapy with me." He licks the white glop off his finger. "I knew the train was going to derail," he finishes. His face, with its chiseled features, is absolutely expressionless.

I must be misunderstanding him in some way. I think he just told me he knew his father would die in a train crash. "Wait, what?"

"My mom and I drove him to the station, which is about an hour away from our house. Anyway, after we drop him off and start driving back home, I wait until we're about forty-five minutes from the train station until I tell my mom."

I stare at Dan. "Until you tell her . . . ?"

"That the train is going to crash."

"How did you know that?" This cannot be true. Yet I don't think he's lying. Whatever I believe, *he* believes what he's telling me. I'm starting to feel a little nauseated.

"I kept having dreams about it."

I'm about to speak, but he holds up a finger. "You're going to say, 'Isn't it possible that because he was abusive you had a general wish for him to die?'"

I nod; that is exactly what the picnic-table psychologist in me was going to say.

"The answer is yes," he confirms. "But the dreams started giving way to a daytime vision. And in that I saw the specifics."

"So . . . you told this to your mom? What did she do?"

"First, she got very mad. She even said, 'Dan, I think this is a revenge fantasy.' But part of her also suspected I was telling the truth. So she pulled off the road and stopped the car. I can still see that whole thing so clearly." He pauses for a moment, staring at his half-eaten bagel. "She took out her cell phone and called Amtrak. It took her forever to get a real person on the line, and by the time someone finally did speak to her, she sounded like a lunatic. She starts telling a reservationist that she needs to stop the train, says she has information that the train is going to crash."

"No!"

"That's what I was thinking: How dumb, right? I said, 'Great, now they're going to think you're a terrorist, Mom.' The reservations lady said she needed to get her supervisor on the line; she also connected the call to the police. Mom just keeps repeating, 'Don't let the train leave. Keep it at the gate.' But when the supervisor got on the phone, he said, 'Ma'am, I need to inform you that the train has already departed.'"

I shake my head.

Dan nods. "Mom screamed. Then she hung up," he says matter-of-factly. "She looked at me and said, 'You waited.' Said it just like that, scared but calm, and I said, 'Yeah, I did.'" He finishes the rest of his bagel, wipes his mouth off with the edges of the paper bag, then crumples it into a ball. "You have some cream cheese on your cheek."

My head spins. I can't believe what I'm hearing, and yet it's become increasingly difficult to deny. "Dan," I say, wiping my hand across my face, "the shooting in the mall?"

"Yeah, I bet that's what Alex was talking about. He saw it before it went down."

WHEN DAN AND I get back to the lab, the others have already returned.

"Where's the professor?" Dan asks.

Pankaj points to the dry-erase board bearing a note from Uncle Brian: *Back ASAP.* He's apparently been summoned to his department chair's office.

"Do you think it had to do with the shooting?" I ask. But from the looks in their eyes, it's clear they haven't yet heard the news.

"Mall shooting," Dan says. "It's all over TV."

"Oh no," Alex says softly, flopping onto one of the stools and closing his eyes. "Was a Henley professor killed?"

I flinch, glancing at Dan. Nobody mentioned that on the news.

Dan shakes his head. "They confirmed one fatality, but didn't identify—"

"It was a Henley professor. He was the fatality," Alex says. "When I saw the aftermath of the shooting earlier this morning, I didn't want to say it. Too scary, too . . ."

We wait for him to say more—but he just stands and shakes his head, then gathers his bag. He starts walking out.

Mara's face has turned ashen. "Do you want any company?" she calls after him.

"No, I'm gonna . . . I just have to, uh . . ." He trails off and shuts the door behind him.

"Told ya," Dan says, looking me directly in the eye.

CHAPTER EIGHT

"Einstein got it wrong," Uncle Brian tells us. "Even geniuses get things wrong. Remember that. Einstein believed the universe was deterministic—meaning the past has already dictated the way things will turn out, that nothing happens randomly or in ways that can't be predicted. He even famously said—and I'm paraphrasing—'That God plays dice and uses "telepathic" methods is something I cannot believe for a single moment.' Yet on the contrary, any physicist will tell you that this was Einstein's biggest blunder. Not only does God play dice; it would appear he quite enjoys it."

I can't help but wonder if this is the lecture Uncle Brian had planned to give us today or if the subject of randomness was inspired by the senselessness of yesterday's shooting.

When he finally returned to the lab after the midmorning break had stretched to two hours, Brian was pale and visibly trembling. An elderly colleague with longish white hair a la Andrew Jackson accompanied him. Brian didn't bother to introduce the man at his side. Instead he mumbled that he'd just learned of the "tragic and villainous murder" of his "dear friend" Professor Graham Pinberg and told us to take the rest of the day off. "And please be careful out there," he said as we gathered our things. "The gunman is still at large."

I didn't hear Uncle Brian come home last night, but this morning I found him drinking his coffee in the kitchen. He stood behind the kitchen curtains, staring out the window. His eyes were a little bleary—they still are—but he seemed determined to forge ahead with the day as planned, in spite of the tragedy. I wasn't sure how much he'd want to talk about his friend, so I asked if the university would hold a memorial service. Brian exhaled heavily, mumbled that there'd be a tribute of some kind but that it was important to keep on with the work in front of us. "Graham was a man whose life was dedicated to the pursuit of discovery, and getting on with it honors him best."

As we drove to school this morning, we saw flags lowered to half-staff throughout the town. We also discovered that a large number of security guards had suddenly materialized on campus. With the "armed and dangerous" gunman still on the loose, their presence had ironically only made me feel more vulnerable.

"Einstein believed in entanglement, though, didn't he?" Dan now asks Brian.

"Yes, that he did," Brian responds.

"Entanglement?" Pankaj repeats.

Brian nods. "That's when two particles that are separated by any distance—even light-years—instantaneously affect one another, as if they were part of the same unified system."

I shift in my seat, barely paying attention to what's being discussed. This whole incomprehensible conversation began when Mara started talking about her tarot cards. She was naturally on edge when she came into the lab—we all were—but then she started babbling about the "challenging read" she'd picked from the deck upon waking up. That set Dan off on some long tangent about the relationship between tarot cards and quantum mechanics. And that's when I started to tune out.

Truthfully, though, I'm much more concerned about Alex—or rather, the absence of Alex. He's been AWOL ever since he fled the lab yesterday. No one has seen him in the dorm, and no one knows what time he got home last night. Or *if* he got home last night, and there's a deranged gunman still at large. Yet I seem to be the only one freaked out that Alex is missing. It's not only distressing; it's *weird* . . .

By 10:10, I can no longer sit still. I feel like I'm going to lose it. But right at the moment that I'm about to blow—as if on cue—Alex bursts through the door.

"Hey, all," he says, his hair wet from the shower, sunglasses hanging from a button of his stylish plaid shirt. "Sorry I'm late."

My jaw hangs open. That's it?

Brian raises his eyebrows. "Care to explain?"

"I need space after these things happen, so I tend to vanish for a while," Alex answers quietly, matter-of-factly. He doesn't look at any of us when he speaks; he just sits on his stool. "It's really hard to know about this stuff before it goes down and then be powerless to stop it, you know?" Mara and Dan nod to themselves. "It was a whole tidal wave of emotion. For a while I was even feeling happy because it was your colleague and not you, Professor. Then I felt guilty for feeling happy because it's so wrong. Someone was gunned down in cold blood. But my mind kept racing, you know?" Alex takes a breath and finds Brian's eyes. "I mean, *what if it had been you?*" He shakes his head.

Brian continues to study Alex for a moment, and we all wait for his response. But instead of offering comforting words or reading Alex the riot act for having disappeared for nearly eighteen hours, Brian picks up a yellow legal pad, flips through several pages, and scrawls some notes.

"Okay, so moving on," Brian says, eventually looking back up at us.

I try to process the weirdness I've just witnessed, but I can't. Maybe Uncle Brian is trying to deflect his own grief by cataloging Alex's response?

"For the tests we'll be doing later in the day," Brian says, "we'll be studying anomalies that arise from human-machine interactions. I want to see if you can bias a machine."

"Bias a machine?" Pankaj asks with a grin. "Easy. Just tell it its job has been outsourced to cheaper machines in a foreign country."

Brian breaks into a grin, and I laugh, but then quickly put my hand over my mouth. Laughter hardly seems appropriate on a day like today. Then again, with this group, I have no idea what's considered "appropriate."

"Bias in the sense of influencing a machine with your mind alone," Brian clarifies.

Collecting myself, I straighten on my stool. "You want us to make a machine do something without touching it?" When my uncle nods, I continue: "Okay, so then that's just impossible. No way can that happen."

Brian shakes his head, but his grin hasn't entirely faded. "Let's not forget the lesson of our man Einstein, Kass. Even geniuses get things wrong."

I HEAD TO THE bathroom at the end of another ridiculous day. No one appeared to influence anything, but Uncle Brian watched us all afternoon and took copious notes. I'm looking at my hands as I wash them in the sink when I feel something slide down the back of my hair. I'm momentarily seized with terror, and my head jerks up. I see Mara's reflection in the mirror. She's standing right behind me.

"Your hair is so pretty, Kass," she says.

I try not to shudder. Who sneaks up behind someone and starts petting her hair? It'd be alarming even without a lunatic on the loose. Mara runs her hand through her own silky black hair and tousles it; she has one of those silent movie–star hairdos you need the perfect heart-shaped face to carry off. Mara's face is so delicate it seems like the haircut was created solely for her. And her wide-set eyes, framed by long, false lashes, make her look like a manga heroine. "Thanks," I manage to reply.

I want to leave, but she stands between me and the door.

"I used to have great hair too," she says, the words tumbling out quickly, "but in a fit of *I don't know what*, I chopped it all off a few months ago—actually, I do know what." She leans in a little closer behind me and lowers her voice. "I was getting too much attention from the male population of Oklahoma, and it got to be disturbing."

Having tried to remain inconspicuous myself for the past two years, I can actually relate. But I'm not buying it. She's up to something.

"Boys don't like the short hair," she goes on. "Or at least not on me, so my plan seems to have worked. Almost too well." She hesitates, and then looks me in the eye. "Let's get out of here. Come on, there's someplace I want to show you."

I have to admit, even though I'm a little creeped out, I'm intrigued by the invitation. Maybe we *can* be friends, after all? Doubtful. But maybe.

"Where?"

"Follow me." She flashes a mischievous smile.

MARA RUNS—BACKWARD—THE WHOLE WAY from the building, yelling that I needed to move faster, faster, faster! I don't know where we're headed, but for some reason I don't think her urgency has anything to do with her fear of the gunman. It feels more like she's rushing me someplace that has a limited-quantity giveaway or a unicorn. Finally she stops in front of the enormous sculpture on the art museum's front lawn.

"Look at *this*!"

I pause to catch my breath. "Yeah," I gasp. "Yeah, it's nice." I wonder if I'm missing something. It's no unicorn.

"They have the most amazing American art here!" As she throws open the museum's doors, I'm tempted to ask her how many energy drinks she's had today; she seems to be operating at three times her normal speed.

A guard asks for our IDs, and as I fish mine out of my bag, Mara pulls hers from the top of her T-shirt. "Voilà," she says to the guard, who, it must be said, seems to have enjoyed the trick. Maybe Mara's overcompensating for the gloom that's fallen over the campus. Maybe she doesn't notice or care. But there's something unhinged in those huge eyes.

I follow her, warily, as she flits through the galleries. After a few minutes, she stands still in front of a black-and-white painting . . . of nothing. Seriously. To me it just looks like black and white paint, possibly the outline of a chair.

"What's going on?" I ask.

"I find this mesmerizing. Look." She points to a segment where the black paint seems to be peeking out from under the white paint. "You assume the artist, Franz Kline, was using black paint on a white canvas, right? I mean, that's the way things usually go. But here you can't tell what's the background and what's the foreground. The eye is fooled because he applies paint in layers."

Where is she going with this? There's no way Mara dragged me here to discuss modern art. But I play along. "Uh-huh."

"We come to a painting believing we understand the rules in advance, right?" Mara turns to me, her brown eyes glittering beneath the fringe of lashes. "The canvas is white; the black goes on top. But in this work it's completely unclear which came first. Maybe it's white paint on a black canvas. We can't know. And that's the point. With abstract expressionism, the artist is telling us to expect the unexpected." She takes a step toward me and lowers her voice. "It's kind of like the feeling of falling in love; you know what I mean?"

"Uh-huh," I say again. I have absolutely no idea what she means. This would be a problem if we were going to be friends. But since I can't follow her leap from paint thrown on canvas to falling in love, I feel pretty confident the friendship thing ain't happening. "I guess."

"Come on, Kass. You've fallen in love, haven't you?" She says this like a taunt. As if she knows my secret.

"Yeah," I reply noncommittally. The problem is, I'm not actually sure of the answer to that question: Is it love if it's only one-sided? Or did the feelings I had for Pete Lewis count as something else? Obsession maybe? I haven't thought of him since I've been at Henley—which must be some kind of record for me since I used to think of him every few seconds. But he was my infinity crush, the boy I'd been dreaming about since I first laid eyes on him in eighth-grade math class. He was the boy whose smile sent me spinning. The boy whose betrayal felt like a death.

"When I'm in love, colors are brighter," Mara says in the silence. "Smells are sharper; my skin is more sensitive; my visions stronger. It's like the emotion pumps pure adrenaline through my body!" She spins around several times, and when she stops, she lets out a "Woo!" She grabs my arm to brace her-self. A couple of the security guards frown in our direction. I don't blame them. Even if there weren't a killer on the loose, even if a member of the Henley community *hadn't* been killed, her behavior wouldn't exactly be museum appropriate.

"Hey, Mara, let me ask you something. You seem a little—"

"Alive?"

Interesting word choice. "Well, that, yeah, but also—"

"Tired?"

"No, I definitely wasn't going to go with tired."

"Oh, good, because the thing is I haven't really slept in the last few days." She twirls once more, limply, and rubs her eyes. "I'm worried it's starting to show."

I force a smile. "Well, you might be a little punchy . . ."

"Like this?" With a laugh, she punches me in the arm. Not lightly. She has a decent jab for a small girl; I rub my bicep. "Sorry, sorry," she says. "I know I'm a little all over the place right now, and *my God*," she says loudly, "I am *so* horny."

The guards are glaring now. I can feel my face reddening. Mara just smiles and waves at them, and they glance at each other and turn away.

"Ever since I stopped taking my medication, I just feel so much freer. Like I said, more aliiiiiiive!" She grabs my hand and pulls me down the hall—away from the guards, thankfully.

"What medication did you stop taking?" I whisper.

"The mood stabilizers."

Aha, I think. I'm no less embarrassed or concerned or freaked, but I'm at least finally cognizant of what's going on. She looks manic because she *is* manic. Clinically. Diagnostically.

"I've been weaning myself off them since I got here because Professor Black told me to stop taking them. But you can't stop all at once or else—" Mara makes a gesture like she's hung herself with an imaginary rope, her head falling to her left shoulder, her tongue sticking out of her mouth. "But it's okay. I've been eating a lot of ginger instead. Its chemical compounds have calming properties."

I nod. The good news is that Mara is beginning to come into

focus for me. The bad news is that, globally, there isn't a large enough supply of ginger to bring this girl back to earth. "Can I ask *why* my uncle told you to stop taking them?" I say. I plant my feet so she's no longer able to drag me along behind her. Her hand slips from my wrist.

With a dramatic sigh, she says, "Fine. The drugs interfere with your brain chemistry. They're *supposed* to do that, that's how they *work*, but I'm pretty sure they interfere with our ability to have visions. Also, my cards said I was blocked, so I knew I had to do something to reverse that. It's what the tarot was telling me. It felt like I'd been trying to swim through drying cement. Now I'm back in clear blue waters." She moves her arms as if she's doing a breaststroke for emphasis.

I glance around to see if anyone is nearby, if anyone is listening.

Mara pulls her cell phone out of one of the front pockets of her bag and slides her finger across the screen. "Don't freak out—I'm not using the phone to call or text anyone, so you don't need to rat on me. But check this out." She flips through the picture gallery and hands me the phone. "I did this series of paintings the last time I went off the meds. That first one is a detail of the larger work."

I peer at the screen: an image of three terrified-looking Asian people. Their bodies appear to be in motion, but it's impossible to see what they're running from. "Can I?"

"Yeah, keep flipping," Mara encourages me.

I swipe my finger across the screen, and the whole picture comes into focus. Behind the three people in the previous image, hundreds of other equally detailed figures are running as well—from a monstrous flood—stampeding through a small seaside village. But there's no escape. Angry waves crash over the bulkhead, filling the streets with seawater. With a shudder,

I realize that the image is so horrifying in part because it is so familiar. I've seen this before. I look up at Mara and my eyes narrow. "What is this?"

"It's a depiction of the disaster in Japan. You remember when they had the earthquake in 2011, which set off a tsunami, which screwed up their nuclear facility in Fukushima?"

"Yeah, sure." It was actually one of the first major world events of which I was conscious. It terrified me. And I remember exactly why: it was the first time I truly realized that there are things we absolutely can't control. "This painting is really good, Mara," I breathe. I expand the image on the screen with my thumb and index finger to focus in on the details. The fear on the victims' faces is palpable. "How long did it take you to do this?"

"Uh," she replies, looking up to the ceiling, "I don't know, maybe a couple of days. I kind of lost track of time. I wasn't sleeping in February of 2011 either. I just worked in a real manic-y burst. Keep flipping, though. I downloaded a photo of the actual disaster, which was a month later, from the CNN website. I think you'll find it interesting."

My fingers feel clammy; they tremble as I do as she says. When I find the CNN photo, it is literally a pale imitation of her painting. The photo is all sea green, brown, and grey. Mara's painting is dotted with the hot pink of a little girl's sweatshirt, the fire-engine red of a motorbike being swept out to sea, and the neon multi-colors of a supermarket sign wrenched from its facade.

I remember this photograph; it haunted me. This was nature's wrath—the picture of chaos—and even at the age of eleven, I was conscious of how the photographer had managed to capture that raw and brutal destruction.

Yet Mara saw it and captured it too. A month before it happened. I start to feel wobbly, dizzy. I lean against the wall for support.

"Did you try to stop it?" I ask her.

"The earthquake and tsunami?" she asks. She gives a little laugh. "Kass, I appreciate your belief in me, but I haven't figured out how to control the weather quite yet."

"No," I snap. "I mean did you try to *warn* anyone?"

"Yes, of course," she snaps back. "Of course I did." In a flash, Mara's mania and joy are gone; now her face is flushed and twisted with rage.

As I try to remain calm in order to calm *her,* I also try to imagine how a teenager would go about warning a foreign country that it's about to experience a devastating natural disaster. "So what did you do?" I ask. "Who did you tell? Your parents?"

"Are you kidding? If I told them that, they would have doubled my meds." She rolls her eyes as if she's embarrassed by my stupidity. "I emailed the prime minister of Japan's office, like, repeatedly." She shrugs. "No one answered. Apparently no one in his office was particularly interested in the weather forecasts of a kid from Oklahoma. And it wasn't like I was going to be able to stop it, so eventually I gave up and started painting it instead."

Footsteps approach. When I glimpse the two unhappy guards entering our gallery, I link arms with Mara. Best to steer her out of the museum before we get booted. I'm hoping she'll chill out once we're back outside in the sunshine. She seems to have relaxed a little, though she's still far from serene. As we walk through the exit, she unwraps a gummy ginger candy and pops it in her mouth. When she finishes chewing it, she stops in her tracks and slips her arm from mine.

"You know that I had an ulterior motive in inviting you here, don't you?" she says. Her voice is surprisingly calm.

Uh-oh.

Before I can utter a word, she states, "I want you to stay away from Pankaj."

I almost laugh. "Stay away from Pankaj? What are you talking about?"

"Don't play coy, Kass; it's really unattractive on you."

"Mara, you're insane." I immediately regret my choice of words, but now I'm angry. My patience has worn thin. "I don't even like Pankaj, and it's pretty clear that he has a raging hate-on for me, so you don't have a lot to worry about on this one."

"I'm serious," she says. She's leaning so close to me I'm wondering if she might get violent. Only now do I see the dark circles under her eyes beneath some concealer.

I take a step back. "I don't even know why you're worried about this. If you like him, take him. He's all yours."

"That's not the point." She glares at me. "Just . . . just remember this conversation."

"Not a problem. You've done a pretty good job of freaking me out here."

"Good," she says, her voice sliding into a grim whisper. "Exactly what I was hoping to do."

CHAPTER NINE

I need to cool down, but I can't. There are so many feelings rumbling through me, I feel like a teakettle coming to a boil. The day is over, and I need to avoid everyone and everything until I can let off some steam. If I can make it up to the observatory and shut the door without Uncle Brian noticing, I think I might be okay.

"Kass?" Uncle Brian calls out as I attempt to sneak through the front door. "I'm in the living room. Come on in."

Perfect.

I know he's hurting, so I try to focus on my breathing, yoga-style, to get into a more Zen place before talking to him. But as per *always*, the exercise not only fails; it seems to make me more anxious. When I walk into the living room, I find my great-uncle sitting in his recliner with his feet up, a large photo album resting on his legs.

He smiles at me, looking over the rims of his glasses. "Did you have a nice afternoon?"

"It was . . . okay." I can't get into what happened right now. "How are you doing?"

"Okay," he echoes with a shrug. "It was a tough day." He nods at the album. "I was asked to gather some personal effects from Graham's office to use in a memorial, and I found a scrapbook he'd kept since our time together as undergraduates at Princeton."

I move to the arm of my uncle's chair to get a better look. He flips back to the front and points to a picture in the center of the page.

Three young men, all clean-cut and in suits, sit together on a staircase. The one on the left appears the geekiest—though between these three, geeky is a relative term—scrawny with black-framed eyeglasses, the kind now favored by hipsters and architects. His hands grip his knees. The boy in the middle appears the most relaxed of the three, like he's just aced a calculus test. And the guy on the right smiles widely and squints at the camera. It's hard to tell if that's because the sun is in his eyes or because he's stoned. I lean in and look at him more closely. "Is that you?"

Brian nods. "Terrible shot. The sun was shining directly in my eyes. The man in the glasses is Graham."

"Wait a second," I say. I step over to the mantel and point at the photo of the three colleagues, the one I noticed when I first arrived. "This is of the three of you too, isn't it?"

"That's right," Brian says. "That was taken after we'd been working together for a while. But the picture in this album is where the story begins. It was taken at Princeton, the day we three were tapped."

He has my attention now. "Tapped? For what?"

"The CIA."

"Ha!" I chuckle before realizing he's not joking. I look more closely at the shot on the mantel and squint to read the words on the seal behind the men: *Central Intelligence Agency*. "You were a spy?"

"No," he says calmly. "I was employed by the CIA as a scientist, as was Graham."

I nod.

But even if he *were* a spy, wouldn't he deny it? That has to be one of the first lessons you learn in Spy 101.

"Princeton always had strong ties to the Agency," he says. "Allen Dulles, class of '14, was one of its best-known directors. Several of the school's most distinguished professors were CIA consultants as well. When we were tapped, it felt like quite an honor."

I nod again, my eyes drawn back to the photo of the three men at Princeton. "Wait, what's the name of the guy in the middle again?"

"Christopher Figg." Brian closes the album. He takes a moment to wipe his glasses with a handkerchief.

"He was the one who ran the summer program here when I was a kid, right?"

"Yes, Camp Dodona."

The image of Mara in her tiny kiddie T flashes through my mind. "Speaking of that camp, can I ask you a question?"

"Certainly."

I didn't want to bring up Mara, but now I can't turn back. I know I need to tread lightly; my uncle personally selected Mara to be here this summer, which means he must think highly of her and her "powers." Still, for my own sanity, I have to get a sense of how dangerously cuckoo she really is.

"So," I say, "Mara's kind of an 'interesting' person, isn't she?"

Brian puts his glasses back on and straightens. "What did she do?"

"Well, she basically threatened me with bodily harm if I didn't stay away from Pankaj."

"I see." Brian nods. "I suppose there's a certain consistency to that. Even as a child she was terribly protective of him."

"Wait . . . what?" I pause. "They knew each other as children?"

Brian smiles. "Of course. From Camp Dodona. Mara's always been a bit dramatic, and she tried to keep you away from him even then."

My heart is pounding all of a sudden. "Pankaj was at that camp too?" I whisper.

"So was his sister, Nisha, though she wasn't in your group," Brian adds. "She was in another program that Figg ran down the hall from ours—one for children with emotional and behavioral issues. I didn't know the other campers in that group. I only knew Nisha because she and Pankaj were siblings and she would occasionally come looking for him." He shakes his head ruefully. "Quite a bully, that one."

"But it's really weird," I say out loud. "I have no memory of him being there at all. He hasn't mentioned it either."

"You were all quite young. And you weren't there for very long." He shrugs. "Memory is slippery."

My uncle is right about that. Memory *is* slippery, particularly if you don't *want* to remember something. Like being bullied. I think again about my only clear recollection of Camp Dodona—the day I left, the day my popsicle-stick house was destroyed and I punched the kid who did it. Then I think about this afternoon at the art museum. I wonder how much of this summer I'll recall in the future . . . and what my response might be if I'm provoked again.

Brian is smiling at me. "It really was a shame you left camp so early. We were just starting to get the first real glimmers of your talents. But that famous 'hit first; ask questions later' streak of yours was also becoming more pronounced, and your father was not keen to let it develop further."

"Me?" I counter reflexively, my hackles rising. "Maybe I was a little impulsive, but let's not forget, Mara's the nutty one." I'm not sure why I'm so defensive about my behavior at that age, but I feel like he's suggesting I'm somehow responsible for provoking her. "She even told me it was *your* idea for her to go off her meds."

I'm expecting Uncle Brian's jaw to drop. Or maybe I *want* him to be shocked and outraged by this revelation: that his handpicked HEAR is lying about such a dangerous act of negligence on his part, claiming that he deliberately told her to ignore her treatment.

When he nods, I start feeling sick. "That's true," he confirms.

"Pardon?"

"With those drugs running through her system, her brain chemistry isn't what I need it to be. For my experiments to work, there can be no interference. I assume you now know that she forecasted the disaster in Japan?"

As he says this, the queasiness spreads. I start thinking about the others. Like how Dan knew his father would die, and how Alex knew about the mall shooting, that a Henley professor would be killed. "So it's not just that your geniuses are so smart; it's that they're all prophets of doom. They all foresee disasters, don't they?"

Brian takes hold of the scrapbook, clutching it firmly in both hands: "Finally a sign you might be smart enough to be here."

I'M FLOATING. AS I stare at the fake stars above me, I question everything from the reality of what I've experienced to what I believe—or rather, how much I'm *willing* to believe.

I excused myself after Uncle Brian's last comment and have been hiding out in the observatory ever since. Night has fallen. If I could stay in my room by myself for the rest of the summer, I would.

There's a knock on the door. I cringe.

"Kass, may I come in?" Uncle Brian asks.

"Give me a minute," I reply, wanting a lot longer than that to compose myself. I struggle off the water bed, take a deep breath then reach for the doorknob.

Standing in the dim light of the hallway, Brian looks anxious. My dad gets the same strained expression on his face when he's on edge. With all the stress of this week, I'm worried my great-uncle might give himself a heart attack, and I want to tell him to calm down. But having tried that line on Dad, I've learned *the last* thing you want to tell a high-strung person to do is to "calm down." It's like lighting a bomb's fuse and then suggesting it not detonate.

When Brian enters the room, he walks directly to the window and scans the street below.

"Kass," he says, "No one arrived here by mistake or through good fortune. In addition to being very bright, all the HEARs tripped the system in some way. Every one." He turns around to face me. "Why do you think you're at Henley?"

I hold out my hands, palms up, with a resigned smile on my face. Is he really going to make me say it out loud? "Because Dad begged you."

This makes Brian laugh for some reason I can't possibly fathom. "You think it was your dad who got you here?"

"Uh, yeah? After I got into trouble and my acceptance to Columbia was revoked, he—"

"That you got caught by the police was simply fortuitous," Brian interrupts. "Good luck on my part really." He must see the flash of anger and confusion on my face, because he gestures to my desk chair. "May I?"

I can no longer hold back. "My getting caught by the police was good luck for you? What the hell is that supposed to mean?"

He sighs and remains standing. "Kassandra, I apologize. That came out less elegantly than intended. What I meant was that I have been asking your father to send you back here for quite some time now, but it was only after your run-in with the authorities that he relented."

What?! No. No way. I shake my head. "*You* wanted me to come here? *Dad* was the one who stopped it? That makes zero sense. It's . . ." I'm about to use the word "crazy," but I stop myself since crazy seems A-OK here. "Wrong. Just wrong."

"I must say, Kass," he says, "I've been very gratified to see that in the last two years specifically you've started using your abilities in such a constructive way."

I swallow. "What are you talking about?"

"I know about all of your exploits as the anonymous vigilante. 'Ally X,' righter of wrongs. That's why I needed you back. That's why you getting caught was such a surprisingly good"—he pauses, a gleam in his eye—"roll of the dice for me."

Though I've never fainted before, this could be my moment.

"What baffles me, though," he continues, "is how the police were able to catch you? Why did you get caught this last time? Do you even know the answer to that yourself?"

My head shakes, involuntarily. I don't want to sound too full of myself, but he *is* right. It never occurred to me that I'd get busted. I think the realization that I got caught, that I'd slipped up somehow, was even more upsetting to me than getting handcuffed with those extra-strong garbage bag ties and thrown in the back of the police cruiser.

"No one else knew I was responsible for the other stuff," I finally manage. "I acted alone and anonymously, and I was always in and out before anyone noticed. That was something I was really proud of . . ."

"I would imagine."

"So how do *you* know?"

Brian takes off his glasses and tucks them into his shirt pocket, glancing again at my desk. I relent with nod. He sits, and I ease down onto the edge of my water bed, mostly because I'm not sure if my legs can support me for much longer.

"Let me ask you something first, Kassandra. Why is it, do you think, that you were able to get away with your shenanigans for so long? And how is it, do you think, that you've been able to slip in and out of so many places without being noticed?"

I lift my shoulders. "Because I've been really careful." It's true: as a planner, I've measured distances, triple-checked schedules, kept detailed logs of people's comings and goings. "I spent a lot of time—" I stop at Uncle Brian's headshake.

There is, of course, another answer.

Every meticulous planner knows that, despite all the hard work, shit happens. Regardless of how finely tuned your plan is, something will go wrong. Someone leaves his house a minute early or a minute late. There's a freak storm. Bad traffic. Gluten. Yet I always managed to stay one step ahead of the unexpected. It wasn't that I didn't make mistakes. It was something else. And what I think Uncle Brian is trying to get me to admit is that every time the risk of getting caught lurked, I got a feeling—literally, a physical sensation—that told me to get the hell out of wherever I was.

"Because I'm really lucky?" I offer.

Brian sighs. "Luck had nothing to do with, and you know it. It's your ESP."

I stare at him blankly. In this shadowy room, with the fake stars overhead and the oversize telescope and my body gently bobbing up and down on a water-filled mattress, I once again feel as if I've entered some hallucinatory dreamscape. I do not have ESP. Maybe the other HEARs do—I've allowed myself to accept that possibility, given the seemingly indisputable evidence—but *I* do not. I am here because my father called in a favor.

"You felt the danger, am I right?" Brian presses. His voice is still calm, but I hear urgency. "Your body was flashing hazard. Kass, everyone has moments of foresight. People know who's calling before they pick up the phone; mothers sense what their babies need through coos. That expression, 'Your ears must have been burning'? These moments happen occasionally for most people. But there are some who can channel that sensitivity much more precisely, and far more often. You showed great aptitude for this even as a child in our summer program. No one recognized your talent aside from me—not even you—which is why it's so lucky I have you back now."

There's that word again. "Lucky." I feel like shouting that line from *The Princess Bride,* "I do not think it means what you think it means."

"No, lucky is not the right word," he says, as if reading my mind. Maybe he is, for all I know. His voice falters when he speaks again. "It's fortuitous. And it makes Graham Pinberg's senseless death all the more tragic. Tragic and ironic. With all the talent I've gathered here this summer, that I couldn't stop his murder . . ." Brian's head droops and he shakes it back and forth.

I turn away, staring down at my hands in my lap. "I'm sorry about your friend," I murmur. "I really am, Uncle Brian. But I need you to explain this to me. I don't understand how this works. If I'm supposed to have ESP, why don't I have it all the time? And if it's so strong, why didn't I have any sort of clue about it?"

Brian pats his hands on his knees and stands. "Those are some of the questions we've been working on for a good long time, Kass."

"And?" I say, unable to hide my impatience. "What have you

come up with so far? I feel like I'm supposed to know how you're going to respond to that."

"Ah, ESP humor," he muses, a smile flitting across his face. "Always good for a laugh. Graham was a fan too. And yes, of course I've come up with some theories about this. But you're only first learning that you possess these abilities, Kass, so it's important for you to explore them without outside influence. It's also important for me to study how they flourish and manifest from this point forth."

I lift my eyes. "So the rest of them? Dan, Mara, Alex, Pankaj . . . they all have these same abilities too? That's why you picked us?"

"Everyone's brain is slightly different, so everyone has a slightly different capacity." Brian walks over to the telescope and bends slightly at the waist. He squints into the eyepiece. "Yes, there are overlaps in your abilities, but you all have unique blind spots too."

I try to follow, but can't. "I don't understand what you mean."

"Maybe it's better explained as farsightedness." He looks up from the scope. "Think of it as being able to read a movie's subtitles but not being able to read your text messages if you hold your phone too close. We've discovered that something similar is true for people with ESP. Some people have a hard time forecasting what will happen to those with whom they're closest. Often people can't predict things about their own families for this very reason. They can't see them clearly because they can't be objective. These are the blind spots. The x factors. And given what happened to my friend, you can imagine that this area of study is very important to me right now."

I nod, thinking about him, thinking about the rest of my family. I've never been able to guess what my parents are thinking—about anything. "But obviously that wasn't true for Dan," I say.

"True, though one could hardly say he was close to his father," Brian replies. "And just to confuse matters, we've also found exactly the opposite can be true too: the closer you are to someone, the more accurate your predictions can be."

This is making me feel insane, and now I really want my uncle to leave so I can curl into the fetal position and shut out the world. But he doesn't take the hint. Apparently communicating my thoughts to him is not part of my alleged psychic powers.

And then, just like that, he shuffles toward the door.

"As I said before, I believe we're nearing our breakthrough, Kass. It's dependent on you and your friends here, which is why having you together in the lab this summer is such a gift." His posture stiffens as he reaches for the knob. "And with Graham gone . . . it's also what makes the university's hearing on HEAR's closure all the more vexing."

"Wait . . . what did you just say?" I clutch the edge of the bed frame to steady myself. "HEAR's closure?"

"I was planning to tell you all before the tragedy, but yes, the fate of my lab is to be decided at the next meeting of Henley's Internal Review Board. Years of research will come down to what the trustees choose to do in that one afternoon."

"Why would Henley close your lab?"

"The powers that be don't believe in my work. And, just as vitally, they don't like *me*. You may find this hard to believe, but I am not the most beloved professor on campus. Graham and I used to joke about it. My lab got more attention, but he said he liked to have me around anyway, because his popularity rose by comparison."

There's no point in trying to contradict him. I don't know enough about Henley, and I don't doubt him either.

"But if I can present the review board with some interesting new data at this critical meeting, and show them that it won't take very much money to keep us up and running—a hundred thousand dollars at most—I'm hopeful they'll relent."

I blink, not sure that I've heard him correctly. I was assuming he'd say something in the range of millions. "A hundred thousand dollars? That's it?"

"I've secured an outside grant from an interested party, but it's up to the university provide the rest."

I rub the bottom of my chin and consider this. There seems to be an obvious answer to his dilemma. "Uncle Brian, Dad invests loads of money in science and tech start-ups. I'm sure he'd be happy to help you. Why don't you just ask him?"

"No." He shakes his head vigorously. "Out of the question."

"I really don't think it'd be a problem—"

"No," he repeats, cutting me off. "Taking money from your father for this is the one thing I can never do. And it's not appropriate for us to discuss. Understood?"

Before I can even nod, he's out the door.

CHAPTER TEN

I can't remember when I first heard the term "mind virus," though it might have involved a lolcat meme of a kitten wearing a lime-rind helmet. But now I can't stop thinking about it. Since Uncle Brian dropped the ESP bombshell on me—*I have ESP? . . . I have ESP . . . I have ESP!*—I feel infected. I flash on the idea more frequently than I blink.

I'm also tired and wrecked, but sleep is impossible.

How can someone have ESP and not know until she's told?

There are so many counterintuitive problems with that question, I feel like my head might explode as I try to work through them.

At 4 A.M., I clamber out of my sloshing bed and go online.

I don't know what I'm looking for exactly. I think of how Dan researched the group, so I decide to start with him. He seems to be doing incredibly well on the experiments we've performed, and I imagine a thorough Google search should turn up some decent information. But all I get are stories about another Dan Taylor: the owner of an auto body shop who was convicted on multiple counts of insurance fraud.

Then I search for train derailments two years ago. I quickly discover Dan's mother's name and start digging around on her instead. *Bingo.* As it turns out, Lauren Taylor had her share of "luck" over the years: both epically good—she won a lottery jackpot when "a family member" bought her a ticket for her birthday—and nightmarishly tragic. Not only did her husband die in a horrible accident, but she witnessed the aftermath of a robbery that had turned deadly.

I click on a news interview. "My boy grabbed my sunglasses from my purse and wouldn't let them go," the newspaper quotes her as saying. "So by the time I got them out of his hands and walked in to the convenience store, the gunmen had just fled through the back door. If it wasn't for the struggle with the glasses, we would have been inside too."

The convenience store owner and three customers were shot dead.

I look at the date on the article. Dan was three years old at the time.

I start thinking about the other HEARs. I know some backstory on both Mara and Pankaj, but though I've seen the evidence of Alex's talent, his past is still a mystery to me . . . I type *Alex Hill, Texas* into the search bar. A few unrelated results pop up, but after those there are links about and pictures of Alex as a Boy Scout. Literally, in uniform. He must have been seven or eight in the pictures, but cute and mop haired in a way that forecasts the handsome guy to come. Apparently he tried to warn several members of his troop not to canoe on the lake where they were camping. In a published report, their distraught scout leader was later quoted as saying, *"If I'd just listened to him, those boys would be alive today."*

I also discover an abandoned blog Alex kept until last year, making various calamitous predictions, such as *Ten Car Pileup on the Interstate!* Later, he'd post a link to a story about or a picture of the disaster if it made the news.

I could probably keep searching their histories for hours, but I've learned what I need to know.

I move on to general ESP research.

It turns out reputable scientists have taken the field seriously since at least the 1880s. In the 1930s, J. B. Rhine, a researcher at Duke University, established the parapsychology lab there and professionalized the study of the field with a book called *Parapsychology: Frontier Science of the Mind.* But perhaps not surprisingly, there are many more people on the record trying to debunk ESP and dismiss it outright. They call its supporters everything from "shamans and charlatans" to "crackpots and boobs." Even the National Academy of Sciences has weighed in; in the 1980s they produced a book-length study called *Enhancing Human Performance,* which essentially writes off the entire field as bogus because none of the predictions or "proofs" could ever be replicated in a lab.

Yet Alex knew of a specific shooting before it happened. Dan foresaw a train derailment. Mara sensed a looming environmental catastrophe. How could you possibly repeat any of those things in a lab?

Parts of the *Enhancing Human Performance* report are online, so I dig in. I'm most intrigued by what I find in its preface. I tend to skip prefaces on principle—if it's important information, you should call it chapter one and start your page numbering there. But because it's one of the only available sections, I dig in. I learn that the report was commissioned by the US Army Research Institute.

I know nothing should surprise me at this point. But . . . *the US Army studies ESP?*

I Google further, digging down to the website of the US Army

Research Institute. It's "under construction." A near-blank home page tells interested parties that they can visit the institute itself in Virginia or consult its archives . . . *located in Peabody Library, Henley University.*

That's when I get a twitch. It's less mental light bulb than electric shock. My body convulses, just for an instant. Then it's gone. Granted, I'm anxious and lonely and sleep deprived. But I also recognize this as something different.

I have no idea what it's supposed to mean or signify—if anything—but it gets my attention. And it gets me dressed.

No doubt this archive's convenient location has a lot to do with my great-uncle's research. I also guess that my dad must know something about it. I hit his number on speed dial, but the call goes straight to voice mail.

"Hi, Dad. It's your daughter again. Call me, okay? Please call me. Like, as soon as you get this. And, um . . . just call me. Thanks."

IT'S 5:24 A.M. WHEN I slip out of Uncle Brian's house and head for campus. I hurry through the empty and silent green. When I arrive at the library's doors, I find a boy sitting off to the side, passed out drunk. At least that's what I'm guessing from the wet stain on his T-shirt and the empty beer bottle on which his flip-flops hang. I never thought I'd be happy to stumble across a pasty, wasted college student, but there's something about seeing this kid snoozing peacefully out in the open while a shooter's at large that makes me feel protected here in this ivory tower.

I sidestep the guy and pull the library's door handle. Locked. I peer through the door's window and see nothing but darkness inside. I pull again, harder this time, because I'm mad at myself for not checking library hours, but succeed only in waking Sir Pale Ale, whose eyes pop open.

He scrambles to his feet and puts on his flip-flops. "What time is it?" he croaks. He wipes the back of his hand against his mouth then rubs the top of his head several times.

I check my phone. "It's about ten to six."

A look of confusion flashes across his face. "In the morning?"

"Yeah."

"Thank God," he mutters, scratching his belly.

"Hey, what time does this place open?"

"Eight."

I chew my lip, glancing back toward Brian's house. "Dammit."

"You really need to find an answer that bad, huh?" He stretches and yawns for several seconds like a cartoon bear greeting the morning. I can see his belly protruding from under his T-shirt.

I turn and examine the door's lock to see if I can get in another way. I'm fairly certain I could pick it, but I imagine the door will be alarmed. When I look up at the corners of the eaves, I see the security cameras trained at the stoop.

"Thanks anyway," I mumble.

I walk over to the chapel and sit on its stairs to think for a while. At least it's getting light out. I can see a few security guards roaming the green. But when I close my eyes and turn my face in the direction of the sun, it's like I've hit the sleep button on the computer. Everything spontaneously powers down.

WHEN MY EYES OPEN, the first thing I do is check my phone clock. It's a few minutes before eight. I stroll back over to the library and get into the line that has already formed at the door. Flip-Flops is still there, leaning against the side of the building. He nods to me as I walk in.

Inside, a guard checks Henley IDs. After I flash mine, I head straight for the information desk where a librarian is setting herself up for the day. She takes a big swig from her to-go mug, closes her eyes, and seems to meditate on the caffeine for a moment.

"May I help you?"

"US Army Research Institute archive?" I wonder what she'll make of this request since it feels somehow illicit to me.

"Ask in the Special Collections Room," she replies, unfazed. She points to a room at the other end of the library. "Most of the archive's on microfilm."

"Microfilm, right." I wait, hoping she'll explain what that means. Instead she just nods in the direction of the room, then picks up her coffee mug, closes her eyes, and takes another good slug. Though this woman couldn't be less interested in my research, I wonder if the other HEARs know about this archive, if they know why the US Army would be interested in ESP research, if they know my uncle's lab is in trouble.

The Special Collections Room turns out to be a soaring two-story rotunda. The second floor balcony is lined with curving bookshelves, and the ground floor features reading tables and several glassed-in exhibits featuring books and drawings. At the back is an information desk, behind which is a floor-to-ceiling cabinet containing metal drawers of various sizes.

The girl behind the desk is looking in one of the drawers.

I clear my throat to get her attention.

"Sorry!" she says, turning around. I recognize her as the pretty Brit brunette from the Hounskull Club the other night. "Can I help you?"

"I need the microfilm for the US Army Research Institute archive?" Smiling, I add, "Dumb question, I know, but . . . what *is* microfilm?"

She gives a sympathetic laugh. "Not a dumb question." Then she leans in conspiratorially. "I wasn't sure myself until after I'd worked here for a few weeks. Microfilm and its cousin microfiche are photographic reproductions of images copied at one twenty-fifth their normal size, hence 'micro.'"

"Aha, thanks. So how do I—"

"See what's on them?" she interjects. "Right. In order to see those images, you thread the film through a dedicated machine—a fiche reader—which you'll find over there." She points to three big machines on the other side of the room. "And it magnifies the pictures onto a projector inside the machine. You look at it through a binocular-like eyepiece, like the kind they use in eye exams at the optometrist."

I nod, suppressing a groan. "They don't have this information stored anywhere else too, do they? Online or a DVD or something?"

"Not yet," she replies. "We're working on scanning the archive. Though the library looks impressive, we haven't quite made it to the twenty-first century yet." She waves her arm at the drawers of cataloged material behind her. "Truth be told, we've barely reached the twentieth century. Just give me the call numbers for the archives you want, and I'll get them for you."

"Okay, thanks." This would be a lot easier if I actually knew what I was looking for. "I guess I'll start with whatever's first in the army archive."

"Sure." She walks to her computer terminal and types something in. Finding the corresponding call number in one of the drawers, she hands me the box of film. "Good luck."

"Thanks." It takes me a while to figure out how to thread the film, but once it's in, I give the front dial a spin and watch the now magnified pages fly across the projector. When I start turning the wheel more slowly, I catch glimpses of words and phrases until I finally strike gold: Brian's name whirs by.

I turn the dial to focus on the image and begin reading the

report—or as much of it as I can. A lot of words and phrases, even entire sections, are blacked out.

In the preparation of this report, we owe a great debt of gratitude to Star Gate lead researcher, Dr. Brian Black. Dr. Black was instrumental in helping us ██████████. And without the willingness of ██████████ to cooperate with the US Army's ongoing exploration of ██████████, we are convinced that ██████████.

I spend the better part of the next hour my eyes pressed so closely to the film reader that my pupils start burning. I don't find anything else with Brian's name in it.

Some of the pages read like the way he talks, which makes me think he might have written them himself, but the rest concern the army's own research into ESP. They describe predictions from "subjects" identified only by their initials and match them to corresponding articles about disasters—every imaginable horror, from avalanches to explosions in coal mines. Another section compiles the program's failures: forecasts so ridiculously off the mark that the comments made afterward suggest that they put the institute itself in jeopardy.

I push my chair away from the viewing machine and rub my bleary eyes. I don't know what I'm supposed to make of any of this. I take a few deep breaths, eyes still closed, trying to process what I've read—

A brief shudder of nausea ripples through me. It leaves a tingly wake as it passes.

I squeeze my eyes shut tighter, desperate to flush the feeling out, and in the darkness of my mind's eye, I see a sniper.

But this shooter isn't in a mall, and the environment doesn't look like it's anywhere on or near the Henley campus. The sniper is standing in a nondescript room, setting up a rifle on a window ledge. When he peers through the scope of his weapon, I can see the scene below: a crowd of people on the street is gathered around one man.

The man at the center is the one shaking hands with the others.

The man at the center is the one running for office.

The man at the center is the one whose head explodes after the sniper pulls the trigger, fragments of skull blasting apart in a shower of blood and brain matter.

My eyes snap open. My head jerks forward. I can't breathe. Four letters appear to me: UCLA.

What the hell?

I blink hard several times and try to scrub the image from my mind. Is this the same shooter who killed Graham Pinberg? Someone else? And UCLA? *University of California, Los Angeles?* Is that where this takes place, on the other side of the country? It doesn't make sense, but questions keep coming: Who was the man who was shot? A teacher? An administrator? When does this happen?

Disoriented, I look at my phone to see how much time has passed. I'm late for lab. I've got to get out of here as quickly as possible. With trembling fingers, I rebox the microfilm and hand it back to the pretty Brit at the desk.

"Did you find what you need?" she asks.

I can't even muster a nod. "I have no idea."

CHAPTER ELEVEN

I run as fast as I can from the library to the Merion Building. But when I reach the lobby, I skid to a stop in front of a makeshift memorial for Professor Pinberg. There are clusters of bouquets and votive candles underneath his framed photo, which hangs on the wall. Next to his picture, someone has taped a piece of paper scrawled with the following inscription:

THE LAW OF CONSERVATION OF ENERGY:
The total amount of energy in an isolated system remains
constant over time. A consequence of this law is that energy can
neither be created nor destroyed: it can only be transformed from
one state to another.

R.I.P. Professor Graham Pinberg, gifted scientist, inspiring
teacher, beloved human.

My throat catches as Graham Pinberg again becomes *real*: an actual person and not just a random shooting victim. I think about the loss of this man who meant so much to so many.

I hurry on to the lab, wondering what I'll offer as an excuse for my tardiness, trying to convince myself that in the grand scheme of things it really doesn't matter if I'm a few minutes late. But when I enter to see that Uncle Brian still hasn't arrived, I heave a sigh of relief.

All the other HEARs are sitting on their stools.

"I lost track of time at the library," I blurt, feeling the need to justify my lateness.

Pankaj laughs. "At the library? A likely story, Legacy."

I see the glint in his eye as I take my own seat. It's like he knows something—something about *me*—and I feel exposed, like I did when he saw my bear, Henry. Pankaj keeps smiling, hands pressed against the table in front of him, revealing the definition of the long, lean muscles of his forearms. The right sleeve of his black T-shirt is carelessly pushed up, giving me a peek at a strong bicep too. My eyes linger there for a moment longer than they should. When I finally look away, I'm embarrassed, like I've just seen something I shouldn't—something private, something intimate.

"And what were you doing at the library?" he asks.

I hesitate. I want to know how much *they* know about my uncle, but I'm not sure how much I should reveal. If I've learned anything from my past activities as "Ally X," it's that by staying quiet you put yourself at less risk; you face less exposure. As soon as you open your mouth, you subject yourself to misinterpretation, especially by people you don't know well or people you don't know you can trust.

"Well, I was looking at the pretty picture books," I say sarcastically. "Just like I'm sure you did when you were there, Rocket."

As Pankaj stares back at me from under those sideswept black bangs, I wonder what he *was* doing at the library the night I arrived on campus. It's not as if he needed to do any work for classes or research for Uncle Brian.

Our eyes fixed on each other, it feels like we're in the middle of a tug-of-war.

"That's strange," Mara interjects, her tone clipped and her voice a notch louder than it should be. "After our trip to the museum, I sensed you didn't like looking at pictures, Kass. I thought you found the whole thing really intimidating."

"You're intimidated by art?" Dan asks.

"By artists," Mara replies for me. She peels a piece of ginger candy out of its wax paper wrapper and pops it into her mouth, almost daring me to respond.

"It's because most artists are seriously unhinged," I say. "But the way they twist and misinterpret obvious signs and signals is always really interesting to me."

Alex leans forward in his chair. "So, Kass, here's what you missed when you were at 'the library.'" With his mocking tone, he manages to poke fun at both Pankaj's teasing and my supposed studiousness. "I was just telling these guys that when I was roaming around the campus, you know, after the shooting, I ran into this girl I'd seen around once or twice before. I guess she could see how upset I was and we started chatting. She probably just felt sorry for me."

Yeah, right, I think. I'm sure this girl's motives were that pure.

"Anyway, she invited me to a party in her friends' room tonight. Should be fun, and I want you guys to come with."

"Who is this mystery girl?" Mara grumbles.

"Her name's Erika. Comp lit major. Silky brown hair, sea-green eyes, and a British accent that's to die for."

I'm tempted to ask if it's the Hounskull girl, the one who works in the Peabody Special Collections Room, but at that moment, Uncle Brian walks in—with three empty wineglasses.

"No, I haven't been drinking," he says dryly by way of a greeting. He places the glasses on the front workstation. "But as someone who's traditionally found his solace in work, especially during difficult moments, I hope you'll understand why I need to stay focused on our project. It's through experimentation and hard work that we make discoveries and unearth logic, and these things seem in short supply at a time like this."

We all nod in understanding. Brian catches my eye. In that moment, I also get that he wants to proceed as if the program's not in jeopardy, as if its survival is assured. So I give him another nod to let him know I'll keep his confidence.

"Thank you," Brian says. "Now, you may also wonder, will I be filling these glasses with wine? I'm sorry to tell you the answer is no."

"What if I do *really* well?" Pankaj jokes.

"Then paradoxically you'll experience failure, and you'll be even happier the glass is empty."

"Huh?" Pankaj turns to Dan. "Did you understand that, or am I somehow drunk already?"

Brian laughs. "The failure I refer to will be that of the glass itself." He picks one up by the stem and holds it out for our inspection. "No visible chips or cracks, a nice weight, not even a stray lipstick mark . . . But this glass is covered with fissures and defects that are invisible to the naked eye. Keep that in mind." He sets the glass down. "Every material, from glass to concrete, has a natural frequency at which it vibrates, a 'resonant frequency.'" He walks over to the whiteboard and writes the term in all caps. "Imagine a tower of Jell-O is sitting on a tray. What happens if I send energy into it by giving that tray a shove?"

"The Jell-O starts jiggling," I say.

"Right, and if you shove it hard enough, eventually you'll be able to get it to break apart. Of course, every object has a different resonant frequency, so you'd have to send a great deal more energy into a slab of concrete to get it to jiggle like Jell-O. Now, what other phenomena produce vibrational energy?"

"Sound waves," Dan says.

"Very good."

"Professor, should we start warming up our vocal cords?" asks Alex with an amused nod at the glasses.

"That is not what I have planned."

But suddenly I think I know what he does have planned. "You want to see if we can shatter these glasses with our brain waves, don't you?"

He smiles at me. "Correct."

Before anyone can respond, protest, or even laugh, my phone rings. As the telltale "Big Poppa" ringtone blares, my eyes widen in panic. Guiltily, I shove my hand into my bag to silence it.

"Kassandra," he says, "when you find your phone, I want you to tell your father that he should refrain from calling you again, even if he is simply returning your calls."

I feel my head nodding as my fingers wrap around the familiar shape and yank it up to my ear. "Hello?" I croak.

"Kassie! So glad to reach you."

Dad. The sound of his voice causes a small lump to materialize in my throat. But Uncle Brian fixes me with his stare, and I can't unlock from his gaze.

"Dad, I'm really sorry, but I can't talk now." My uncle rolls his hand to remind me of the message I need to deliver. "Oh, and, um, parents can't call while we're here, so I gotta go. Sorry."

"Kass, are you all right? Please—"

I hang up and slip the phone back into my bag. My hands shake. I hear myself breathing heavily and try to be still and silent.

"I did wonder who'd be the first to break that rule," Brian says dispassionately. He turns back to the wineglasses.

"Who'd you guess?" asks Alex.

"I had odds on Kass. But back to our work. As I was saying, your goal is to shatter one of these glasses with the energy your brain waves emit. I'm going to make it easy on you this morning and let you put your heads together on this one, so today you'll be working in teams of two. However, it seems only fair that, because Kass broke the phone call rule and was late today, she'll go it alone."

Glorious. My cheeks feel as if they're on fire. Still, something dawns on me: Uncle Brian came in after I did. He should have no way of knowing I was late . . .

"Mara, you work with Pankaj. Dan, you team with Alex." Brian hands each team a glass, then gives me the one that remains. He reaches into a cabinet and pulls out five pairs of safety goggles. "Better safe than sorry," he adds, handing them out.

We move to stations well apart from one another. I set my wineglass in the middle of my table, grateful for the distraction, grateful that there's no attention focused on me right now, ready to work. But I'm starting to feel midmorning fuzzy from lack of sleep. I put the lab goggles on, close my eyes, and try to focus on quieting my breathing. Keeping it even and soft. As the repetitive inhalations and exhalations fill my ears, I feel that electric twitch again.

The sniper.

Once more, I'm witnessing the execution, an act of violence I cannot place, recognize, or comprehend. I'm left only with the visceral feeling of a witness: terror. It's not the mall shooting; it's political. It's not recent either. In the aftermath, I stay with the gunman. He stows his rifle in a bag then dashes down a stairwell and into an alley, empty but for one abandoned car. The assassin flings open the back passenger-side door and dives inside. A driver, previously concealed, bolts up behind the wheel. The car is in motion even before the sniper has the chance to yank his door closed.

As the car peels onto the street, I see the CONSUL license plate bearing the code for the United States.

The baseball-capped driver looks in the rear view mirror to check if anyone's following. I know the face; I've seen it before. But it isn't until the man takes off his cap and a ponytail tumbles out that I recognize the driver as Chris Figg, my uncle's colleague and the director of Camp Dodona.

When my eyes pop open, I find myself staring at the wineglass in front of me.

It shatters with a loud and frightening resonance.

CHAPTER TWELVE

To get to Alex's friend's party, I need to enter the university through Amory Gate, at the north edge of campus. Its imposing size and ornate filigree design make it an iconic reminder of how beautiful and daunting this place can be. And as I approach, I remember my first encounter here, when I received that hard shove for attempting to exit through its middle arch. Though campus custom does permit me to *enter* through the central access point, I'm not taking any chances tonight. I scurry through the door on the far left side, unable to shake the feeling that people are watching and waiting to pounce.

I'm still trying to figure out how to process the vision of my former camp director at the wheel of the getaway car for an assassination. I wasn't about to trouble Uncle Brian with it. To start, I have no idea if it even happened or whether this powerful "brain wave" was just the result of my imagination running wild. But what was very real, and what remains in the front of my mind, is the shattered wineglass and the energy I produced to destroy it. I felt like a live wire for the rest of the afternoon.

That was one of the reasons I decided to go for a run before the party this evening.

It was my first since I arrived at Henley. In my old life, running was a bit of a religion for me. It not only made me feel better; it made me feel smarter. There's hard science behind that too: running causes brain-cell growth. So I did cross-country in the fall, indoor in the winter, and outdoor track in the spring. And though I discovered I liked being part of a team—being part of a group instead of acting independently was novel for me—I joined because it forced me to run every day. Considering my other major "extracurricular," possessing stamina and the ability to sprint seemed like very good things indeed.

Ironically, before today, the last time I sprinted was the day I got caught breaking into Sean Mitchell's car: the crime that landed me here.

IN RETROSPECT, I SHOULD have turned around and gone straight home after my conversation with Pete Lewis.

I didn't *exactly* lie to Mara when the topic turned to love. Pete was boy I'd been in love with for as long as I could remember.

I'd gone looking for Pete that afternoon and found him by the soccer field before his practice. A classmate of ours had been assaulted after passing out at a party, and Pete's friend Sean was the perpetrator. Pete knew it too; rumor was Sean had shown friends the video on his cell phone. But when I asked Pete to do the right thing and stand up for the girl, he not only refused; Pete told me not to worry about it. "It really wasn't a big deal," he said, and he added that the girl had always liked Sean. As if that made it okay.

His response enraged me, and it destroyed my illusion of the person I believed Pete to be. I'd spent years thinking I was in love with this boy. But the "Pete" I loved was kind and smart and had a sense of right and wrong. He bore no resemblance to this heartless and witless asshole. It was all so clear, so plain now: I was in love with a fantasy, not the real person. I'd been deluding myself about him from the start.

I knew I needed to calm down. I knew I needed to regroup and recover. But though I felt sick to my stomach, I decided that if Pete wouldn't help, I would make things right on my own. I knew Sean kept his phone in his book bag, and he always locked his bag in his car before practice. I would get into the car, take the phone, and anonymously turn over the evidence to the authorities.

Straightforward enough.

I didn't count on the squad car.

Though I knew the local police cruised the school grounds on a semi-regular basis, I wasn't thinking properly or "seeing" straight. So I somehow missed the approaching patrol car. I was sliding the wire lock pick through Sean's window when the police car rolled to a stop in front of me. The police officer called out to me and I panicked. Then I started running.

Jumping out of his car, the cop pursued me on foot. I ran for the familiar territory of the woods behind the school. I knew I'd opened a good distance between us, but I couldn't resist the urge to look back to double-check.

Another mistake.

Turning, I failed to see the root of a tree directly ahead of me, and a fraction of a second later, my arms were dog-paddling the air as I went slamming into the ground. It was a bone-rattling fall, and as I scrambled to my feet, the officer threw his body at me, making me his tackling dummy. It took him a three count before he was able to catch his breath and huff out the words: "I . . . said . . . 'Freeze' . . . bitch!"

I tried to explain. The problem was that I was the one who'd been caught in the act of committing a crime, and by the time Sean was "strongly encouraged" to hand over his phone, the video he'd taken had magically disappeared. No evidence of the assault remained. An official search warrant was required to try to retrieve the file, so the powers that be decided on a deal: official charges wouldn't be pressed against Sean or me. However, *my* "obstruction of justice"—running away from the police on school grounds—was crime enough to get me expelled.

I spent my run this afternoon mentally rehashing the whole incident, regretting what I could and should have done differently. Who would have guessed my need to sprint now would somehow feel every bit as strong as it did in the past?

THE PARTY IS IN a baking-hot suite on the second floor of a senior dorm. It's in full swing by the time I arrive. The guys who live here have tricked the place out nicely, and they've even set up a small bar next to the fireplace where the keg sits. A combination of stolen road signs and neon beer ads adorn the walls along with a giant Henley banner, navy blue stitched with gold.

My eyes immediately find Pankaj sitting at a poker table in one corner of the room. I don't see the others, so I meander over. Pankaj has changed his clothes since earlier in the day. Instead of the black T, he's in a short-sleeved ivory-colored guayabera shirt. He looks cool, almost elegant, and there's a calm intensity in his amber eyes. I can practically picture him in a party scene in an alcohol ad.

The poker table is one of those authentic green-felt deals, and it looks like it's been passed down from student to student for decades. You can probably date it by the rings left by wet beer cups. The three other guys at the table are all beefy, and they all sport Henley-branded athletic wear. There also are two girls at the table. One's wearing a baseball cap slung low on her forehead. She's studying the game with an intense look of concentration. The other is the preppy Brit from the library, who I'm now positive is the one who invited Alex, though Alex is nowhere to be seen.

When the hand is called, Pankaj lays out his cards for the others to see. He smiles at the guy directly across from him. The guy doesn't smile back.

"Well," Pankaj says, "I guess that's how it goes." He reaches into the center of the table and sweeps up not only the pile of chips but also an expensive-looking watch.

Not good, I think. When personal belongings become part of the pot, it tends to mean two things: (1) a player is desperate and out of money, but still eager to gamble; (2) that same player is getting hustled. That's when trouble starts. Especially if alcohol is involved.

The guy's cheeks flush. His hairline is soaked with sweat. I can't tell if this is because it's insanely hot in the room, because he's drunk, or because he's hot, drunk, *and* angry. The guy's got about forty pounds on Pankaj, some muscle, some flab.

"You cheated," the guy hisses.

"I don't know what you're talking about, man." Pankaj's tone is calm as he shakes his head. "I was sitting here playing, same as you."

"You were counting."

"Which is technically not illegal," the British girl says. "Just frowned upon."

"He was counting cards," the guy repeats to the other two guys. He pushes his chair back and stands. "So you either give me my watch back right now, or—"

"Or what?" one of the other guys interrupts with a menacing grin. It seems like he already knows the answer to his own question. He stands too, as does the third guy.

"Or I'll make him sorry."

"I understand why you're upset," Pankaj says. "This is a very nice watch." In a fluid movement, he takes it from his right hand and slides it over his left hand, clasping it on his wrist. "If you want to try to win it back, I'm happy to keep playing."

I glance around the room. I wonder how many of this guy's friends will join in on the "make him sorry" promise. It doesn't seem like an especially violent crowd, but heat, beer, losing, and testosterone is never a great combination . . . I move to the nearest window, look down at the ground floor below, and yank the window up as far as I can.

"Thanks," the Brit says to me, trying to fan herself with her hand.

"I know, right? So hot in here." I walk back to the table as things appear to be getting even more heated.

"You have ten seconds to take my watch off your arm and give it back to me," the first guy barks. "One . . ."

Pankaj, who's also now on his feet, seems unfazed.

"Two . . . three . . ."

I look at the guy. I am certain when he gets to "nine" he's going to hop over the table and deck Pankaj. I don't think this is nearly as obvious to Pankaj, though.

"Six . . . sev—"

"My contact! I just lost my contact!" I shout. "Can anyone help me look for it?" I bend down, purposely knocking into a few people near me to create a distraction. Only one person makes an effort to help, but that's enough. The time and space allow me to dart forward and grab Pankaj's hand. "Follow me," I whisper, yanking him down to a crouch so the crowd obscures us and then pulling him back to the open window. "Jump!" He flashes me an *are you crazy?* look, requiring me to add: "It's two flights, you baby! Jump!"

His poker rivals rush from the table. Their chairs crash to the floor behind them.

"Gangway!" Pankaj whisper yells, then hops out the window. I vault out behind him. It's only in midair that I realize it actually *is* pretty far to the ground. When I land, I fall onto my back with a thud.

"What the hell?" someone shouts above us.

Followed by: "Where'd he go?"

Pankaj leaps to his feet and helps me to mine, dusting the dirt and grass off his ivory linen shirt. "You didn't have to do that. I had everything under control and—"

"Quiet!" I whisper. My back is aching, and my sides are bruised, but I ignore the pain. We're still right below the window, right at the edge of the building, far too close for comfort, but because I'm unfamiliar with the environment, I don't know if we should try to make a run for it now or stay hidden. A second later the question is answered for us. The heavy wooden dorm door slams open, and out comes a stampede. It's hard to tell how many of the guys have mobilized, but the odds of outrunning them have just plunged.

My eyes scour our surroundings in a panic. The nearby shrub is just big enough to conceal one of us. I stop thinking as instinct and adrenaline take over. With one hand I grab the top of Pankaj's arm; with the other I reach for the back of his head. I yank him to me because I need to make this believable; I need to make this appear spontaneously passionate and sloppy. I kiss him hard, pushing him into the shrub and shielding him from the group of guys who gallop past us.

"Show your face, asshole!" the watchless loser yells into the night . . . not in our direction. Several of his friends are screaming taunts of their own. They're still close by, but moving farther away. There's also a high-pitched voice screaming inside my head: *We do NOT kiss first. This is NOT. WHAT. WE. DO!* And then another tone comes through, this one lower and calmer. It's the voice of my inner strategist, who is confident enough to tell my inner Miss Manners to shut up. I basically smother Pankaj to prevent him from being seen.

"Get back here, dick!" another voice calls out. "And give Pat his watch back!"

I know Pankaj wants to show himself; he wants to prove that he can take whatever it is they throw at him. I also know that this isn't going to be a fair fight; there are too many of them. With every shout, Pankaj squirms, and I can feel the tug of his pride and his need to his defend himself. I understand it, I even respect it, but I am not going to let this happen, so I inhale deeply and press myself against him more urgently.

At a certain point, a magnetic pull takes over, and we're drawn into one another with what feels like a furious click. His lips are on my cheek, my tongue, my neck. There's no space or air between us. The force keeps us pinned to one another . . . until I realize that the air is still and silent.

My heart is pounding. My clothes are mess; so are his. The lovely linen shirt is now totally wrinkled, grass stained, and smudged with dirt. I have no idea how much time has passed. Either the unhappy meatheads have run far enough away that we can no longer hear them, or they've abandoned their mission and headed back to the party.

Pankaj blinks at me. He runs his long hand through his hair. It's trembling slightly. "You know, you're pretty good at that, Legacy," he murmurs.

"I come from a long line of perfectionists," I say, realizing the bobby pin that was holding my hair back now hangs uselessly at the side of my head. I can only imagine what I look like—and it's not perfection.

He laughs. "There might be something to this whole genetic inheritance thing after all." After a peek at his new watch, he shakes his head. Then he unclasps the watch and slides his hand out of it. "Here," he says, holding the watch out to me. "You've earned this."

"No way." I reposition the bobby pin, dust off the dirt and stray leaves still stuck to my shirt, and stand straight. "I couldn't possibly. You won that fair and square." I cock my right eyebrow at him. "Didn't you, Rocket?"

"Welllllll, that might depend on your definitions of 'fair' and 'square.'"

I smile. "So," I say, "I guess we're not going to be heading back to the party?"

His eyes go to the second floor window, and he shakes his head. "No, I think I might head back to my room. Do you . . . Maybe want to come with me?"

Before I can answer, flashing lights start blinking in front of me. They float across my field of vision in blue and orange striped bars. Almost immediately I feel dizzy. "I uh." I wobble backward.

"I mean, it's no big deal," he replies, trying to backtrack.

"No, it's that I'm starting to feel . . ." I don't exactly know how to describe it. "It's weird. I started seeing these multicolored, flashing lights."

"Floaters? I get them too. Usually at the beginning of a migraine. Is your head hurting?"

"No, but I'm starting to feel a little nauseous."

"I will do my best to assume that's unrelated to my invitation."

I manage a laugh, but I'm starting to feel worse. "I think I should head back to my uncle's house . . ."

"Do you want me to walk you?"

I shake my head. I'm happy he asked, but I'm worried that

at any minute I'm going to hurl. The only thing that makes throwing up any more uncomfortable than it already is is yakking in front of someone else. "That's okay. You don't have to."

"I know I don't have to," he responds. "But you saved my ass back there. The least I can do is hold your hair back and avert my eyes if you barf."

There is genuine concern for me on his face, and I cave. Despite my desire to act brave, I *would* like the escort. He extends his arm, and I take hold of it. It's exactly as strong and steady as I imagined it to be.

CHAPTER THIRTEEN

By the time Pankaj and I reach my uncle's house, a headache has taken over my entire skull, the pain echoing inside. We've been walking in silence; I'm not feeling well enough to banter, and besides, I don't want to say anything stupid or that I might regret. He doesn't seem that interested in banter either. We stop in the shadow of the front walk.

"Thank you," I say. It comes out as a whisper.

Pankaj smiles, leans in, and gives me a soft kiss on the cheek. "Feel better," he says as he squeezes my hand. "And sweet dreams." He turns and walks back in the direction of campus.

I watch him disappear down the road before heading for the front door. Under the florescent glow of the porch light, I start rubbing my eyes to try to get the pain in my head to subside. Incredibly, the more I paw at my eyes, the more I seem able to keep the throbbing at bay. I reach into my pocket to retrieve my key, and I feel something smooth and metallic collide with my right hand: the not-so-fairly-and-squarely won watch. I half smile, half wince, sliding my hand through the steel wristband, and clasp it on my wrist.

As I look down at the watch's face, I'm seized with such an intense sensation of vertigo it feels like I've just been let go after being spun in circles. I grip the doorjamb, shutting my eyes tightly to stop myself from crashing to the ground.

That's when I see the explosion.

A fireball shatters windows and blows the doors off a small white house. Its orange-brown clay-tile roof buckles with the blast. The body of a woman flies out of the house, limbs limp, like a tossed rag doll's. Seconds later, two men—one wearing an aqua T under a white sports coat, the other dressed in a Hawaiian shirt—stumble out of the gaping hole that was once the door of the burning building. They're coughing violently, covered in black soot and blood. The man in the sports coat scans the area as he staggers around the debris-strewn street. He seems to be looking for movement, for any sign that the bombers are still nearby. But the only motion is in the distance. Windblown foreign flags wave and snap at the base of an enormous statue—a sixty-foot-tall figure of a man in a broad-brimmed cowboy hat.

The second man out of the building, the man in the Hawaiian shirt, has run directly for the woman. He gathers her in his arms and presses his ear to her heart. Her eyes are lifeless. He pulls away, his mouth open in a silent, anguished howl . . .

And then I'm released from the vision's hold. The headache is gone too. Stranger still, as I slide the key into the lock and twist, another sensation fills me: euphoria. I feel a rush of something wonderful, totally disconnected from the horror I just witnessed. It's as if the pain grew like a soap bubble to create the vision and then popped, sprinkling everything with a rainbow-tinted afterglow.

I close the door behind me and hurry to the mantel in the living room. To that picture of Uncle Brian and that woman . . . and just as I remembered, he's sitting in a café in an all-too-familiar Hawaiian shirt. Having focused only on Brian and the woman with whom he was so clearly in love, I failed to notice before what was in the background of the shot: a looming silhouette of a man in a broad-brimmed hat.

"Uncle Brian?" I call out. I head back into the entry hall. "Uncle Brian!" I shout with more urgency.

"Kass?" His muted reply floats down the stairs. "I'm in my room."

I glance at my new watch. It's past midnight. I'm late for curfew, and I've probably just woken him, but I don't care. I need answers. *Now.* "Okay, I'll come up there."

"No," he shouts back quickly. "Give me a moment. I'll be right down."

I head back into the living room and sit in his chair. As I wait, I try to catalog all the various tchotchkes on the bookshelves and windowsills, the random items a person collects over the course of his life that paint the story of who he is. Or the person he tries to convince others he is. Now that I'm focused, I notice that there are a lot of items from Latin America: a small brightly colored wool rug (the kind the hippie kids wear as ponchos); a fuzzy little llama sculpture; woven baskets; and candle holders.

"Do you approve?" Uncle Brian says as he shuffles into the room, catching me mid-inventory.

"Is it all from one trip, or have you traveled to Latin America a lot?"

He tightens the belt on his robe then runs his hand over his face. The skin under his eyes is puffy and pink. His face looks haggard, his body tense. "Is that really what you wanted to ask me?"

I shake my head. "I'm sorry if I woke you."

"You didn't." He pauses, puts his hands in the pockets of his robe. "I haven't really slept much since Graham was murdered, if you want to know the truth."

Seeing my great-uncle in this state, I no longer have the stomach to pump him with questions. So I sit there, mute, as he stands over me, waiting for me to say something.

"Um, I was just wondering if they'd made any progress in the investigation?" I ask lamely. "Like, are they any closer to finding the person or figuring out who did it?"

Brian shakes his head. "Not that I'm aware, no. I realize this must be very upsetting for you too."

I nod. That much is true. "I just hope they catch the guy soon." This too is true.

Brian nods. "Why don't I make us some tea? Hopefully it will soothe us both."

"That sounds great, thanks." I stand and follow him into the kitchen. But in the light, I pause, realizing just how dirty my clothes are from my roll on the ground with Pankaj. "Uh . . . I'm just going to change into my pj's," I mumble, heading for the stairs. "Be right back down."

"Take your time," he replies. "I'll put the kettle on."

As I climb the steps, there's twitch in the reptilian part of my brain. It's the part that acts before it thinks. I'm *aware* I'm about to do something ill-advised. But even my superego isn't strong enough to stop me from doing it.

I look at my new watch and give myself six minutes.

After loudly padding into the observatory, I strip off my clothes, throw my nightshirt over my head, and exit silently. (Watch check: 5:20 remaining.) Back in the hallway, I start moving on my toes, placing my feet slowly and gently on the floor in front of me. Once I'm up the stairs on the third floor, I switch to my soundless and stealthy fox walk, touching each foot lightly to the ground so that the outside edge hits first, then rolling the foot inward until the whole surface area of the sole is down.

There are doors to my left and right, both partially open, and one at the end of the hall, which is closed. I assume that's Brian's bedroom, so that's the door I walk through (4:53).

The hardwood floor is partially covered by a worn Persian rug, and a large bed takes up most of the back wall. On the nightstand rest a glass of water on a coaster and a heaping stack of books, each with a bookmark jutting out of its pages. There's also a small wooden desk in front of the window and a corkboard hanging on the wall to the left. For such an eccentric, he has a disappointingly normal bedroom . . . at least at first glance. Unsure what I'm looking for, I slink over to the bulletin board.

Tacked up is a Polaroid photo of my uncle, who looks like he's in his thirties, ice skates hanging off his shoulder. He's holding the mittened hand of a young woman—the same woman from the picture downstairs, the same woman killed in that explosion. Though they're standing together at the edge of a crowded rink, they're looking at each other as if they're the only two people in the world. They are the stars of their own epic romance. Written in neat block letters in the white space below the image is a quotation: *"Gravitation cannot be held responsible for people falling in love."—Albert Einstein.* There's an asterisk under the quote followed by the words: *"But it CAN and MUST be held responsible for my fall on that ice."—Ellen Rios.*

So that's her name (4:21).

Still unsure of what I hope to find, I poke my head into the closet. The heap of junk at the bottom makes it look like Uncle Brian's been in a perpetual state of "throw everything where no one can see it" housekeeping.

Unless . . .

Unless that's the point. Getting on my hands and knees, I dig through the pile until I find small safe he's hidden here (4:08). My new lock pick is ideal for this type of work, but it's in my bag downstairs, and I can't risk the exposure of going back to get it. I need to make something work here, so I scan the room. On Brian's desk is a single paper clip. That'll do. Once I straighten the clip and refashion it into a tension tool, I pull the bobby pin from my hair and bend the end, turning it into a pick (2:34).

It takes me longer than I hoped to get into the safe, but eventually I hear that telltale click, and the door swings open (1:47). I rifle through the papers inside until I find a file with a tab marked UCLA. My pulse quickens: the letters from my first vision. I flip open the folder.

Reading the front page of the report inside, stamped with the word CONFIDENTIAL in red ink, I discover that UCLA doesn't stand for University of California, Los Angeles, as I assumed. It's an acronym for something else entirely:

> *Though controversial, the CIA's use of the UCLAs (Unilaterally Controlled Latino Assets) in Nicaragua in the 1980s proved a highly effective tool of governmental destabilization.*

My head spins. I try to process this information. What the hell does "Unilaterally Controlled" even mean? It sounds shady, wrong, and racist. Though my visions now have some context, they feel even more unclear and unsettling to me. Both the assassination of the candidate and the bombing must, in some way, be related to these tools of destabilization. And Brian was somehow connected to these various tragedies, if not directly responsible. More than ever, I need to know the role he played then and the role he's playing now.

"Kass!" Uncle Brian shouts from downstairs.

I look at my watch: 0:23. *Damn it.* "Be right there!" I shove the report back in the folder and return it to the safe, throwing the clothes and junk back on top before shutting the closet door. I tiptoe down the hall and hit the stairs, flying down to the second floor before assuming a casual pace. When I get to the bottom step, I see I have two seconds left, though it feels like a year's been taken off my life.

Uncle Brian is steeping the tea when I enter the kitchen. "Sugar?"

"A lot," I manage, somehow not gasping. "Thanks."

Handing me the mug, he looks me in the eye. "Now, what was it that you were so keen to speak to me about when you came home?"

I take a sip of the tea before responding; I need to compose my thoughts. But I also don't want to stall anymore. I need to know who this man really is. "I want you to tell me about your time with the CIA," I say. "Specifically I want to know about Unilaterally Controlled Latino Assets." I'm uncomfortable even saying the words. "What does that even mean?"

Brian takes a step back, his eyes widening with surprise. "How did you—" But he stops. "How much do you know?"

"I've had two visions. Two *really disturbing* visions." I put the tea down on the counter. "You were in the second one. A building you were in blew up. What's UCLA, Uncle Brian?"

Brian's eyes close and he swallows hard. I wonder if he's picturing the scene again too. "The UCLAs were elite teams the CIA put together. They had allegiance only to us, putting the CIA ahead of their own governments and families; that's what 'unilaterally controlled' means. All of the team members, the "assets," were Latino, so—Unilaterally Controlled Latino Assets." He looks down into his mug and stirs his tea. "I worked with them in Managua, Nicaragua. Graham Pinberg, Chris Figg, and I were down there helping them strategize in the fight against the Sandinistas. Graham didn't last very long; didn't suit him. He didn't like the climate. But more pointedly, he didn't like the work we were doing. So he left the Agency and found a job here at Henley."

I nod, feeling somewhat encouraged. He's not trying to hide anything from me, and he seems to be telling the truth. "What about the woman?"

Brian nods. "Ellen. She was the reason I stayed." He pauses momentarily and takes a sip of his tea. "She was the leader of our unit. She was brilliant, she was beautiful, and she was shrewd. She was also the love of my life."

"I'm . . . I'm so sorry." I have a million questions, but don't know what to ask first. "Why did they bomb your house?"

"It was in retaliation for a political assassination."

I nod again. Just as I suspected, the visions *were* connected.

"The US government sent the CIA into Nicaragua to promote 'regime change.' That's what the government does when it wants to get rid of its enemies. So it was our job to assist assets commit acts of sabotage," Brian continues, taking another sip of his tea. "We then trained them to create unrest and undermine governments throughout Latin America."

"By gunning people down?" I ask, first thinking of the vision and then getting a mental flicker of Professor Pinberg's memorial in the Merion Building.

Brian shakes his head. "No, assassinations were rare. The UCLAs generally blew up refineries, ships, and bridges. The idea was to create chaos, especially at the ports, because they were of great economic importance. It was all in the name of stopping the 'dire threat' of communism." His face darkens as his tone turns sarcastic, his eyes far away. "Sadly it's just another dark and ugly chapter in US history. But I left the Agency after . . . Ellen." He shakes his head. "I had to leave after that. I stopped believing in the mission. And I'd come undone."

I lift my own mug to my lips. I want him to keep talking, but

I also don't want to give him the third degree. He's suffering, clearly—not just over the present, but over the past—and I wonder how long he has been.

"So then you and Figg came here?"

"When Graham learned what happened, he reached out to me and suggested I join him at Henley, but Chris stayed on at the Agency. He still had the stomach for it, and he had a particular genius for the work." Brian's tone shifts when he says this; it sounds like less than a compliment. "But it was Ellen who continued to influence me. In fact, she's been the guiding light in my work here at Henley."

I shake my head, not understanding. "What do you mean by that?"

"I told you we were exploring various aspects of ESP. I'm sure it's been difficult to understand the purpose of many of the experiments I've been conducting, but they are all pieces of a larger mosaic. You see, my goal is figuring out how to amplify the neurological response to improve telepathy and strengthen visions. I won't get into the neuroscience now, but essentially I'm trying to create a booster. Imagine going from terrestrial to satellite radio: you'll have access to more channels than you ever dreamed possible."

I've been watching my uncle's lips move, but I basically stopped listening after he said he was more or less creating *an ESP booster shot.*

"Does anyone at Henley know that this is what you're working on?" I ask.

"No, not even Graham."

"But this is huge! Why not tell them at that big Internal Review Board meeting you have coming up?" I'm surprised he hasn't thought of this solution himself. It seems so obvious.

Brian shakes his head. "I can't do that, Kass."

I make a gesture of bewilderment. "Why not?"

"Because if I tell them how close it is to completion, my research could be co-opted. By people I don't know. If it falls into the wrong hands, the results could be deadly."

"More deadly," I say without thinking.

He pauses. "More deadly," he repeats sorrowfully.

CHAPTER FOURTEEN

I wake up early, drenched in sweat, my mind racing after a jumble of strange and upsetting dreams. The only one I can remember clearly involved jumping out a series of windows with Pankaj, and each time we landed more painfully and more tangled up in each other. Apparently our adventure at the party last night made quite an impression on my subconscious. I decide not to delve too deeply into what my mind makes of all this.

Though I itch to get back into Uncle Brian's room, even *I'm* not rash enough to sneak in while's he's still in bed. I put on shorts and a T-shirt, lace up my sneakers, and leave a note for Uncle Brian saying I'll meet him at the lab at nine.

I start my run with a series of intervals, sprinting as hard as I can for short bursts of time. Slowly the BDNF, the brain-derived neurotrophic factor, kicks in. BDNF is a protein that protects you from stress by repairing and resetting the brain's equilibrium, which is why running will genuinely calm you and improve your mood.

Yes, there really *is* science behind it.

So while I feel much better by the time I walk into the lab at 8:57 A.M., the peace of mind is short-lived. Mara enters behind me, chomping loudly on raw ginger. Pankaj and Dan are already seated; Alex and Uncle Brian have yet to arrive. I glance at Pankaj, but his eyes are down as he studiously doodles on a sheet of paper in front of him.

"What happened to you guys last night?" Mara points between Pankaj and me. "I saw you as I came in, and then it was like you both vanished from the party." She puts emphasis on *vanished* as if it implies wrongdoing. I silently curse my great-uncle for encouraging her to go off her meds.

"I had to make a quick exit," Pankaj says, continuing to avoid my gaze, his hand moving in front of his face to brush back his hair. "I think I might have pissed off one of the hosts. I decided it was better to slip out before he broke my arms."

Mara turns to me.

"I got a really bad headache and had to get out of there," I answer, which is not even a total lie. I take my seat, feeling like I've just outsmarted a riddle-asking sphinx.

"Oh, really?" she says. "That must have been awful."

"Yeah, it was—" I don't get to finish the thought because suddenly Mara's behind me, and the force of her hands on my shoulders stuns me. Breathing ginger down my neck, she kneads my muscles with her thumbs as if trying to manipulate dried-out Play-Doh.

"Oh, that's, um . . ." *Incredibly painful.*

"My mom's a masseuse," Mara replies evenly. "The tarot cards suggested things would be especially stressful today, so I just want to make sure everyone starts off as relaxed as possible."

"Thanks," I say, as her left hand grips the base of my neck and the right pushes my head forward. As she jabs at pressure points behind my ears, I wonder if her mother received training at the

Swedish Institute for Massage and Spearfishing. "So," I grunt, "did you have fun at the party?"

How much does she already know? How much can she sense about what happened between Pankaj and me? I can't help wondering if this changes anything between us. Between *any* of us.

But Mara keeps her own cards close and gives nothing away. "Well," she says, "I didn't feel invisible at least. But I don't know if that's good or bad."

"Bad," Dan states. "I didn't think it was fun. It made me uncomfortable."

"Dan"—Mara rolls her eyes—"you're just going to have to get used to the fact that you're very good-looking, and people are going to stare at you."

Pankaj and I exchange a quick smile. I turn and see Mara is smiling too. But Dan's lips are tightly set. He shakes his head.

"I don't like it. Feels exposed, dangerous. And then when I looked for you guys and couldn't find you, I got worried. Thought something bad might have happened."

I wonder if he too might have been encouraged to go off meds. "Dan, I'm really sorry. I didn't mean to worry you. I just started seeing flashing lights, and it felt like—"

"Like you were getting a migraine?"

I blink at him. "Yeah, do you get them too?"

Dan nods. "They're the worst."

"I get them sometimes too," Mara says. She finally releases me from her grip with a last karate chop to the shoulders. I wince, and I hope once the pain of the massage wears off I'll feel more relaxed, if only for being freed from her claws.

"I get them before bad stuff happens," Dan clarifies.

"You want me to give you a reading, Dan?" Mara asks. "We can see if the cards show any of the danger you're feeling."

Before Dan can answer, Alex enters.

"Everyone have fun last night?" he asks. His voice is slightly hoarse. From the blissful smile on his face and the way he sprawls on his stool, it certainly looks like *he* did.

Brian follows close behind with a plastic bag from the local card store. He closes the door behind him. "Our supplies for today," he announces with a forced smile. He shakes the bag playfully, but the gesture is wooden. It's as if he's working off a script, going through the motions because he's too anxious to do otherwise.

"What's in the bag, Professor?" Dan asks.

Brian pulls out what looks like a set of flash cards, along with multiple decks of playing cards.

Alex turns to Pankaj. "You in the market for another watch? Because this might be your lucky day."

"We have some card sharks among us?" Brian asks.

"Depends what your definition of shark is," Pankaj and I say simultaneously.

Brian and Alex laugh. Dan and Mara narrow their eyes.

I sneak a glance at Pankaj.

"Jinx," he says, staring right back at me.

Brian peels the protective plastic covering off the large flash cards. "These are Zener cards. Each is printed with one of five symbols: a star, circle, square, a cross, or wavy lines." He puts them down and then picks up a deck of the regular cards, standard Bicycles. "These you're probably more familiar with."

"Some of us maybe *too* familiar." Alex tilts his head toward Pankaj then winks. "Desai, you and I need to chat later," he whispers.

"It should be clear now that you all have slightly different skill sets," Brian continues. "At this point we don't know why, other than simple biology—we all express variation. What we're looking to uncover and work on today are your deficiencies.

If, say, you don't speak a particular language, the best way to become fluent is to converse with a native speaker. In the last experiment, Kass was able to shatter a glass by herself. But perhaps with a teammate, you might be able to send it flying across the room."

"*At* someone?" Mara asks coolly.

"Sorry, sorry . . . bad example," Brian says, waving his hands. "The theory is, if two of you train together, you'll reinforce each other through limbic resonance. You'll work in harmony to achieve even greater things. So with these cards, our ultimate goal is not merely to see which one comes next but to *influence* which card comes next." He pauses. "Think of it as an electric current. Who knows how a light works?"

I put up my hand. "You flip a switch, and then there's light?"

"My niece the comedian." Brian walks over to the whiteboard. He sketches a battery and a light bulb, then two wires connecting them. "The flow of electricity is called a current, yes? To harness that electricity, both wires are needed to complete the circuit from battery to bulb." He retraces the connecting wires then adds hash marks to the top of the light bulb to indicate it's now lit. "My hypothesis is that if two people with ESP work together, they'll form a circuit, and the metaphoric light bulb"—he taps his pen against the bulb—"turns on."

OVER THE NEXT TWENTY minutes, we each take twenty-five turns trying to guess which Zener card Brian will draw. I get twelve right, thirteen wrong.

I cringe. "Looks like my guessing skills are worse than average."

Dan shakes his head. "Statistically, guessing averages would come to five right answers out of twenty-five or twenty percent," he says. "Your average was closer to fifty percent."

"Yes," Brian agrees. "Onwards."

Mara and Dan each get nine. Annoyingly, Pankaj ties my score of twelve, but surprisingly, Alex gets only five right. Then again, considering how much (i.e., how little) sleep he got last night, maybe that should have been predictable.

"On to part two," Brian says. "Alex, you'll work with me. Mara and Dan, I want you to work together today. Kass, you team up with Pankaj."

I can feel Mara's eyes on me. I know she's thinking I engineered this. *Not my idea!* I scream to her in my head.

Yeah, right, I hear her say. *I warned you.*

Her voice comes through so clearly in my ear, it feels like she's directly behind me again. I whirl to face her, but she's across the room, glaring at me icily.

Did you just say something to me, like, telepathically? If so, name your favorite animal.

I wait for a few seconds. I try to anticipate Mara's response. I assume she'll say something ridiculous, like cockatoo or praying mantis. But I hear nothing beyond the sound of my own voice in my head.

Pankaj motions me to a table by the window. "I'll go first," he says. It's our first real moment alone, and I wonder if he is going to mention anything about last night. "Don't screw me up, Legacy. I'm pretty good with the cards, so if my percentages go down thanks to your 'help,' I'll be pissed."

His smile tells me nothing. I hold the cards out. If this is the way he wants to play it, fine. "It hadn't occurred to me to mess with you, *but now* . . . You ready, Rocket?" I shake my wrist to readjust the placement of my new watch.

We've been going back and forth with the cards for a while when Alex wanders over to us. I glance at him, puzzled, and then suddenly realize Uncle Brian is gone. I've been so focused on Pankaj, I didn't even register that he left.

"Professor Black said he needed to make a call," Alex says. "Something about his 'very important board meeting.' Then he just cut out of here."

I'm still not sure if the funding issue and the lab's potential closure is a secret. But it seemed strongly implied that I was not to discuss it. On the other hand, considering the nature of the group, it's likely one or all of them know anyway. It's also possible at least someone here knows how things will ultimately turn out.

"Pinberg's death still has him pretty shaken up, huh?" Pankaj asks me quietly.

I shrug. "I guess so. That and . . ." I bite my lip.

"And what?" Mara and Dan demand in unison.

I shake my head.

"Hey, stop giving Kass here the third degree," Alex says with another one of his winks. He winks so often it's beginning to strike me as less charming than gimmicky. He turns to Pankaj. "So, kid, about last night. Big score for you, huh?"

I feel my cheeks going red, dismayed that Alex saw us making out. But then it dawns on me that Alex is referring *not* to any perceived hookup but to the watch Pankaj won in the poker game.

"As Kass has learned," Pankaj replies, "I'm good at cards."

"Erika was mighty impressed that you got the vintage Rolex off Pat," Alex says. "I heard he got a little, um . . . *agitated* when you won."

"Agitated?" Pankaj snorts. "He wanted to break my legs."

"Come on," Alex protests, "he's a Henley student, not a barbarian. He would have broken *one* leg at most!"

"Fair point." Pankaj laughs. "But hey, at least I impressed your new girlfriend."

"You actually did," Alex says seriously. "In fact, she suggested you to come to the high-stakes game at the Century Club tonight. What do you say?"

Pankaj rolls his eyes at Alex. "Much as I'd love to dip into their bank accounts, there's only one problem: I can't afford the buy-in for a high-stakes game. You see, I'm what's classically called 'poor.' You'll explain to Erika the concept of 'poor,' right?" He makes exaggerated air quotes, his amber eyes gleaming.

In the tense silence, an idea comes to me.

An idea of how to right a wrong.

"If I'm not mistaken," Pankaj says without so much as glance in my direction, "it looks like Legacy has a notion?"

"I do," I reply. "Alex, how high stakes are we talking?"

He shrugs. "These guys have bank. They're trust-fund kids. Serious money."

"Good. That's what I thought." I turn back to Pankaj. "You're in the game. I'm going to stake you."

That finally wrenches his attention from Alex. "What did you just say?"

"You heard me. On two conditions: One, we are going to practice every spare minute before the game to make sure you're in top form. And two, you can keep twenty-five percent of the winnings, but the other seventy-five will go to the lab."

"You mean put the money to saving it?" Dan asks.

"You really think he can win all the money Professor Black needs?" Mara asks, making it clear we're all in on this "secret."

"Why not?" Alex asks rhetorically. "Our boy here's got game, and besides, the 'poor' always just seem to try a little harder, don't they?" There's an edge in Alex's voice, one that's perhaps unintentionally revealing. Alex hasn't said anything about his own home life, but that doesn't mean his family isn't just as disadvantaged or screwed up as Pankaj's.

Pankaj hears it too, and his expression softens. He nods. "If we surprise him with the money by using our talents, seems like it's an even bigger win."

I nod, liking the plan even more. Uncle Brian might not be willing to take money from my father, but if it's from me, a fair trade for all he's doing for me this summer, maybe he'll accept. "So it's a deal." I put out my hand to shake Pankaj's. "Consider yourself staked, Rocket."

Alex pokes his index finger into Pankaj's chest. "Looks like someone has a sugar mama."

"Let's think of me more as his boss."

Pankaj purses his lips as if considering his options, but I know he's already made up his mind. "This idea of yours is crazy, Kass. You know that, right?" I nod. "Good," he continues. "Because this is the kind of crazy I can get behind. Especially since it helps me live by my guru's mantra: you can't win unless you play."

"Who's your guru?" I ask.

"The announcer for the Pennsylvania Lottery."

Alex's smile widens. "So I'll tell Erika you're in, Pankaj?"

"The rocket's all in," he replies, finally taking my hand and shaking it, a smirk playing across his lips. "Thanks, boss."

CHAPTER FIFTEEN

The vision was blurry.

But both Pankaj and I saw *something*.

Here we are: the five of us in a lazy circle, cards laid out. For the last hour, we've been huddling together on this narrow dock outside the Henley boathouse as the sun falls behind Sinclair Lake. Now time has stopped. The entire universe has shrunk to just Pankaj and me. I can tell from his searching eyes that neither one of us caught more than the premonition's nebulous wake: someone in our group is supposed to die. And it could be either one of us.

All that was bothering me so much until mere seconds ago—whether or not Pankaj was cheating and, more important, whether or not he was being obvious enough about it to get caught—no longer matters. *Unless cheating tonight somehow leads to his death?* Needing more information, I feel something wriggling in that reptilian part of my brain. It's ironic: the longer I'm at Henley, the harder I'm finding it is to restrain myself. There's something about being in this place that's making impulse control impossible.

"You know, Mara, I'm so curious about all the stuff you do with tarot cards." I try to sound off-the-cuff casual, but the words come out awkward, in a high register. "Can you get really specific information about things?"

She stares back at me for a moment, maybe studying me, questioning my motives.

"Ask Pankaj," she replies, turning away. "He thought tarot was total crap when I gave him his reading."

"Wait, come on. You have to give me a break," he says in apologetic tone. "Where I'm from, there are psychics on every corner. You can find them between every check cashing place and liquor store, and they all promise to help people find the path to riches. But all they do is take your money and spout BS. I would know because my sister ran that kind of racket for a while. And she's a straight-up con artist."

"Harsh," Dan says.

Pankaj laughs bitterly. "That's actually one of the nicer things I can say about Nisha. Anyway, I assumed if Professor Black had recruited someone with *my* background to his program, everyone else here would know how to work a scam too." Pankaj turns to me. "But Mara wasn't looking for any money." He pauses. "Besides, she nailed a lot of the *details.*" He hits the last word with an odd emphasis.

Mara sets her jaw, but says nothing.

I won't allow myself to become distracted by whatever's going on between them. "So . . . *how?* How do you do it and get all the details?" I ask.

"It's quantum mechanics and particle physics," she snaps, as if that's an obvious answer when it comes to tarot card reading. "*I* don't do anything."

"Come on, that's not exactly true," Pankaj says.

"Well, yes, it's up to the person reading the cards to interpret the events, but quantum forces drive what cards appear. So it's possible to draw the same cards in front of two readers and get two radically different accounts of your life. One could be all right, the other all wrong."

"Then how do you know what to believe?" I press.

Alex laughs. He's stretched out on the dock, sunbathing with his eyes closed, as if he doesn't have a care in the world. "That's the question, isn't it?" he says. "How do you *ever* know what to believe?"

This whole carefree genius playboy shtick of his is infuriating to me at the moment. "Well, *I* believe that if Pankaj doesn't win big tonight, we're screwed. But my uncle, who'll lose his lab, is screwed most of all."

Alex doesn't respond. Dan stares at me, as if trying to compute what's going on in my head. Mara just turns away, gazing out on the lake, watching the sun ripple off the water. But when Pankaj's eyes home in on mine, I hear his voice in my mind again, as clearly as I heard him moments ago . . . as clearly as I heard Mara in the lab this morning.

I think I know what Mara was trying to say, he tells me silently. *ESP is like a mirror. And as the reflection is filtered through your perception, it becomes warped and imperfect, just like life.*

Warped and imperfect, I echo, *just like life.*

I know we're both thinking about the vision we just shared. One member of our group won't survive the summer. And of the four who do, three will join together. But neither of us has any clue as to the membership of that group or purpose of those selected.

STANDING AT THE OPULENT marble arched door of the Century Club, I notice that both Alex and Pankaj seem tense. Hard to blame them.

In a final moment of pregame styling, Alex runs his fingers through his hair. He's especially well coiffed tonight and wears a blue blazer with a pastel tie that's pulled rakishly loose around the neck. He's also spent a lot of time applying cologne; the scent of a spice garden wafts from him as powerfully as the smell of fries in a McDonald's parking lot. Though he's trying hard to convey his usual unstudied, casual, cool vibe, what's most apparent is that he's trying *really* hard. His desire to be liked by Erika is achingly clear. It's sort of sweet.

Pankaj has also dressed up (at Alex's insistence), and the borrowed blazer makes him fidget, even though it fits him perfectly and accentuates his broad shoulders. He's annoyed at Alex for making Dan and Mara feeling unwelcome tonight. Earlier, Alex said only Pankaj and I could come to the game, and he gave the universal lame excuse to explain their exclusion: "It's not my decision." He said space was limited and I was only allowed to come because I was fronting the money. But it wasn't hard to guess the real reason Alex didn't want Dan and Mara here. He was worried they might embarrass him—Dan with his social ineptitude and Mara with her unpredictability.

Alex takes a deep breath. The door knocker is a bronze lion head; he grasps the ring in its mouth and bangs it against the back plate.

A few excruciating moments later, Erika opens the door. "Well *hello*," she greets us in that refined British accent. She smiles at Alex. "My, we're fancy, aren't we?"

I somehow expected her to be dressed in a ball gown or in clothes from the recent Ralph Lauren collection. But her untucked button-down is slightly frayed at the edges and distinctly unfussy. I glance at Pankaj, who frowns. He didn't need to "dress" at all. I frown too, but with envy. Erika is one of those lucky girls who looks great whatever she wears. Whenever I "dress to impress," I wind up looking like a demented sorority girl, somehow always managing to mess up some stupid but crucial detail. Tonight, for instance, I'm in a dress that features a small guppy pattern. I cinched it at the waist with a belt whose clasp, I've only now realized, looks like a whale tale. *I'm like a walking seafood platter.*

"Just on time. Come in," she says.

"Uh . . . hi. Great, thanks." Alex leans in for a glancing kiss on the cheek. But Erika turns too quickly, and he is left hanging midair.

"Follow me," she calls over her shoulder.

We trail Erika up the grand staircase to the left of the door. The club's interior is as old-school elegant as I imagined: large portraits of former members line its oak-paneled walls, and the ceiling is decorated with ornate wood and plaster detail—a Fitzgerald novel come to life. We're led into one of the libraries upstairs, all mahogany bookshelves, soft lamps, and leather couches. A few desks face large Palladian windows.

But my eyes are drawn to the large round poker table placed in the center.

Most of the guys—and the other players are all guys this evening—are already seated when we enter the room. They too are dressed super casually, as if a "high-stakes" game in fact is just the opposite to them; it's something they play so regularly, it's of no consequence whatsoever. They glance up at Erika.

She clears her throat. "Everyone, this is . . . Sorry, what's your name again?"

"Pankaj."

"This is Pun . . . Wait, say it again."

"You can call me Punk."

Erika smiles. "I think I can handle that. Punk, this is Connor, Quartie, Veck, Heath, Trip, and Andre." Alex and I are not introduced, but I'm just as happy to remain anonymous in the background. "Do you guys want a drink before we start?"

"No thanks," I reply.

Pankaj shakes his head. *That would be all I need, a fuzzy head on top of all the rest*, he communicates silently.

My head jerks as I hear his unspoken words in my mind as clearly as if he'd whispered them in my ear. Luckily nobody is looking in my direction. All eyes are on Pankaj.

How are we doing this? I ask.

He gives a subtle smile. *Not a clue.*

"I'd love a drink, thanks!" Alex says, a little too eagerly.

"Hard alcohol's in the bar at the back, or the taproom is on the ground floor, to the right of the stairs," Erika replies. Her tone is brusque.

Alex's smile falters. "Oh, okay. Maybe I'll get one later."

Pankaj takes his seat at the table.

"Let's start," Connor says. He's skinnier than the others, and his large white, short-sleeved Izod polo shirt looks borrowed from his father's closet. "We're playing no-limit Texas Hold 'em. Trip's button."

Trip, ginger haired, nods and shuffles the cards. He's spent a lot of time in the sun, perhaps rowing with the Henley crew team; his face and neck are tan, and he's sprayed with freckles across his cheeks and nose. Veck, on his left, wears classic Ray-Ban aviator sunglasses and a sleeveless green Patagonia fleece. He puts in a stack of five $100 chips. The player to his left, Heath—the largest guy at the table (the one who looks like he might feel quite at home in Roman gladiator garb)—puts in two stacks of five $100 chips.

I know from my dad's weekly poker games that these are the "forced" bets, the small blind and big blind respectively. They encourage you stay in the game rather than fold right away if you draw bad cards. The logic is that if you've already put down a substantial amount of money, you may as well just play out the hand. Of course, $1,000 seems like a lot of money to put down right off the bat, but that's why we're here. Big money.

Still, something about this evening has already begun to bother me. Maybe it's the gratuitous privilege. Maybe what I'm feeling is simple fear. Maybe it's concern for Pankaj and his level of comfort. *His* face, however, remains neutral. Score one for Pankaj.

Gladiator Heath turns over his cards to reveal a queen of spades and jack of spades.

Pankaj smiles. He's holding a pair of sevens, with a third seven showing in the center of the table, and the three of a kind is good enough for the win.

"Well done, new guy," Erika cheers from the sidelines. "And, gentlemen, I'd encourage you to keep your time pieces away from our man Punk."

Alex laughs, but Erika ignores him, her eyes on the game. He scowls, and his eyes dart furtively toward the stairwell. Cards soon start flying around the table again, and when I look at skinny Connor, I get a feeling he's got the hand to beat.

Pankaj looks around the table and also seems to zero in on Connor. After glancing back down at his own cards, he folds. Moments later, Connor scoops up the pot.

I focus my thoughts, concentrating on Pankaj.

Well, well, well, the boy might have some sense in him after all.

Pankaj casts a sidelong glance at me. *And the girl might have noticed that sooner if she hadn't been so focused on my butt. Which, I'll grant you, is awesome.*

I stifle a smile. *You think Mara and Dan are okay?*

He puffs out his cheeks as new cards are dealt; he's worried about them too. I don't want to be a distraction, but with this new channel of communication, it's impossible to keep my feelings to myself. Even partial access to each other's thoughts seems as useful as it is awkward, if not horrifying. Previously, I only ever had to worry about blurting out something I'd regret before I could think twice. It's possible that Pankaj will now know what I'm thinking as my thoughts are still forming.

From what I can tell, though, he isn't experiencing the same fears. He's not even focused on me. He's in the game, "*all* in," just as he said.

The longer I watch him the more impressed I become; he's cool under pressure, and as I know very well, when you're playing for someone else, that's not only important; it's difficult. His pile of money—our pile of money—continues to grow.

I'm fairly certain that he's not counting cards. Of course, he *is* probably using his psychic abilities to intuit what the other players have in their hands. So depending on your definition of "cheating," you could make the argument that he's not playing a completely clean game. But those are details. His opponents wouldn't believe the psychic stuff anyway. Besides, this is all for Uncle Brian, for preserving the research that might one day allow Pankaj to use his talents for something more constructive than a poker win.

Alex, on the other hand, seems nervous. His eyes keep flitting around the room, and he looks between Erika and the table several times a minute. I can't read what he's thinking. If there really is an open channel of communication between those of us with extrasensory abilities, Alex doesn't seem to be on our party line.

Hey, how much do you have at this point? I ask Pankaj silently.

He pretends to study his hand as if unaware of my question, but his thoughts boom back at me. *Kass, you don't count*

your money when you're sitting at the table. Damn, girl, there's even a
country music song about that.

"Punk?" Erika says, tilting her chin up at him. "Your bet?"

"Sorry!" He tosses a few chips in the pot.

I've distracted him, and I know this for certain when he loses
the hand.

That one was my fault, I think at him. *I apologize.*

It's okay. It is your money, after all.

Veck gathers his winnings, smirking behind his sunglasses.
"Finally!"

A few other people have come upstairs and now stand around
the table, watching the action. Since they all look entirely at
ease, I'm guessing they belong here.

"Who wants whiskey?" a guy calls out from behind a small bar
near the fireplace.

I almost laugh when I recognize him; it's Flip-Flops, the guy
who passed out in front of the library. He's more fresh faced
tonight (maybe because he hasn't started drinking?), and clean-
shaven. His eyes meet mine briefly, but he doesn't appear to
remember me at all.

Veck spins his forefinger in the air counterclockwise. "Shots
all around."

Flip-Flops nods. He reaches down and places seven shot
glasses on the top of the bar, then carefully pours out the brown
liquor. He brings the shots over to the table, two by two, and the
squish-thwack sound of his footgear seems to echo in my brain,
making me feel vaguely ill.

When he sets a shot glass in front of Pankaj, the pain hits.

It's like a corkscrew stabbing through the side of my head. It
literally feels as if metal has twisted into my skull. I wince and
almost lose my balance. I sense people are starting to watch me,
and in a panic I start coughing. Loudly.

"Kass, are you okay?" Alex asks.

I shake my head.

Pankaj stands and hurries over to my side. "Kass?"

As he pats my back, I whisper, "Don't drink it." I let the cough dissipate.

What's going on? he asks silently.

We need to get out of here.

"Do you need some water?" Erika asks. She turns to Flip-Flops. "See if we have some water back there."

"Sure thing." He jogs back to the little bar and ducks underneath the counter. His head emerges a few moments later. He's holding a cup full of dark red liquid. "No water, just cranberry juice. Sorry about that. Here ya go."

Another flash of pain. No way do I drink this.

"I'm so sorry," I say, smiling weakly and hacking some more. "Allergic to cranberries. I'll just get some water from the bathroom."

"Take a cup from here, and if you want ice, the kitchen's down the stairs and back to the right," Erika replies.

"I'm going to sit this round out and go with her," Pankaj says, nodding a thank you. "Apologies. I'll be right back." He starts to escort me toward the stairwell.

"Alex," I choke out. "Come with us?"

Alex doesn't respond. He's concentrating on two men in dark suits sitting on one of the leather couches. I didn't see them before, but it's impossible not to notice them now: they're at least twenty years older than anyone else present. These guys don't look like professors; they're too slick. Alumni? Parents? Or something else?

"Back in a minute," Pankaj adds, putting his hand on Alex's arm. "Come on."

"Oh, yeah. Sorry. Sure." He sounds like we've pulled him from a trance.

The three of us are silent until we're down the stairs and in the empty kitchen. Once I'm convinced we're alone, I turn to them. "Something's not right," I advise.

"I agree," Alex replies.

"I think they put something in your drink," I tell Pankaj.

"Who do you mean? Which *they*?" he asks.

I look at Alex, but he's locked on Pankaj. "Have you felt or noticed anything strange?"

"No, not really. I've been trying to stay focused on the table. Why? What are you thinking, man?"

Alex shakes his head. "The whole night's been weird in my opinion." He leans against the counter. "Can't tell yet, but something's off; that's for sure."

"Kass, you think it was one of the other players who put the thing in my drink?" Pankaj asks me.

"I don't think so." I try to lower my voice even more. "Who are those two old guys sitting on the couch?"

"That's what I was trying to figure out." Alex lowers his voice too. "I've seen them on campus before. Listen, I know this will sound paranoid . . . but remember our very first experiment? I mentioned I thought we had a tail. I wasn't kidding. I mean, I know I'm starting to sound like Dan with his conspiracy theories, but—"

"So you're sure it's not just another one of the players trying to take me out, or something?" Pankaj interrupts. "Like, to protect his investment?"

Alex makes a dismissive *pffft* sound. "Are they overprivileged assholes? Probably yes. But I don't think it goes further than that."

"Maybe the old guys are just the club's private security force," I suggest. Some of my father's wealthiest associates have private security teams. The best of them just blend into the background.

But if you're a middle-aged man in a suit, it's a lot easier to blend into a crowd of middle-aged men in suits than a club full of preppy college kids. "Maybe parents want them around in the aftermath of the shooting?"

Neither Alex nor Pankaj seems impressed with this theory.

"So what's our move?" Pankaj asks.

"I say we get out of here. Just go. It feels too dangerous to stay."

Alex nods. "Yeah, you guys should definitely take off."

"You're not coming with?" I ask, frowning. "I meant *all* of us."

"No, I'll stick around . . . try to get a handle on things." Alex swallows and glances toward the ceiling. "Plus . . . Erika." His face flushes with an embarrassed-looking smile. "Look, I'm sorry, okay? I *am* a teenage boy. My hormones rule my life. There. I said it."

"Okay, just promise us you don't drink anything you don't pour yourself," Pankaj says. He turns back to me. "Come on, Legacy. Let's roll."

"Wait!" Alex calls after us in a low voice as we head for the door. "What about your winnings? You have a lot of money still on the table."

Pankaj taps his pocket, which is bulging. Amazing: he somehow managed to swipe his cash before leaving the room. "I told you my mama was a grifter," he says.

"I thought you said your sister was the grifter," I whisper.

Pankaj's hand is already on the doorknob. "Her too. Where do you think we learned our tricks?"

CHAPTER SIXTEEN

"It's not a lot," I tell Uncle Brian as I spread the cash before him on the kitchen table. "But don't worry. It's just the beginning."

He gives me a quizzical look as I push the money closer to him.

"It's to save the lab," I add, but his expression remains unchanged. "It's only five thousand dollars, but consider it the first layaway payment."

The term "layaway" was Pankaj's. So was the idea to turn over what little we'd made tonight in the first place. I admit I didn't even know what the word "layaway" meant until Pankaj explained it to me on the walk home.

"Layaway, my wealthy friend, is also known as payment on an installment plan. You put down a deposit on an item as a pledge that you intend to buy it. But since you don't have all the cash up front, you pay the rest when you get the money together. For its part, the store takes the money and reserves the item for you. It shows good faith and trust on both ends. My mom signs those little IOUs like a movie star giving autographs at a film premiere. Your uncle will get it."

Now I'm not so sure. Brian not only seems *not* to get it; he seems disappointed and annoyed. I gamely plow forward in the silence nonetheless. "It occurred to me that we have some advantages working in our favor, so we might as well use them, right? Atlantic City isn't all that far from here. I mean, if we spend a few days there, we should be able to win more than enough to make the hundred thousand you need." My eyebrows rise in excitement as I nod along with my own great idea.

Brian absently rubs his palm into his forehead in circles; it almost looks as if he's extinguishing an invisible cigarette. "Kass, you're suggesting that you and the other HEARs use your abilities to restore funding to my lab through gambling?" His voice is gravelly. He sighs, and his hand drops to his lap. "That is . . . very kind of you."

I shake my head. "It's no big deal."

"I know." He laughs cynically. "But what I don't think you realize is that, to present it to the university, the money must come from a respectable source. The provenance of the currency is very important at a place like Henley. If cash were the sole issue, there are easier ways of acquiring it. I could have you pick stocks, for example."

He says this last part with purpose, and it hits me like a punch to the gut.

Picking stocks is what my dad—my very, very successful dad—does for a living. Not only did he short the market during the financial crisis; he's always one of the top hedge-fund managers on those "highest earning" year-end lists. Everything written about him mentions his "smarts," his "nose for sniffing out value," and his "uncanny timing." He always jokes that these are just sexier ways of saying he works all the time and gets lucky.

I'm suddenly thrown, now quite certain my father has been

beating the market not because of his intellect or intensity but because he shares my gift.

Uncle Brian nods at me. "Some families have a genetic predisposition towards obesity; others, athleticism and certain types of cancers. Some family members get it; others do not. But this is our predisposition."

How did I never know this? Why didn't my father tell me—about him *or* me?

"So obviously *you* have it," I say accusatorily, wondering what else my dad may be hiding. "Does my mom have it too?"

Uncle Brian shakes his head. "No, your mother doesn't have ESP," he mutters. "And neither do I."

"Stop lying!" I yell, sick and tired of being shielded from the truth.

"Kassandra, I am not lying. I do not have extrasensory perception. Not anymore." He places his hands on the kitchen table and pushes himself up. "Come with me."

I follow him into the living room. He stops a foot away from the mantel, the altar on which stands the picture of him and Ellen Rios.

"You lost it because of her?" I ask, baffled.

"I lost it when she was murdered." He stares at the picture. "I never had the vision that you were born with. My innate ability was much weaker, not much greater than the average person's. The difference was that I was *aware* of it. And unlike most people, I didn't chalk it up to 'good parking karma' or believe my luck was made by some talisman like a rabbit's foot. But when I was with Ellen, those largely latent talents became activated, practically supercharged. I *did* have a gift like yours. And when Ellen died, that part of me died with her."

I swallow, half-tempted to reach out to him, to hug him. I

don't. "You didn't get any sort of warning about the bomb?" I whisper.

His head droops. "Yes," he murmurs. "Though I completely misinterpreted the vision I received and pursued a lead that went nowhere. All the while, the attack was being planned for our home office. These false readings or misinterpretations of visions, these 'failures of intelligence,' as they're known . . . they happen all the time. But I've never been able to forgive myself for it."

"And you never had another vision after that?"

"No."

He takes the framed photo in his hands. I want to ask more questions, but he's already a million miles away. I start twisting my signet ring. I stare down at it as he shambles out of the room and back upstairs, still clutching the photo. The etching on the onyx in the center of the ring is an image of a temple. My dad claimed it was a family heirloom, and I never bothered asking more about it; the family inheritance piece didn't really interest me. Now I can't help but wonder if there are more inheritances from my family I have yet to discover. Or if the temple signifies something . . .

If there's an answer to that question, my gut tells me there are more clues to be found on the third floor.

FOR AN HOUR AND twenty minutes, I lie in wait on my water bed. If Uncle Brian suspected I was about to undertake an exploratory mission, hopefully the long delay has assuaged his concerns and he's gone to sleep. I slide out of my shoes and stretch and flex my feet, popping the noisy cracks out of my toes. Then I reach into my backpack and feel the Zippo lighter and the mini LED flashlight I keep in the side pocket for emergencies.

When my dad discovered the lighter shortly after I bought it, I told him I needed it for an art project. ("Project Set Off Fire Alarm," though that detail I kept to myself.) Dad seemed skeptical, but at the time, I assumed he worried I'd become a smoker. The lighter and flashlight have proven invaluable tools on various missions in the past, so I always keep them handy. It's only the flashlight I need tonight.

I inhale and exhale deeply, summoning my inner ninja before sneaking back to the third floor. The door to Uncle Brian's room is closed, and the main light is off. Whether or not he's still awake and reading, I can't tell, but I won't risk going near the end of the hall to find out. Of the other two rooms on the hallway, the door to the right is open. That's where I'll go first—always take the easy way out (or in) if offered.

I creep through the door and shine the flashlight across the walls. The bookshelves are filled with cans of spray starch, extra light bulbs, a mug full of pens, and a sewing basket. To the left is an ironing board with a stack of handkerchiefs on top awaiting pressing. It's a glorified laundry room—pretty unglorified, actually—there isn't even a washing machine. Nothing seems out of the ordinary on preliminary inspection; several framed paintings hang on the pale yellow walls. I run the flashlight over the carpet edges to see if anything looks loose. I even search for hidden panels—he did work for the CIA, after all—but find nothing.

When I swing the flashlight over the bookshelves one last time, I spot a shadow behind one of the cans of starch. The shadow is a container the size of a pill bottle made of opaque black plastic with a grey flip-top lid. I can't imagine what kind of pills would require such secrecy, so I shake the bottle to hear if there are any left. Rather than the rattle of pills, it produces the sound of something solid.

I uncap the container. As the rolled brown strip of plastic slides out, I realize I'm holding a film canister. I uncurl the strip and shine my flashlight at it. Faces are dark and the backgrounds are light, exactly the opposite of how they're supposed to look. It only now occurs to me why strips of film are called negatives.

"YOU LOOK LIKE ASS," Pankaj says when I walk into the lab early the next morning and find him sitting there alone.

He's right—I haven't slept—so I don't have an immediate comeback. It doesn't help that he looks pretty good himself. Maybe even more than pretty good. Whatever.

Since I couldn't sleep, I considered calling my dad at 3 A.M. to vent. I wanted to tell him the big family secret was out and demand that he tell *me* all he knew about his abilities and mine. But I didn't call. Something stopped me. Part of it was rage—righteous rage, if I'm allowed to call it that. I was afraid of what I would say. I also knew that if I pressed him on why he'd lied to me about this for my whole life, he would find an excuse. *I never lied to you, Kass. I just never mentioned it. There's a difference*, he would say, and then he'd assure me whatever he did or didn't tell me was to protect me and my innocence. All for my benefit.

But this is so much more than just a sin of omission. This is deception about something very personal, something that exists inside of *me*, that is part of *me*. This goes far beyond the lies all parents tell their children: that the tooth fairy exists, that everything will be okay.

Besides, I know there's nothing he can do at this point. If my father was ever able to protect me before, that's no longer the case. There's no way he can save me now—or whichever one of the five of us is supposed to die.

"Apologies for the comment," Pankaj says in the silence. "But don't take it the wrong way, Legacy."

I take a seat at a different workstation and turn to face Pankaj. "How could I possibly take 'You look like ass' the 'wrong' way? There's really only one interpretation for a statement like that."

Pankaj smiles. "That I'm a jerk?"

"I'm beginning to see the downside of this mind-reading business."

When he laughs, I can't help myself. I start laughing too. And I have to admit, the laughter feels good. Thankfully the others have yet to arrive, so I don't have to be self-conscious about it. How is it that this cocky con artist—this kid who's so dismissive of my background that he still calls me "Legacy"—can lift my mood in an instant?

"I promise I wasn't trying to be mean," Pankaj says as he walks over to my workstation, leaning across it. "Seriously, what's going on? How did it go with the money and your uncle last night?"

I shrug, and because we're still alone, I consider telling him what I learned about my dad. But for once, I'm able to stop myself. Before confessing anything to anyone, I need to learn more about his abilities myself. "It's all related to family drama, I guess."

"Ah, family drama," he repeats. "I know it well. As I may have mentioned, my family is award-winningly dysfunctional. My sister, Nisha, is perpetually up for 'worst performance' in social situations. She has a particular skill for making people uncomfortable and scared. I spent my childhood sleeping with one eye open. So, yeah, I get that worrying about family stuff can suck the life-force right out of you." His voice softens. "I'm being serious, Kass. You can talk to me."

"There is so much about all this that I can't even begin to understand." I wave my arms around the lab. "I mean, why would you close a lab that's doing research on ESP? If we can find a reliable way to predict events in the future, we can stop things like disease, conflict, and environmental disasters . . . just to name a few."

Pankaj lets out a whistle. "Wow," he says.

"Wow?"

"You don't seem to get how dangerous this is."

"What are you talking about?"

"Kass, scientific advances almost always come with moral ambiguities." He pauses but I wait for him to continue. "Okay, ever heard of J. Robert Oppenheimer?"

I knit my eyebrows, not sure where he's going with this. "Father of the atomic bomb. Manhattan Project guy, right?"

"Right, the guy whose creation, the nuclear weapon, killed or injured somewhere around two hundred thousand people in Japan. Oppenheimer said that in the moments following the first successful test of his bomb, he realized the dark consequences of his work; the world would not be the same, his invention could end life on a massive scale. He said he thought of the words from the Hindu scripture, the Bhagavad Gita: *Now I am become Death, the destroyer of worlds.*"

"Yikes. How do you know all this?"

"I'm smarter than I'm given credit for," Pankaj says. "Maybe I'm *a lot* smarter than I'm given credit for."

"You hide it really well."

He laughs. But as I picture the famous photo of the mushroom cloud over Hiroshima, he looks down and his expression grows serious.

"Look," he says, "I mention this because advances in science come with all kinds of consequences, good and bad. And your uncle, he's . . . troubling."

"I'm not following."

"Kass—"

"He's the J. J. Dyckman Distinguished Professor of Applied Engineering at Henley University," I interrupt. "He got you out of jail. What's troubling about that?"

Pankaj sighs and brushes his hair away from his eyes. "Nothing about him has been ringing any alarm bells for you?"

I hesitate. Lots about my uncle rings alarm bells. But for some reason I feel defensive; this is my family, after all. "No," I lie.

"I guess that's your blind spot," Pankaj says with a shrug. "You can't see him, not really."

I snort. "You're making it sound like he's a serial killer or something!"

"Not a *serial* killer . . ." he says, but not in a "that's completely out of the question" tone of voice. "I am saying that his motives in testing ESP and our minds are in no way as pure as he claims. Especially not for someone with his background."

I get a tingling at the back of my spine. "How much do you know about his background?"

Pankaj takes my left arm and turns it to glance at my Rolex, the one he won for me. It hasn't left my wrist; I even wear it in the shower, even though I'm not entirely sure it's waterproof. It's 8:50. We have ten minutes until the others arrive.

"Follow me." He hurries out of the lab before I can protest, so I trail him down the hallway to the stairs. He opens the door and descends two flights before exiting on a basement level and strides quickly to the end of a bare cinder-block hallway lit with harsh fluorescent bulbs. He stops in front of an unmarked door. After glancing around to make sure we're completely alone, he leans close and starts to whisper.

"Kass, I want to tell you something. I waited until now because I wasn't sure you were ready to hear it. But as soon as I landed on campus a few weeks ago and shook hands with the professor,

I knew something was off. I started digging right away. When you all went to dinner that first night you were here, I was in the library doing research on him. It actually felt like I was getting somewhere when Dan found me and forced me to come out with you guys."

So *that's* why he was so pissed off that night. He flashes a rueful grin, as if reading my thoughts, which for all I know, he is. I sigh. "What did you find?"

"One roll of microfilm had images copied from your uncle's old lab notebook. For whatever reason, someone had taken pictures of every page in that notebook to make the film. But I couldn't make heads or tails of most of it because it seemed to be about drug development and testing."

"Something to magnify the brain's response to ESP?"

"Exactly. I found lots of notes that were case histories of some sort. They all included a photo of the subject then listed bizarre details about their love lives, like 'S, twenty years old. Not interested in food. Hears conversations in rooms where she's not present. In love for sixteen days.'"

"That's . . . weird."

He leans closer to me now; his amber eyes seem to take up my entire field of vision. "No kidding. They were *all* like that. 'K, seventeen years old. Increased heart rate. Sweaty palms. Correctly predicted path of tornado. Told girlfriend of six weeks he loved her.'"

"Are you trying to tell me that my great-uncle is studying love? That *love* somehow magnifies ESP?"

Pankaj's eyes are searching now; he knows how ridiculous it sounds. "Like I said, I needed more time, but one of the things in your uncle's file was an article by Freud. It's about how the brain works differently when it experiences obsessive feelings of love. That was followed by a sheet of paper with only three words, in your uncle's handwriting: *Blinded by love.* And when I started thinking about it, there was a certain logic to it. When people are blind, their other senses sharpen and become more acute, like their hearing and sense of smell, right?"

I nod. My heart is pounding, and I'm not sure why. "Right."

"So if you're in love and your brain is being flooded by all these different chemicals and neurotransmitters, you may have a certain tunnel vision, but it may well give you *extra*sensory perception too."

What he's saying also aligns with Mara's contention that when she's most emotionally engaged, her "vision and her *visions*" are stronger. And then, of course, my uncle's own words echo back to me: *But when I was with Ellen, those largely latent talents became activated, practically supercharged. I did have a gift like yours. And when Ellen died, that part of me died with her.*

But on the other hand, my own experience with Pete Lewis doesn't fit the pattern. He broke my heart, and then I completely missed the looming disaster. I don't necessarily want to bring Pete up, but I need to understand this.

"What are you thinking?" Pankaj asks, perhaps out of politeness. I can't help but wonder if he already knows. I glance at my fancy Rolex. It's 8:58, two minutes before we need to be upstairs and pretend nothing's going on.

"Okay. So right before I got busted by the cops, I was hanging out with the guy I'd been obsessed with."

"Oh," he says evenly. "And?"

"And being with him not only *didn't* tip me off that something bad was about to go down; it pushed me to do the very thing that got me caught."

Pankaj shrugs. "I guess that's not so surprising either, is it? People who are in love do crazy stuff all the time. They're more 'suggestible' when they're in that state." He looks down.

"And there are always stories about the stupid things people do because they've been spurned by their lovers."

I swallow hard, embarrassed. "So it's a double-edged sword," I say out loud. *All that chemical stimulation can make you hypersensitive, but it can also make you reckless.*

Pankaj heads toward the stairwell. "We should head back to the lab. But later this afternoon I'm going to go back to the library and check out more of his files on the microfilm."

The word reminds me of the little canister of negatives burning a hole in my pocket. "Hey, do you know any places around here where I could get film developed?"

He smiles. "You use a camera that's not part of your phone? Do you do Civil War reenactments too?"

"No . . . I just have some old negatives I want to get processed. No big deal."

"What's on them?" Pankaj scans my face.

I know he immediately understands that I've stolen the film from my uncle. He also understands that the research project that he'd gotten started when I first arrived is about to become even more intense.

"Go now," he says. "I'll hang back here for another minute so we aren't seen walking into the lab together. At the end of the day, we also leave separately. But you'll meet me in town at five P.M. in front of that CVS on Horner Street. Got me?"

I nod. "I got you," I say over my shoulder, and finally start to feel somewhat better.

CHAPTER SEVENTEEN

At 5:01 that afternoon, Pankaj and I are stepping through the sliding glass doors of the CVS. I pause, breathing in carpet freshener and recycled air-conditioned air.

"I don't want to sound too paranoid, but I'm wondering whose eyeballs will see the pictures before we do," I whisper to him.

Pankaj shrugs. "I did some Googling at lunch, and aside from the Henley photo lab, which we *definitely* don't want to use, this is the only place near here that develops thirty-five millimeter film. I think it's our only option."

"I'm sure it'll be fine," I reply, trying to force myself to believe it.

A pale guy with unnaturally black, slicked-back hair mans the register in the photo center. Though he's wearing the regulation red polo and khakis, his sideburns and tats (red dice, vintage camera, forties pinup model) betray his rockabilly style. His name tag reads ZANDER. We stand there for a moment waiting to get the guy's attention, but his eyes are down as he looks at something just below the counter.

"Uh . . . *Zander?*" I finally say.

He looks up, dazed. "Dude, sorry about that." He waves his phone at us. "Just watching the latest news update on that shooting." He gives a "world's gone crazy" eye roll. "Anyways. How can I help you?"

Interest piqued, Pankaj holds up his index finger. "What did the news say? Did they find the shooter?"

Zander shakes his head. "No. Turned out to be a fluffy feel-good piece about a victim getting released from the hospital. No mention of the loose gun nut." He leans over the counter, closer to us. "I think it's 'cause they've run out of leads and just want the public to relax."

Pankaj and I nod back.

"So, I have some negatives for processing?" I put the roll of film on the counter, continuing to hold it for a moment as I try to make up my mind about the guy.

"Old school," he says, taking the roll from my hands. "Okay, no problem." He takes a pen and starts filling out an order form. "How many copies of each do you want? And do you want glossy or matte?"

"Just one set. Glossy's good."

"When will they be ready?" Pankaj asks.

"Like two to three weeks."

"Weeks?" Pankaj replies. "How is that even possible?"

"I know, right?" Zander flips his hands out, exposing the tattoo on his inner arm: a boxy black camera with LEICA emblazoned on the lens cap. He gives a sympathetic look. "It's like they send them for processing in China. Actually, that would probably be faster. But they have to go to a lab in Georgia."

I try to get a read on this guy. He clearly digs old-time photography. And while I sense he's not above helping himself to stuff off the shelves of this store, I also pick up an honor-among-thieves vibe. In short: I see him helping us. "You wouldn't be able to do it any faster, would you?"

"Kass, he just said they have to send them to Georgia."

I shake my head. "I'm just thinking that Zander probably knows his way around a darkroom." I throw a smile at him, the smile that says, *I have faith in you; you can do this; you* will *do this!* "I'll pay you whatever you think is fair. I just need these back fast. Like, as soon as possible. Can you do that?"

His eyes dart around the store, making sure his manager's out of earshot. "Fifty bucks, tomorrow morning?" he breathes.

"Deal." I flash another smile. "And we'll keep this between us."

Zander nods and pockets the negatives. "Cool."

Pankaj and I head for the door.

He waits until we're outside before saying anything. As he steers us back to campus, he shakes his head. "Must admit, Miss Black, that was impressive. How did you know to ask if he could print the pictures? You get some sort of read on him?"

Though I'd like to take credit for sixth-sensing it, I tell Pankaj the truth. "Well, I *did* get the feeling he was inclined to help us. But his tattoo sealed it. I just put two and two together."

He nods. "Legacy might be smarter than I've given her credit for."

"A lot smarter, Rocket."

"I HAVE AN IDEA," Pankaj says as we walk back up Horner Street. "It's a good one." He grabs my hand and drags me to a side street off the square.

I have no idea where we're going, but the block is full of quirky local shops selling things from decorative toddler socks to designer dog accessories. Because the sun is setting, everything is bathed in its pink-and-golden glow, and it reminds me what a great place Henley is—what a great place it *should* be—to go to school.

I keep my eyes on Pankaj when he drops my hand and takes a few steps ahead. He opens one of the shop doors and motions me inside. As I enter and take in the scent of Cece's Ice Cream's freshly baked waffle cones, my mouth starts to water.

"When you're right, you're right," I say. "This may be your best idea yet."

Grinning, Pankaj walks to the counter. "A cone of mint chip, please."

"That's my favorite too!" I exclaim far too gleefully.

"I know. I was ordering that for you. I don't like ice cream." He gives me a serious nod, but as my eyes widen in disbelief, he breaks out laughing. "Kidding! Who doesn't love ice cream?" He turns back to the boy at the counter. "Two cones of mint chip, please."

We finish our ice cream in the shop, and as we're leaving, he again takes my hand. I shiver from the touch and move closer to him as we walk down the deserted block.

"This is probably where your uncle's experiments with mind control would get interesting," he whispers.

As I feel his breath on my ear, my whole body begins to tingle. "Mind control?"

"You know, the dark essence of his life's work."

"Come on, that's not fair. You can't say that." I'm beginning to feel defensive again; I'm the only one allowed to question my family's questionable nature.

"You know it's true. The real reason why he wants people to become suggestible? He wants to be able to control how people act, what they do."

"Stop. That's a vicious, twisted lie . . ." I try to stay focused on my point, but with him so close, I lose track of what I was saying. "What do you even mean by that anyway?"

"Well, say I wanted you to kiss me right now." He doesn't break eye contact with me as he speaks.

I shake my head. *That's not going to happen.* The boy is trouble. I know this, and obviously I don't need any more trouble in my life. He can want me to kiss him, but I won't do it. I did it before, but that was simply to prevent his ass from getting kicked. The fact that he was a great kisser was just a nice surprise . . .

"Sure," he says, dropping my hand and nodding. Then he turns and runs, hanging a left at the first corner, about twenty yards away.

"Hey!" I yell, sprinting to catch up and dashing into the alley after him. Pankaj is breathing heavily and smiles when he sees me. "What was—" I gasp, watching him shake his head as he approaches, backing me against the wall.

And then I'm kissing him. Yanking him closer to me. We move as if we've always known this choreography. My brain feels wiped clean, and I'm aware of nothing but physical sensations. I let my hands explore his back. He kisses the skin on the side of my neck up to my ear, and my whole body warms.

When our eyes finally connect, he pulls back and blinks slowly several times. He flicks his hair off his forehead then brushes my hair off my face. Closing my eyes again, I hear him say, "What if I told you I implanted the idea to do that in your head?"

My eyes snap open. "What? No you didn't. I did that because I wanted to."

"Well, that's really nice to hear, but . . ." He shakes his head and presses his lips together. "You know what? Forget it. Let's just leave it at that."

I roll my eyes. "Tell me what you were going to say."

"Five seconds before we started kissing, you were offended that I'd slandered your uncle. You basically called me a liar, didn't you?"

This is hard to deny because it's completely true. "Well . . ."

"Well, I would be lying if I didn't admit I find it kind of hot that you get turned on when you're repulsed."

"Ew!" My head rears back, smacking the wall. "Ow! Gross!"

"Does that mean you want to kiss me again?" Pankaj asks.

Maddeningly, the answer is yes, though I will not admit it, or even think it if I can help myself.

"Okay, so you're trying to prove what?" I reply.

"That I really wanted you to kiss me," he whispers. "So I was doing my best to put that idea in your head. The experiments your uncle has been running with us—establishing 'limbic resonance' so we can *influence* cards—that's only a few steps away from this."

"But he's doing that because—" And then I get a flash: an idea that not only might make me feel more confident about what my uncle's up to but also might help him make his case to the Internal Review Board.

"What?" Pankaj asks. "What are you thinking?"

"I'm thinking about that archive in the library. It's part of public record, right?"

His head tilts slightly. "What are you suggesting?"

"I want to believe in my uncle's basic goodness. There must be *something* in those files that shows he's looking for a way to help, something that shows *why* he left the CIA and came here to Henley. If we're lucky, we'll prove that he didn't know how his work would be perverted. That he really does have only the best intentions."

Pankaj slaps his hand to his forehead. "I don't know what Kool-Aid you drank—"

"I'm serious. The possibility at least exists, doesn't it?" I bite my lip. "Be honest."

"Honestly?" He pauses, looks at the ground, and when he

finally looks back into my eyes, his face is serious. "I know very little, but here's what I *honestly* think: you're beautiful, you're brilliant, and you're a badass. Kass, I find you blindingly attractive, and nothing else is as true to me."

I reach for him, putting my hands around the back of his neck, and pull him to me. My eyes close, and that's when the pain roars through my head. I see flames. This is the clearest vision I've had yet: fire licks a window frame; I hear the crackle of the wood as it burns; I feel the heat of the blaze on my cheeks.

My eyes open.

Pankaj yells, "Fire!"

"Oh God!" I whisper.

I catch a whiff of what I fear is the smell of burning skin.

"Where is it?" Pankaj asks.

I don't have any idea, I say silently, reading the terror in his eyes.

CHAPTER EIGHTEEN

As we run through the halls of the Merion Building, the disturbing images of the blaze are long gone. In my brain, there's nothing but a low-level hum; white noise replaces everything else. We pound up the stairs two by two and race toward the lab. Finally, as we approach, I hear something: part of a conversation between Mara and Dan.

"... never survive it," Dan is saying.

"I don't know if that's true." Mara sounds almost pleading, as if she's trying to will another outcome.

"That's just how I see it going down," Dan says.

Pankaj flings the door open.

Dan and Mara look like they've been caught doing something they shouldn't.

"Hey, guys," Dan offers, startled. "What's up?"

"Have you seen my uncle?" I gasp.

"Not recently." He glances at Mara, who quickly and dismissively looks away from me, turning her eyes to Pankaj.

I glance at the wall clock and see it's late. There's no reason he'd be here. There's no reason the two of them should be here either . . . and I get another feeling—a physical sensation— different than the ones I've recently experienced, but no less powerful. It's a feeling of exclusion. It's that sense of knowing you're not wanted or welcome in a conversation. Given how Mara has turned away from me, I can't help but recall the vision with the hazy three-versus-one prophecy.

"He left with the guy with the flowing white hair," Dan adds.

"That was Figg," Mara confirms. "We saw him earlier. He's been around a lot since Pinberg died. We figured he had a meeting here with Professor Black. Might have had something to do with the Internal Review Board decision. Professor Black is really worried that they'll cut off his funding and shut the lab."

"I know . . . Will they?" I ask, finally seeking the answer I've been afraid to hear.

They shrug and shake their heads, implying they don't know. I can't tell if this is the truth. I sense more powerfully than ever that they're hiding something from me, but I can't understand why.

"We need to find the professor," Pankaj says to all of us. "Right away."

"Let's just call him." I unzip my bag to take out my cell phone.

"Won't work," Dan says. "The professor doesn't have his cell with him. I saw it on his desk when he was leaving with Figg. I tried to hand it to him, but he wouldn't take it."

"It *was* weird," confirms Mara. "If he didn't want to be disturbed, he could have just silenced it."

"I even made a joke. Well, *I* thought it was a joke," Dan continues. "I said, 'You afraid they'll use it to track you?' He didn't think that was funny at all. He tossed the phone back on top of his desk."

Pankaj shoots me a look.

Mara takes it in. "Why are you two so desperate to find the professor?" she asks.

"We both saw something," he says. "A fire. Here."

Dan's eyes widen. "On campus?"

I nod. "But we don't know where or when."

Mara glances between Pankaj and me. "It was a simultaneous vision? What are you seeing now?"

"Me? Nothing," Pankaj says. "Kass?"

"Nope. All of it's gone: the sight, sound, smell. Gone. Dan, is that what happened when you got your impression?"

He looks confused.

"I mean about . . . your dad?"

"Oh," he says. His eyes go blank, the way they always do when he's thinking hard about something. Then they snap back onto me. "That one hung around for a while. Sometimes I still see it in my dreams."

None of us says a word. For a moment, I regret I even brought it up; the trauma must be hard for him to shake. It's only been two years.

Then something strange happens. Mara takes Dan's hand.

The spontaneous gesture of empathy catches him off guard. Pankaj looks surprised too. I am somewhere beyond surprised. The jealous, threatening, unpredictable drama queen is gone.

"Let's get Alex on this," I say urgently. "Where is he?"

Dan frowns, still puzzling over Mara's hand. "I don't know. He said he had a dinner date with Erika, but then he got back to the dorm really early, carrying a doggie bag or something. He seemed off to me. Upset." He shrugs. "But what do I know?"

"Maybe he saw the fire too," Pankaj says. "You think he was having a vision?"

"It didn't seem that way to me." Dan pulls his hand away and scratches his head. "Maybe that's because it's not how I react when I get one. I'm more matter of fact about these things."

"Well, let's try to find him just in case," Pankaj says. "He could be closer to figuring this out than we are."

Dan nods. "Besides, I don't think Professor Black intends to be found tonight."

IT DOESN'T TAKE LONG to locate Alex. Pankaj and I find him leaning over the pool table in the Miller Student Center, measuring a shot with his stick. As soon as I spot him, I text Dan to tell him and Mara to meet us here. Alex looks up and catches Pankaj's stare.

"Cool if I play?" Pankaj asks.

Alex nods. I'm glad Pankaj speaks first since his greeting makes this sound like a nonchalant run-in as opposed to a desperate stalking. Pankaj picks up a cue from the rack that hangs on the wall and starts chalking it. He waits for Alex to get his shot off, but Alex paces up and down the length of the table making it clear that *he's* in no rush.

"We've been trying to find you," I say.

"Yeah? Why?"

"We need your help with something. We got a feeling something bad's about to go down, and we think you can help us stop it."

Alex backs away from the table. "It's too late." He exhales, his face clouding. "It already happened."

A pit forms in my stomach. "What already happened?"

"I was dumped." He looks back to the pool table as Pankaj starts lining up his shot. "Erika wants nothing to do with me."

I try to stop my eyes from rolling. Given what's at stake, getting rejected by a girl you just met doesn't seem all that traumatic to me. I glance at the entrance and spot Mara and Dan, and I wave them over to us.

Alex leans against his stick. "I really thought we had a

connection. I was already picturing a future together when I started school here."

"Here?" I ask, distracted, panic about the fire kicking in again. "Aren't you going to Harvard?"

"I was, but I asked Professor Black if he could pull some strings. I want to stay here at Henley."

Pankaj and I share a look.

"Um, I don't want to sound insensitive," Pankaj says, "but you guys only just met, and you already planned to switch schools?"

Alex exhales dramatically. "I always fall fast and hard. I don't even know how to explain it, but when something's there, it's intense. It's like there's a straight line from my heart to my head. As soon as someone starts making my heart beat faster, my brain gets taken up too. So whenever I get dumped, I'm wrecked."

The brain on love, I think to myself.

"What was it about her you liked so much?" Mara asks sharply, without bothering to say hello. Whether she just wants him to snap out of his self-pity or whether there's something like jealousy at play, I can't tell.

"She was like this perfect butterfly. Unique and beautiful. I guess I just found her . . . *blindingly attractive*."

The phrase "blindingly attractive" sends a chill up my spine. Pankaj said those exact words to me earlier. My head snaps in his direction, but he's focused on Alex.

"I'm sorry she broke up with you, man, but we kind of have an emergency here," he says. "Kass and I both saw a fire."

"And we know that people are going to die," I add. "But neither of us knows where or when it's going to happen. We thought you might be able to channel something?"

Alex slowly nods. "I'll try."

Mara watches Alex intently, as if she's analyzing him. "Do you need anything?" she asks. "Like a pillow, someplace to lie down?"

He shakes his head. Without saying anything more, he skulks over to one of the leather club chairs in the corner. The four of us watch as he leans forward, putting his elbows on his knees and shading his eyes with his hands. Tears start rolling down his cheeks. Pankaj nudges me.

Could it be he's crying because of the intensity of the vision? I ask Pankaj silently.

He gives me a hopeful shrug, though I'm not quite sure what to wish for anymore.

"I'm sorry, you guys," Alex says when he finally rises from the chair. "I didn't get anything. So I think you should just follow your instincts. If you think something's going down, be really careful, okay?"

"It's okay," I say, though I wish he would try harder. I want to push him, but I know there's no use.

"What now?" Dan asks.

Mara leans against the pool table. "I have a thought. I'm most receptive when I'm emotionally plugged in." She glances at Pankaj then looks at me. "You guys said you had a joint vision. Were you doing something that produced an emotional response?"

"We were sharing a pizza," I blurt.

"And that caused a joint vision?"

"It was really *amazing* pizza," I say.

She grimaces. "Okay then. You need to repeat the experience exactly. Go back for more 'pizza,' and see if it brings you back to that place."

I'm surprised. Shocked, really. It is quite clear that Mara doesn't buy the lame pizza line. And that would seem to suggest she's giving me the go-ahead to be with Pankaj. But the longer I look at her, the more I get the sense that she's giving us these instructions while holding her nose; Pankaj and me getting together is the lesser of two evils in her mind, which makes me wonder how evil the other option must be . . .

"If the pizza's really that good, I want to go too," Dan says.

"No," Mara snaps. "We don't know how much time they have to get this right, and any outside interference could throw things off. We can't risk it at the moment."

Dan crosses his arms over his chest. "Fine. But you guys better bring me back a slice or two, okay?"

I look at Pankaj. *Did you put the thought of trying that in Mara's head?*

I definitely would have if it occurred to me. Then out loud, Pankaj announces, "We should get going."

I nod, not knowing which of my feelings to trust and walk over to Alex, whose cheeks are still wet.

"You're going to be okay," I say, squeezing his arm. "You're going to find someone else who's even better and who appreciates you for who you are."

"Thanks, Kass." He forces a smile. "I know I have to do a better job getting my emotions under control. I just . . . I know it's ridiculous. I hardly knew her. This is just the way I am. We all have our stuff, right?"

I nod. "That we do."

AS SOON AS THE door to the student center closes behind us, Pankaj says, "Well this is an outcome I didn't expect."

"No kidding. And that Mara is telling us to do this? You think she knows what we were really doing?"

Pankaj is nodding before I even finish the question. "Oh, she definitely knows what's up. Alex may be the best telepath—when he's channeling things properly—but Mara's the one with the best understanding of the way it all works. If anyone can see the order beyond things, it's Mara. She's tuned in on that deep Jungian level. She's tuned in on the particle level."

I'm now too curious not to ask. "So what did she tell you when she gave you your reading?"

We walk in the direction of the Henley Gardens, and since we don't have a particular destination, this seems as good a place as any.

"She nailed my family, knew about some really tough stuff with my sister, Nisha," Pankaj says. He steers us to a bench that's partially obscured by the branches of a dogwood tree and brushes away the fallen petals before we sit. "She kept mentioning how important my mom was, and that I needed to listen to her." He rolls his eyes. "And then she said that I'd meet a dangerous girl who'd try to seduce me in a secluded wooded area."

"Dangerous, huh?" I say, cuffing him on the arm.

"She was pretty adamant about this girl bringing about my demise."

I catch a slight waver in his smile, and the expression betrays his confidence. He's wondering if I'm the threat. "Am I scaring you?"

"Yeah . . . but in a good way."

We say nothing for a moment, looking around at the flowers and shrubbery and trees and everything that is not each other. The fact that we need to get back to the "place" we were, as Mara put it, consumes us—and I think it's fair to say we're both terrified. I've started feeling shy and self-conscious on top of that, wondering if Pankaj has ever truly been attracted to me or if he and Alex just came up with a set of lines together. I'm midspin in this wheel of insecurities when I realize Pankaj is staring at me.

"What?"

He doesn't answer. Instead he simply leans in and kisses me.

When I pull back, thinking I should apologize for something (though I'm not quite sure what), he puts his arms around my waist and pulls me close. The gesture makes me feel singular, special. Doubt dissolves. I close my eyes and feel the heat radiating between us.

Then I start smelling smoke. The vision comes: flames, curling paper; sparks and shards flying skyward. The smell is so pungent that my eyelids squeeze tighter on instinct to prevent the smoldering ash from getting in. I hear Pankaj trying to communicate something over the roar of the inferno.

Body.

"Body?" I cry out loud.

"Yes!" he says. "Pea! Body! The library . . . Peabody Library's on fire."

We start running across campus in the direction of the library. I fish my cell out of my pocket and call 911.

"Nine one one; what's your emergency?" a nasal female voice answers.

"Fire! There's a fire at Peabody Library on the Henley campus."

"Fire, ma'am?" the operator responds calmly. "I'll send the fire department over right now and alert the campus authorities. Can you tell me where it started?"

I pull the phone away from my mouth and ask Pankaj, "Where'd the fire start?" He shakes his head at me.

"Ma'am?" the operator presses.

"Sorry, I don't know. But please come quickly."

"Hang up," Pankaj whispers. I follow his order. "Good," he says. "I was worried that you were going to say it hadn't started yet."

"Has it started yet?"

"I don't know," he says out loud. Silently he adds, *But if there's any chance of salvaging what we have here, let's hope not.*

CHAPTER NINETEEN

In the distance we hear the scream of a fire engine. We're out of breath when we arrive in front of Peabody, and I crumple from our sprint, grabbing my knees with my hands.

Pankaj looks at the building, pacing around me, elbows out with his hands on his waist. "We should go in . . . yeah?"

I can't tell if he's asking or telling. I don't see anything that looks like it's on fire, and though I pick up the scent of something in the air, I don't think it's smoke. "I don't normally advise running into a burning building, but I don't think anything's burning yet."

"So we should go in . . ."

Again the statement, which is maybe a question, dangles between us. The wail of approaching sirens makes it progressively harder to think.

"It's probably our last and only chance," I say. "Let's do it. Let's go." I walk to the library's door and hold it open for Pankaj. "After you."

"You know I'm going to deduct points for sending me first into an inferno . . ."

Weirdly everything seems normal as we enter the lobby. Students are reading in the reference room at the left; librarians are scanning books at the checkout counter; and grad students and professor types are milling around, looking a lot less happy than they should. For everyone else—those who don't know "better"—this is a day like any other.

Behind us, the library doors smash open.

We turn and watch eight firefighters, decked in long black coats and pants piped with yellowy-orange reflective tape, as they stomp into the building. They consult with the guard at the front then disperse in teams of two.

"They're doing a size-up," Pankaj whispers. "Checking things out to see what they're dealing with. Is there anything else we can do at this point?"

I look around, and as far as I can tell, we've done everything we can. "Since the fire department is already here, should we take another look at the microfilm?"

Pankaj nods.

A minute later, as we enter the Special Collections Room, we see that Erika's on duty. She smiles as we approach the desk.

"Hey, Punk! Hi . . . you," she says to me. "I'm sorry. You know, I don't think I ever caught your name. I hope you're feeling better?"

"It's Kass, and yeah, thanks. Feeling much better," I answer. "Alex isn't doing so well, though."

"Ah." She purses her lips. "He told you I ended things."

"Kind of came spilling out of him," Pankaj responds.

Erika shrugs. "I'm sorry; I know you're friends. He's just so intense. He wouldn't leave me alone. He was here all the time, and he—" She stops herself, possibly realizing that pleading her case to us isn't the right thing to do. "I just thought it was fairer and kinder to end things before he got attached."

Too late, I think to myself.

"Anyway," I say, "we'd like to take a look at the microfilm for the US Army Research Institute archive."

A strange smile crosses her face. "Funny, there's been a lot of interest in those things recently. I just checked two boxes out for some older gentleman who was here earlier."

Pankaj stiffens beside me.

"You wouldn't happen to remember his name, would you?" I ask.

"Not off the top of my head, but I can find out. He was a bit of a wanker actually." Erika walks over to the computer and types an access code. "C. Figg."

I turn to Pankaj. *Why was Chris Figg here?*

Strange, Pankaj instantaneously replies.

"How many boxes can we take at once?" he asks Erika.

"Officially two." She leans across the desk then whispers, "But being a FOE grants you special privileges."

"A foe?"

"Friend of Erika."

"We've got FOEs in high places," Pankaj mutters.

"Every FOE says that," Erika replies with a wink.

She and Alex had the winking thing in common, at least. Maybe there's hope for the two of them yet . . . But before I allow myself to get more distracted by wondering if butterfly-beautiful Erika is now flirting with Pankaj, or allow myself to get irritated by the possibility, I clear my throat.

"We'd love to take a look at however many you can snag without getting yourself in trouble."

Erika nods and heads back to the cabinet. Two firefighters enter the Special Collections Room while her back is turned. They sweep through the space rapidly, seeing neither smoke nor fire. "Here you go." She hands a few boxes of microfilm to

Pankaj and me. "You know how to use the fiche reader . . . ?" Her voice trails off, her puzzled eyes now on the firefighters who are regrouping in the library's main lobby.

"Yeah, thanks," I reply. I walk to the reader, drop my bag, and sit down. "Too bad Alex freaked her out," I whisper to Pankaj. "She actually seems very cool."

He grunts in agreement. I haven't even gotten the microfilm out of the box when Pankaj suddenly grips the back of my chair.

"Oh no!" he says, alarmed. "They're gonna leave."

"What?"

"The firemen didn't find a fire, so they're going to leave. Look." He nods in the direction of the picture window. Two of the firefighters are still conferring in the middle of the lobby, but the rest are trickling out the front doors.

"What do we do? We should keep them here . . . right?"

"I don't know." He looks as stumped as I feel. "What if this is like a Mara-versus-the-tsunami scenario? Did she tell you about that? She started getting visions *a month in advance*. We could be off by a month . . . or more."

He's right. Of course he's right.

I'm hit with a woozy wave of embarrassment. That possibility hadn't even dawned on me before. I grip my stomach, trying to massage away the sick juice that's now churning inside me.

"You're really white," Pankaj says.

"Excuse me?" I manage to croak. "My whiteness has nothing to do with my ditziness per se—"

"No." He shakes his head. "I mean all the color just drained from your cheeks. You look like you're going to pass out."

When he says this, it clicks. My gut isn't churning out of embarrassment or anger; it's warning me: danger looms. "It's soon . . ."

"When?"

I shake my head in frustration.

"Got it," he says. "At least you're getting something. I'm not getting anything." Pankaj chews his lip. "We need the firefighters to stick around. And if we want them to stay, we're going to need to give them a reason."

"You think we should tell them about our vision?" I ask, not wanting to.

"No, no chance they'd believe us. I think we need to give them a real reason to be here. We need to start a fire. Just something small. Easily containable."

My head shakes before I can get the words out. "No, absolutely not. That's a terrible idea. Plus, do you know what would happen if we got caught?"

"Kass, when has that ever been a concern of yours when you were trying to do the right thing?"

I stand and pocket the microfilm I'm holding. "Okay, fine, so then one of us has to find an out-of-the-way spot with no surveillance cameras." Strange how that happened so fast—I'm not only going along with his stupid plan; I'm now the one engineering it. "The other needs to convince the firefighters that there's a blaze they missed in their walk-through."

Pankaj massages his temples.

"What?"

"I just had an awful thought. What if our fire gets out of control? What if *our* fire is the one that becomes the inferno we saw, and *our* fire is the one that kills people?"

I flash to what Uncle Brian mentioned about the 'imperfect' nature of ESP: incidents with tragic consequences—probably just like this—where, owing to "failures of intelligence," the worst conceivable decisions were made. Are we really about to risk doing the same?

"No, you're right. We can't do it, it's too risky. And insane."

"Okay." He nods. "Okay. But what other option is there?"

I see flashing lights. I turn my head to look for the police car arriving on the scene. But there isn't one. When my head begins to thunder, I know the flashing lights are appearing only in my field of vision.

"Kass?"

I shake my head. "It's near. Something's going to happen very soon. I think you're right. I think the only way we can stop a major crisis is by starting a mini one." The trolley problem pings through my mind: If you kill an innocent man by pushing him onto the tracks of an oncoming train, you can save five other people from certain death. Do you do it? Rationally, the answer is yes. But that doesn't make shoving that poor guy in front of the train any easier. "Which part do you want to do?"

"You'll have more luck convincing the guys to take another look around," Pankaj says. "So I'll try to find a place where—"

"Bathroom," I interrupt. "No cameras, no books."

He nods. "Give me as much time as you can to find the right spot." He starts walking away, then quickly turns back. "Problem." He flips his empty pockets inside out. "How am I supposed to start a fire?"

I reach into my bag and pull out the Zippo lighter.

Pankaj almost smiles as he takes it. "That thing I said about you being a badass? *Namaste.* The light in me bows to the lighter in you."

We head for the door of the Special Collections Room. I wave at Erika and mouth, *We'll be right back.* She nods. I watch as Pankaj takes the staircase down to a lower level, then study the firemen for a moment as I feel the adrenaline coursing through me. My heart beats fast; if I'm going to do this, I have to do it now.

"Excuse me!" I call out, running for the firefighter who looks most senior, the one wearing the red helmet.

He turns his head as he's pushing through the door. "Yeah?"

I follow him as he walks outside where his men and truck are waiting. "So the fire's out already?"

"There was no fire," he replies. "False alarm."

"But I saw it." Not exactly untrue. I stare directly into his eyes. *Fire in the C-floor women's bathroom. Fire in the C-floor women's bathroom.* "That's why I was asking. I didn't see any of your guys go down to the C floor."

He looks from me to the fire truck. "You guys hit the C-floor, right?"

"Yeah, Captain," one of the men replies. "Of course."

Fire in the C-floor women's bathroom. Fire in the C-floor women's bathroom.

The captain's eyes widen, and he turns back to the library. He stares at the building for a minute then charges for its door.

"Captain?" the guy yells. But the captain doesn't answer. Instead he throws the door open and rushes back inside because he suddenly has the idea that there's a fire in the C-floor women's bathroom. Within a fraction of a second, several of the other men have mobilized and rush back into the building. Following them in, I watch them run down the stairs. After what feels like an eternity, Pankaj comes back up.

"Where?" I ask.

"C floor."

I feel elated, until I realize I've made a very stupid error: he wouldn't have gone into the women's room. "C-floor men's room?"

"Yes. *And no.*"

"What does that mean?"

"I lit some paper towels, but . . . I couldn't do it."

"So what did you do?"

"I threw them in the sink. I couldn't stop thinking that I'd wind up setting the fire that would kill people, and I . . ." He trails off.

I close my eyes. My stomach flares in pain. This was so incredibly foolish; Pankaj was right to try to stop me. But it's too late now. We screwed up. The firefighters are stomping back up the stairs, boots heavy on the steps, and the captain is heading directly for me, his face twisted in a scowl.

"We found charred paper towels in one of the sinks," he snaps. "But that wouldn't produce enough smoke to set off an alarm. So unless you set them on fire yourself, I'm not sure how you'd know that anything was on fire at all."

Neither Pankaj nor I answers. I am staring at the floor now, my pulse pounding in my ears.

"Falsely reporting a fire is a criminal offense," the captain is saying. "And setting a fire is arson, which is a felony."

Pankaj clears his throat. "Sir, I'm sorry. You have to—"

A thundering boom rips through the air. It's followed by the sound of shattering glass and collapsing debris, and I can hear nothing more. The floor rocks beneath my feet. My eyes widen; the side windows of the library have been blown out in a thunderclap of destruction. Instinctively, I wrap my arms around my face, one over my eyes, the other covering my nose and mouth.

"Mother of God," the Captain whispers.

I catch a glimpse of him slapping down the visor on his helmet and dashing toward the blast. Alarms blare and the library's quiet calm has dissolved into chaos. I see sneakers, shoes, legs rushing past.

Pankaj grabs my hand and yanks me out of the building. His hair and clothes are covered in soot. Outside of Peabody, in the plaza, everyone is wide-eyed, shell-shocked. Some of the people are scuffed and bloody too.

"Did we do this?" I whisper.

"No," he says, continuing to tug me away from the madness. He wipes smudges of ash off my face then pulls me into a hug.

When we let go, I feel something wet on my T-shirt.

I glance down and see a dark crimson stain creeping across the cotton. I can't tell if it's Pankaj's blood or my own, but I don't feel any pain.

"Oh my God, you're hurt!" I gasp.

Pankaj looks down. He puts two fingers through the slice in his shirt.

"Huh," he replies, with bizarre calm. I wonder if he's in shock. When he lifts up his shirt we see the laceration. Thankfully it seems to be a fairly small cut, but it's bleeding profusely. "Huh," he says again, squeezing the wound and picking out a shard of whatever it was that hit him.

"Kass! Pankaj!" Alex is running toward us.

I sweep him into a hug.

"Are you guys okay?" he says breathlessly, stepping away. "The vision just came to me, and I ran here as fast as I could."

"I'm all right." I nod toward Pankaj. "But he's injured."

"Oh no! Are you in pain?" Alex asks him. "Here, lean on me. We should get you to the hospital."

Pankaj shakes his head. "No, it's not bad. Once I clean the blood off, it won't seem like anything."

"I think you should go to the ER," Alex insists, and I nod.

"No," Pankaj replies with a slight edge in his voice. "I'm not going to the hospital. Can't. No health insurance." When I give him a look, he adds softly, "Anyway, I'm okay. I promise. It's just a cut." He glances back at the library. Its slate facade doesn't appear to have sustained too much damage, but a fire is raging inside; we can see the glow of flames through a dense curtain of thick black smoke. "I think the blast came from the Special Collections Room." His voice is shaking. "Where we just were, Kass . . ."

My mouth drops open.

I feel sick, light-headed, and it has nothing to do with ESP. Before I can speak, I see a firefighter coming out of the library with a body draped across his back.

I catch a glimpse of brunette hair.

It's Erika. Her head lolls on her neck. "Is she—"

I look at Alex. His face is blank, frozen. It's as if his blood has stopped circulating; there's no life behind his eyes. "I don't think she could have survived that," he says. Then, "She doesn't survive it."

He turns away. I put my hand on his shoulder, but he's rigid, and he doesn't soften or relax at the touch.

You see scenes like this on the news. You play through them in video games. Schools run crisis-simulation drills for moments like these. But nothing can prepare you for this: the smoke, the blood, panic, destruction, screams, fire, sirens, death.

Pankaj takes my hand and moves me away from Alex to give him space.

Alex wraps his arms around his chest as if trying to comfort himself. "I got this awful feeling a few minutes ago," he finally says, still facing away from us. "But I thought it couldn't be true. I was so sure we were going to get back together. I *saw* us getting back together."

"I'm sorry," Pankaj says. "I'm so sorry . . ."

Blinking red and blue lights animate the images of the chaos surrounding us. Sirens continue to wail. I look to Pankaj. The expression on his face twists from sympathy to confusion, then to abject horror.

"Oh no," he says. "No." His left hand rises and slowly lands on the top of his head. "No, no, no, no, no." He points toward the library entrance.

Alex and I whirl around. Another firefighter is carrying a

second body out of the terrorized library—a body with a telltale mop of dark hair.

It's Dan.

Alex's eyes go wide. As if in a dream, I feel my legs start to pump as I race back toward the pandemonium on the heels of him and Pankaj. An ambulance screeches to a halt in front of us. The back door flies open, and a gurney materializes. The firefighter gently lays Dan down. Time seems to slow, warping to a crawl as I approach. My head hovers above the bloody face and soot-covered, closed eyes.

"Dan! Dan!" I yell.

"I need you all to step back," a paramedic says.

Alex and Pankaj follow the order, but I can't pull myself away. I squeeze Dan's hand.

"Dan, it's Kass."

He struggles to unstick his eyelids. "Kass," he manages. "I saw—"

"Dan, you're going to be okay. Everything's going to be okay."

He coughs and a trickle of blood streams from his lips. His eyelids flutter closed.

Panic electrifies my brain. "Stay with me, Dan. Stay strong. You can do it."

"Danger." Dan's voice is a feathery croak, almost inaudible. I lean in closer to his lips. "It's close."

That's the last thing he says.

CHAPTER TWENTY

I'm not even through the front door when Uncle Brian sweeps me into a hug. His face is tortured, his clothing disheveled. His unkempt white hair sticks up in every possible direction. "Kass! Thank God! Thank God, thank God you're okay."

I'm not okay. I am numb. I am a zombie. It's disturbing, or it should be, because I should be feeling something, *anything*. But all I feel is hollow. "You heard about the explosion," I say.

"Of course I have. Everyone knows." He steps back, gripping my shoulders and looking me in the eye. "I had the dreadful thought that you were there when it happened."

I nod. "I was. We were."

"*We?*" This part he doesn't know. This part I have to tell him.

That's when the tears start. I nod, sniffling, feeling a dam break inside me. "Pankaj and me and Alex and . . ."

"And they're all okay too? Is everyone . . ." He doesn't finish the sentence because he can see this isn't the case. "Who?"

"Dan." It isn't until I say his name aloud that I am certain it's true. He's dead.

When the EMTs pushed us aside and loaded him into the

ambulance, they shut the door and then sped away, sirens howling—racing to save him. In my shock, I allowed myself to think of Dan as "gone," but my brain will no longer tolerate the euphemism. This isn't temporary. Dan is gone forever.

"Dear lord." Brian puts his hand to his heart. "Where is Dan now?"

"I don't know. I don't know where they took him. I don't know where the ambulance takes you. Maybe . . ." I can't say it—*the morgue*. I feel gutted. Dan was innocent. He was blameless. And he didn't go looking for trouble the way the rest of us seemed to. There is no way to explain or make sense of this.

There is only that vision. The blurry chronicle of a death foretold.

Again, I think of that uncertain, unformed vision Pankaj and I shared. Three of the four survivors will band together. But what it means for the fourth—and who the fourth is, or why she, he, *or me* gets left out—is even less clear than the vision itself . . .

Uncle Brian reaches out for me, pulling me once more into an embrace. "That poor child," he murmurs as his body rocks back and forth. "This is terrible. Awful. How does something like this happen?"

I shake my head. My body trembles with silent sobs.

"I have to contact his mother. She needs to hear this from me. I need to find his home phone number. He didn't give it to you by any chance did he?"

I pat my pockets for my phone, and I realize for the first time that, though I salvaged the microfilm, I left my bag and phone in the library. "Pretty sure my phone got blown to bits in there," I tell him, my voice hollow. I think about that room, and the fact that it's no longer there. My knees nearly give out. I cling to my uncle's arm for support. I wipe my eyes and meet his troubled stare. "Pankaj and I saw it."

"Saw what? What do you mean?"

"We *foresaw* it. We knew something was about to go down. We called the fire department so they'd be there when it did."

He takes a step away from me. "You *both* had visions about the fire?"

I nod. "But neither one of us knew where or exactly what would happen."

"Did the visions come simultaneously, or did one of you have it and then communicate it to the other?" There's a slight shift in Brian's tone. He sounds less like a concerned relative than a curious investigator.

"Same time, I guess." My jaw tightens. "Dan's mom?" I remind him. "Aren't you going to call her?"

"Yes, yes, of course, in a minute." He pauses. "Kass, I have to ask you: Were you and Pankaj being intimate at the time?"

"What? No!" I shake my head and back away—right into the front door. I'm so thrown by this question that I feel ill. "No. I mean, why would you even *ask*?"

"But you two are in love, yes?"

"No, I am not in love with Pankaj. I mean, I like him, but I am not in love with him! Why would you even ask me this now?" My fists clench at my sides.

"My mistake," he says, sounding unconvinced. "It's just that from my research I know the brain changes when we have strong feelings for someone. There's a chemical release in the caudate nucleus, which gives a person focus, stamina, and vigor. And it also makes them highly receptive to suggestion."

Hearing this mini-lecture now, this confirmation of Pankaj's suspicion, stirs even more anger and grief in my heart. It feels like my body temperature has risen by ten degrees in the last five seconds. "Can we talk about why the Special Collections Room was bombed? And who did it? Because I know at least two of the people who were blown up, and I'm thinking it has something to do with you and your archive."

The expression on Uncle Brian's face now, the horror in his eyes and ghastly paleness of his complexion, reminds me of what Pankaj said about Oppenheimer. Perhaps this is what Oppenheimer looked like when he saw the mushroom cloud: *I am become Death, the destroyer of worlds.* "You're sure it was the Army Research Institute archive?" he asks. "And it was a bomb? Not a gas leak of some sort—"

A loud, old-fashioned telephone ringtone cuts him off. Uncle Brian fishes his cell phone out of his breast pocket and frowns at the screen. "Your father," he mutters.

"Dad?" I say, the word coming out as a sob. "Can I—"

"Hello, William," Brian answers, holding up a finger for silence. He turns his back on me, striding toward the living room. "She's fine. Yes, I can imagine how terrifying it must have been to hear the news . . . She was in the library when the fire began, but thankfully the fire department was already on the scene and evacuated people very rapidly . . . How did you—Ah, a Google Alert. Yes, that makes sense . . . William, let me ask you: Did you have any other inkling?"

I'm not sure why I'm surprised Uncle Brian is taking this opportunity to probe Dad's ESP, but it annoys me. *Hello?* My father is calling to find out *about me*, not to participate in a telephone survey. I race after Uncle Brian, grab his shoulder, and spin him around, holding out my free hand so he can give me the phone.

"I see," Brian says to my dad, staring at me. "Interesting."

I begin tapping my foot, arm still extended. "Can I talk?" I bark.

"William," Brian says, "Kass would like to speak with you, but I think it's best if I just convey her message to you. She wants to tell you that she's fine and she loves you and Lucinda very much."

My eyes bulge. "No, that's not what I—"

"Of course. I'll let her know." Brian pushes the END button. "He says he's very glad you're okay and that he and your mother love you very much too."

I shake my head furiously. "What the hell? You know I wanted to speak to him!"

"Kass, we made a deal when you got here—"

"You don't think this counts as extenuating circumstances? Two of my friends are dead!"

"But *you're* fine." He looks me up and down. "Not a scratch on you."

"That's not the point!" I yell, feeling hot tears filling my eyes. "And I am not fine. I am far from fine."

"It's important that your parents learned you're not injured. It's important that you know that *they* heard about the explosion and they're sending you their love. But beyond that there's nothing to say."

I gape at him, flabbergasted. "Love isn't always about big romantic gestures, you know," I hiss. "It's also about just hearing someone else's voice."

"I know that, Kass. And *that's* the reason I didn't want you communicating with your father."

I run my hand through my bangs, enraged. "What are you talking about?"

"Because he loves you, if he hears your voice, he'll know."

"Know what?"

"That he's no longer the only man in your heart, even if you won't acknowledge it yet." In my moment of stunned silence, Brian adds: "You're welcome."

CHAPTER TWENTY-ONE

You forget how noisy everyday life is until everything stops. Background conversation, laughter, a bike passing, shoes shuffling . . . these are the sounds you take for granted until they're absent. And today, the morning after "the incident"—the day after Dan died and life for the rest of us changed forever—it's devastatingly quiet. It was like this after Professor Pinberg was shot too.

The rapid accumulation of these hushed days, of violent tragedies at Henley, is more than alarming. Many students are starting to pack up and leave, cutting short their summer terms. I can't blame them. Our lives keep getting punctured by catastrophe, then official comment, then silence: a roller coaster of shock, solemnity, and mourning is beginning to feel like a devastating new normal.

I am staying at Henley, of course—at least if Brian's funding holds through the summer—but the reality and horror of what's happened is somehow drowned in my own feeling of failure.

I knew there would be a fire, yet I couldn't save Dan's life.

I pick up the local paper on the way to the lab. *The fire left two dead, Erika Fellner, 21, a rising senior at Henley University from London, and a young man, 17, whom police have declined to identify until his family can be reached.* It also quotes the firefighters on the scene. According to them, the explosion in the library's Special Collections Room was likely the result of a natural gas leak. Leaving it at that feels like shoddy reporting to me.

Most departments have called in their faculty to discuss how best to handle student concerns. Uncle Brian, however, has been called to the university president's office. I don't know whether it's to discuss the HEAR funding issue or the fact that he lost a student. But I know that the lab is the one place he won't be this morning.

I texted the others to meet me here.

It's time for us to put our proverbial cards on the table. It's time to lay bare what each one of us knows, what each one of us really thinks about my great-uncle, and how we're going to move forward.

PANKAJ AND ALEX ARRIVE at the same time. Alex glances at the newspaper I've brought before he sits. He gives himself a spin on the lab stool then looks at Pankaj. "How are you feeling? How's the wound?"

"I've had better days," Pankaj answers grimly, cringing as he eases down. "You?"

"That sounds about right." Alex shakes his head. "It's weird. I've never felt like this. I mean . . . it's like a hole. I don't think I've ever been this sad. Or this numb."

Mara shuffles in. Her face is blotchy from crying; there's no need to ask how she's feeling.

"Gas leak," Mara spits as she sits down, with a disdainful nod toward the paper. "Who do you think planted that story?"

"Probably the terrorist who planted the bomb," Pankaj

replies. He winces, lightly rubbing his fingers across his black T-shirt on the spot over his wound. "And I'm willing to bet it's the same terrorist who shot Professor Pinberg at the mall."

I stare at him, caught off guard. This is new, this theory. I can't help wonder if his injury made him somehow more sensitive in some way. But whether it increased his ability to see connections or merely his desire to draw conclusions, I can't tell.

"What makes you say terrorist?" I ask.

He shrugs. "Acts of terrorism aren't all that hard to commit. I don't want to say any idiot can pull one off, but lots of idiots have. Look in the right places, and you can find bomb-making recipes to cook up in an Easy-Bake Oven."

"He's right," Alex agrees, rubbing his swollen eyes. "Back in the Boy Scouts, we used to blow stuff up in the woods all the time. Any one of us could do it, probably with our eyes closed."

"Right, but why an act of terror?" Mara presses. "I'm not saying I disagree with you; I'm just wondering why you don't think it's the enemies of Professor Black."

"I'm not saying it *isn't* them," Pankaj says tiredly. "I mean . . . the purpose of terrorism is to terrorize people. You scare them enough so they stop what they're doing. Professor Black is working on something that's threatening or considered threatening by a lot of people. Maybe someone is trying to tell him to stop. That's why they killed his friend at the mall. And when that didn't work, they upped the ante."

Alex's mouth drops open. "You really think that's what's going on?"

"What else could it be?" Pankaj asks with another shrug.

"I don't know . . . I think you're part right," Alex says, staring off into space. "But I think the mall shooting was totally unrelated. I mean, this is America. Shootings in malls and office parks happen all the time. Give people easy access to guns, and that's what you get; a personal vendetta becomes a bloodbath," he says with disdain. "But bombing a college library is a different story. A college library is a symbolic target. You take out a nation's best and brightest, you're a hero to whatever screwed-up group with a screwed-up agenda you're trying to impress."

I have to admit I'm as surprised by Alex's idea as he was by Pankaj's. "You think the library has *nothing* to do with my uncle?" I ask him.

"Random and reasonless except in the mind of the angry zealot behind it."

Chaos theory, I think.

"There's tons of online chatter about it." Alex quickly types something into his laptop then turns it around for us to see. We slide off our stools and gather around him.

At the top of a website called Poison Control is the image of an X-rayed fish. In the fish's belly is a man, swallowed whole, who appears to be struggling to get free. Beneath the picture is the site's slogan: "Your Antidote to the Mainstream Media." Tabs to news on 9/11, Osama's "burial," the Boston Marathon bombing, and vaccines are on the left side of the screen.

Mara leans in first, her eyes darting across the screen. "What is this?"

"It's a conspiracy website," Alex replies. "I couldn't sleep last night, so I started doing some poking around online. Here." He scrolls down the home page until we see an image of Amory Gate with the caption *Henley University Library Bombing: Information Warfare.* "Whoever writes for Poison Control specifically blames the 'New World Order,' for planting the bomb."

"What's the New World Order?" I ask.

"Apparently it's a repressive group of elites that seeks to rule the world." He opens another window and pulls up Reddit. On that site, theories abound about which terror organization did it and why. "I almost feel bad for the National Counterterrorism Center," Alex says, "because they have to look at all this stuff and then sort out claims of responsibility."

"You think there will be *multiple* claims of responsibility?" I ask.

"Oh yeah, of course." He nods. "When a bomb goes off, loads of groups come forward so they can get the glory."

"That's sick."

Alex tries to smile but can't. "Sick is a euphemism for what it is."

"So how do they figure out who really did it?" Mara asks.

"Well, they start by examining the signature of the explosive device—determining if it contains dynamite, C-4, fertilizer, or other high-grade explosives—and then based on the signature, they compare it to the group's previous activities."

"You know a lot about this," Pankaj remarks.

"Like I told you, I was a Boy Scout," Alex says. "I got merit badges in chemistry and crime prevention." Mustering a grin, he adds, "Also Indian lore and wood carving, which is why I'm never without my trusty knife." He flashes the three-finger Boy Scout salute. "Be prepared!" He sighs, and the grin fades.

As I stare at the conspiracy site and think about Alex's words, it occurs to me that if perpetrators leave evidence behind at the crime scene, fingerprints are probably on their advance work as well. I reach into my pocket and retrieve the box of microfilm I've been carrying with me since I was last in the library. "I took this because I thought it would show that my uncle was trying to help people with his work. But now I'm thinking it might give us clues about who his enemies might be."

"Interesting," Alex says, sliding off his stool. "Yeah, let's go find out."

"I bet you they have microfilm readers in the Elliot Center," Mara adds. "That's where the Film Department is."

At the word "film," I remember something else: we need to get back to the CVS to pick up the pictures my new friend Zander was developing.

"The Elliot Center," Pankaj repeats, touching his midsection. "There's a CVS near there, right? I need to stop in there to get some more Band-Aids."

I don't need to hear his voice in my head to know we're on the same page. "I'll go with you . . . I need tampons," I add, to quash any suspicion.

"Okay," Mara says impatiently, heading toward the door. "Alex and I will head over and try to find one of the microfilm machines."

"Great, we'll meet you in the Elliot Center in twenty minutes," I say.

BEFORE I ENTER MY PIN into the CVS ATM, I scan my surroundings even more carefully than usual. But the pall over Henley has been cast over the entire town, and it's quiet here in the store too. There are very few other customers.

The machine spits out cash, and Pankaj and I head toward the photo center. Zander sees us approaching, nods slyly, and reaches under the counter.

"Didn't know if you guys were going to come with all the crazy stuff going on," he says.

"Yeah, well." I shrug, not wanting to get into it.

"Pretty disturbing stuff." He slides the envelope of pictures across the counter. "Fifty."

"Let's ring these up," I say, placing Pankaj's box of adhesive bandages on the counter. "I'll pay for the whole thing in cash."

"Good call." He rings up the bandages on the cash register

and then places everything in a white plastic bag. "So that comes to $7.89 with tax."

I hand him three twenties. "Keep the change."

WE HEAD STRAIGHT FOR the Elliot Center, occasionally glancing around to see if anyone's following us. But it isn't until we arrive at the building that we're stopped. Two guards sit behind a white folding table just beyond the door.

"Open your bag," one tells me after he pats me down.

I glance at Pankaj, who gives a slight nod; we have nothing to fear from the rent-a-cops. They're only here to make sure we're not terrorists ourselves. So I open the plastic CVS bag, and the guard peers inside before letting us pass.

Pankaj points to the end of the hallway.

"Right here in the open," he suggests when we get there, sliding down the wall to sit directly below the eye of the building's security cameras.

Once I'm seated next to him, I take the pictures out of the bag. The first photo is of a motel sign: THE MANOR INN WELCOMES YOU! The next is a shot of the motel itself: one of those prefab, cookie-cutter buildings, the kind that look like the person who designed them had the artistic skills of a second grader.

"Did I just pay fifty bucks to have my uncle's vacation pictures developed?"

"I don't think so," Pankaj replies, pointing to the next photo.

My breath catches in my throat. It's a picture of a dead girl—a child, maybe five years old. There's a hideous gash on the side of her head and neck. Her lips are violet blue. "Oh my God," I whisper. "You don't think this is real, do you? I mean . . ." I don't even know what I mean.

Pankaj takes the picture out of my hands and scrutinizes it. "It doesn't look fake."

I shake my head and start shuffling through the rest of the photos. None of them are in a motel; most are in a classroom of some sort, but it's not a warm and welcoming elementary school. There are no construction paper letters or inspirational posters taped to the walls, no displays of student artwork. It's clinical, antiseptic . . . like our lab. The rest of the photos are mostly candid shots. Almost all feature a naughty-looking blond boy, smiling from ear to ear as he punches, pushes, or trips other children.

"Damn," Pankaj says, "what is up with that kid? He looks like he's possessed."

"What about her?" The very last photo is of a little Indian girl wearing a frilly pink dress. She stands apart from the other children, who seem spooked. "Looks like a tough little cookie."

Pankaj gives a short laugh. "She reminds me of my older sister at that age. That I managed to survive Nisha's reign of terror is a minor miracle. This girl even looks like her—or maybe it's just the crazy in the eyes."

That's when it hits me. The answer's so clear. "Pankaj, this is Figg's camp for the kids with behavioral issues . . . That *is* your sister."

"What?" Pankaj seizes the photo. "No, it can't—"

"You both spent time here, right?" I interrupt.

"Uh, *no.*" He chuckles, shaking his head. "I was not a camper in a program for screwed-up kids."

I wag my finger. "You weren't in the group for the disturbed children. But you *were* a camper here. You were in the group with Mara and me."

"Kass, I *think* I would remember being in a camp with you and Mara."

"I don't remember you being there, either. But Uncle Brian told me you were."

Pankaj's head shakes in disbelief as he continues to stare at the picture. "I mean, yeah, this does look a lot like Nisha. I *guess* it's possible she was here. But why would I have no memory of *me* being here?" He turns to me again, and his amber eyes reveal his vulnerability.

"Because memory is slippery," I say, repeating what Uncle Brian told me. "Especially when trauma's involved."

Pankaj hesitates. "Kass, if you know something, tell me," he pleads.

"I don't." I shake my head, adamant. "I don't know anything, I swear."

But he and I both know these pictures are clues to the answers we seek.

His phone pings with a text from Mara: on 2nd floor.

"Come on, we need to find Mara and Alex," he says after a moment. *Let's keep this to ourselves*, he adds silently, though he didn't have to. It's understood.

CHAPTER TWENTY-TWO

We race up the stairs to find Alex and Mara sitting side by side against a closed door.

"No microfilm readers," Mara says as she hops to her feet. "But the good news is that we found a screening room. Unfortunately," she twists the doorknob, "it's locked."

Alex stands and claps his hand on my shoulder. "But there are advantages to having sketchy friends, aren't there?" He gives me a wink.

No use trying to argue; he's right. I glance back toward the stairwell. Though there were security guards and even some students milling around on the ground floor, the second floor seems deserted. I quickly pull my keys out of my pocket and insert the tension wrench into the bottom of the keyhole, jiggling the rake in the top of the lock. When I feel the pins drop, I twist the knob, and the door swings open on a darkened room.

I turn back to the others. "Okay, *my* job here is done. Now which one of *you* can thread this weird old film through a movie projector?"

"Me." Mara holds out her hand. "I can."

I'm doubtful, but I shove my keys back into one pocket and pull the microfilm from another. "All yours."

She takes the film from my hand and vanishes into the shadows.

Alex follows, flicking on the lights. Pankaj and I exchange a wary glance and creep in after them, shutting the door behind us. The room is smaller than I expected, strewn with folding chairs and with a large screen at the far end. Several projectors, everything from a multimedia LCD to a Super 8mm film projector, sit on a table near the door.

"One of these should to the trick," Mara says, perusing the devices. She settles on the one that looks oldest to me and feeds the film through it. She pushes various levers until we hear a locking sound. "Good," she says, flipping on the projector's light. Images blink across the screen.

"Nice!" Pankaj exclaims, sounding relieved something's gone right.

Alex flicks off the lights.

But a moment later the picture turns back to black. The spinning wheel makes a slapping sound as the tail of the film smacks the metal reel.

"Sorry, my bad for jinxing it," Pankaj mutters.

"I just need to find a way to slow it down," Mara says, mostly to herself. After a few minutes of tinkering, she looks up. "It'll be herky-jerky, but this should do it."

Images flash in front of our eyes: nondescript buildings, shot from various perspectives. It looks a lot like Google Street View. I can't fathom why someone thought these places were important enough to catalog.

"They're targets," Alex says, answering my unasked question.

"What makes you say that?" I ask.

"Because if I were planning an attack, this is exactly the type of information I'd want too."

None of us has an answer for that, but we all nod.

Next, there's a flowchart of hierarchy for the Counterintelligence Center Latin America team. I lean forward in my chair. Deputy Director Ellen Rios is at the top. Graham Pinberg, Brian Black, and Christopher Figg are below: "Analysts." Next to Graham Pinberg's name is a small *x* along with a hand-scribbled note reading, *Resigned 10/13/83*. There's nothing surprising or illuminating in this, and I slump back in my chair until the next document comes up:

079977

DEATH CERTIFICATE
DISTRICT OF COLUMBIA HEALTH DEPARTMENT
BUREAU OF VITAL STATISTICS

№ 14016

INFORMATION NOT LISTED DOES NOT APPEAR ON ORIGINAL RECORD.

FULL NAME OF DECEASED (First)	(Middle)	(Last)
Ellen	Alma	Rios

ADDRESS (Street and Number)

SEX	RACE	MARITAL STATUS	DATE OF BIRTH (Mo., Day, Yr.)	AGE
F	W	Single	8-24-1948	36 Yrs. Mos. Days

OCCUPATION	BIRTHPLACE
Civil Servant	Philadelphia

NAME OF FATHER	BIRTHPLACE
Rafael Rios	Camden, NJ

MAIDEN NAME OF MOTHER	BIRTHPLACE
Towers	Atlanta, GA

DATE OF DEATH	CAUSE OF DEATH
7-11-1985	Natural Causes

NAME OF PHYSICIAN	ADDRESS
H. J. Cameron	----

PLACE OF BURIAL OR REMOVAL	BURIAL DATE
William Penn Cemetery	7-14-1985

UNDERTAKER	ADDRESS
Manny Shoemaker	564 Ridgepike Road

INFORMANT	ADDRESS
----	----

I hereby certify the above to be a correct copy of a Death Certificate filed in this office.

_____   _____
(Date Issued)   (Registrar)

82-158 (Rev. 6/82)

My eyes go directly to the cause of death box. Though I wouldn't know how to state the "cause" of death when someone's blown to bits, I'm pretty sure it should be considered anything but "natural."

I look to Pankaj, but his eyes are fixed on the screen as he scans the next document, a letter to Christopher Figg confirming his appointment to the position of Deputy Director of Latin American Operations. The one that follows is an interdepartmental memo stamped CONFIDENTIAL.

Due to BB's erratic behavior the Agency can no longer consider him a trusted asset and recommends his ouster. The committee proposes two potential courses of action:

1. Burn notice
2. Neutralize

Pursuant to the nature of these operations, sign off is required from MKJ. We respectfully urge immediate action, whichever course is chosen.

Pankaj whistles. "They don't kid around."

"I don't understand what that means," Mara says from behind the projector.

"A burn notice is something an intelligence agency issues to discredit an agent or informant," Pankaj replies, flinching as he glances over his shoulder because of the pain in his side. "I knew all those hours I spent watching TV detective shows would come in handy one day . . . Anyway, a burn notice means a person has become unreliable. Maybe they've flipped allegiances or gone bonkers or whatever. So from burn notice forward, all the other agents are literally supposed to trash or 'burn' any information the person provides."

"And neutralizing an agent means offing him." Alex illustrates with a finger slash across his throat. When I start shaking my head, he looks at me with surprise. "Seriously, Kass, that's what it means. Trust me."

"No, Alex, I'm sure you're right about that. I mean *this* doesn't make sense." I point to the memo. "After Ellen Rios was killed by 'natural causes,' Chris Figg took over her position, and Uncle Brian got booted from the Agency for acting crazy."

"Yeah." Pankaj rubs the bottom of his chin. "And that all kind of makes sense given what happened, doesn't it?"

"No, it doesn't. Here's why: If my uncle was really considered such a loose cannon that he could no longer be trusted by the CIA, why would Chris Figg, who had just been promoted within the organization, choose to run a camp with him here?"

Nobody has an answer. I glance around the room; Alex shrugs and crosses his arms over his chest, leaning back in his chair. "They were friends. Maybe Figg felt bad for him. Or maybe he, personally, never lost faith in Professor Black? Maybe Figg knew once he'd recovered he'd start working on something groundbreaking."

"Well, then he was right about that," I mumble.

Mara straightens. "What do you mean?" she asks. "Do you know something, Kass?"

I wonder if *she* already knows what I know. But at this point, we have to share any information we have, redundant or not. "He's working on a drug that will boost visions. A drug to get his ESP back." Again, I scan the room and try to get a read on the others; again, I find them inscrutable.

Alex lets his chair fall forward, and it hits the floor with a bang. "You know what? I'm going to retract my earlier hypothesis about the library just being a symbol for a terrorist. The drug is obviously the motive. That's why all of this stuff is happening."

"But if that's the case, why not just bomb the lab?" Pankaj asks.

"Think about it: the stuff in this archive is literally *history*." Alex's face is somber. "The drug is the future. Literally, it's about seeing the future. So if I wanted to scare Professor Black, I'd start by annihilating his history to show him how easily I can erase any legacy he hopes to leave."

Alex's theory makes a sick kind of sense. But agreeing with it doesn't provide any solace. It just fills me with rage.

"So Dan died because somebody wants to scare my uncle?"

"Is Professor Black scared?" Alex asks me.

I nod.

"Then the plan worked."

AS WE LEAVE THE Elliot Center, Mara suggests we go back to her dorm room "to see what the cards have to say." I don't know that any of us wants a reading, but I'm certain none of us wants to be alone.

Mara's room is pretty much what I imagined: tchotchke and candle filled—with a dream catcher tacked above her bed, a batik dragon on the wall.

Alex flops on the bed, and Pankaj makes himself comfortable on a big bolster pillow on the floor. The boys seem completely at home, as if they've both spent time in these exact positions before. Unfortunately their comfort only sparks discomfort in me. It feels like the union of three has come together, and I'm odd man out. I look at Mara, who's shuffling the tarot cards but scrutinizing my face; it's as if she can see what I'm feeling.

"Kass, let's start with you," she says. "We get the best readings when we have questions to ask. You look like you're seeking something, which means you're receptive to finding an answer. If you have nothing to ask—if you assume you already know everything—you're incapable of learning anything."

I reflexively want to disagree with her, but I don't think she's wrong. "Okay, fine," I reply.

When she finishes shuffling the cards, Mara carefully fans them on her desk and instructs me to pick three. I point to the cards I want, and she plucks them from the deck, placing them in front of me.

She turns over the first card. It's a smiling Grim Reaper holding a long scythe. On the bottom it says, DEATH.

"The Death card?" I shake my head. "You did that on purpose."

Mara gasps as if I've truly offended her. "You picked it yourself."

"The Death card?" I repeat. "You're saying you in no way manipulated the deck so that this was the one to appear?"

Her posture straightens. "I would never do that! Do you *really* think I'd be that insensitive after what just happened to Dan and Erika? Anyway, it's not literal. Death's message is about change. You have to shed long-held beliefs if you want to gain new energy and new life." She fixes her eyes on mine. "The only way for you to go forward is to let go of your ego and admit to your mistakes."

I return her stare. *Admit my mistakes?* I'm about to tell her the only mistake I made was letting her anywhere near my "fortune," but she raises a finger.

"But that's just the first card," she tells me. "We need to see what the others say."

"You know what? I think I'm going to stop at Death."

"Your loss," she huffs. "But maybe your closed-mindedness is something you should take a look at."

"Who wants to go next?" I ask sarcastically. "Pankaj?"

"Nah, I'm good from the last one." There's an edge in his voice.

The last one? I'm somehow stung by this, as if he just confessed to kissing another girl.

"I did Pankaj last night," Mara says. She glances at Alex as she reshuffles the deck.

Alex hops off the bed. "Do me."

Mara nods, spreading the deck in front of him, once again fanning the cards carefully. But this time, I notice that her fingers are trembling. Even after all that's happened, I have no idea what's going through this girl's head. Why is *she* nervous? Is she worried she's the outsider?

Alex pulls three cards from the deck and places each one face up in front of her. "All righty then, what can the Moon, the Three of Swords, and the Nine of Swords tell you about me?"

Mara's eyes roam from card to card. "It's an intense draw," she murmurs, her fingernails drumming the surface of the desk. "The first is your past. It's about what's influenced you and the energies that surrounded you. The middle card is your present situation, and the third is about your future possibilities."

"So what does the Moon have to say about Alex's past?" Pankaj asks.

"The Moon is a shadowy figure—in every sense." Mara's voice quavers and she clears her throat. "She's closely associated with our unconscious and the astrological sign Pisces, which is known for being psychic and mysterious."

Alex looks to Mara for something, maybe approval, but her eyes remain on the reading. "That seems to track, doesn't it?" he asks.

"We know the Moon literally turns the tides. Figuratively, she moves us by speaking to our animal instincts." Mara seems to be gaining confidence as she speaks. "See on the card how the crayfish is crawling out of the water and there's a dog and a wolf howling into the distance? These represent the dawning of our consciousness. They also embody our deepest fears."

Alex sniffs, unimpressed. I can't blame him. Not only has he always been skeptical of the tarot stuff; Mara's "reading" is general enough to fit anything or anyone.

"Of course the Moon also lets us dream our way out of these scary situations. If you were on a sinister path, you could still change it. Jung believed the Moon represents our 'shadow self,' or the unconscious mind. He thought the happier the person seems on the outside, the darker the person's soul. He also believed that this shadow was prone to projection."

"Like this?" Alex makes bunny ears with his fingers, letting the flickering candlelight cast its projection against the wall.

Mara shakes her head, now entirely self-assured. "No, meaning you turn your own personal insecurities into perceived failings in others."

"What?" Alex says incredulously, throwing his hands in the air. "You're only saying that because you're a lousy reader!" He sounds angry, but then he winks. "Get it? Perceived failings . . . ?" He and Pankaj laugh. "Okay, so that's the Moon card. What's the Three of Swords?"

"It suggests you've experienced heartbreak."

The smile drops from Alex's face. "Let's move on to the next card."

She nods, and her eyes are sympathetic. "The Nine of Swords is really similar to one of the Major Arcana cards, the Hermit. It suggests you're trying to work through some conflict alone, to protect yourself. Look at the image: a woman with her arms crossed, trying to shield her heart. And here, you see the owl? The owl represents wisdom. There's knowledge and support close at hand. It means you can get help if you seek it." She finally looks up at him, her voice soft. "You should seek it."

Alex rolls his eyes. "Okay, thanks, Mara."

She sighs. "It's just what the cards say."

A long silence settles over the candlelit room. I look at Pankaj, who gives a strained smile. "Switching topics," he says. "What's the latest with the professor's Internal Review Board meeting? Did they postpone it?"

"I don't think so. In fact"—I look down at my watch—"I think the meeting's scheduled for about two hours from now."

"You're kidding? Professor Black doesn't get a pass for having one of his students die?" Alex sounds offended. "You'd think he'd get a reprieve for at least a year."

"Like when your roommate dies, and you automatically get straight As?" Mara says.

"That doesn't happen; that's just urban legend," Alex says dismissively. "I don't know. It just seems like *something* good should come from Dan's death. Right?"

But no one answers. Apparently none of us can find an upside.

CHAPTER TWENTY-THREE

It's a little before four o'clock when I arrive back at Uncle Brian's home, and I find him knotting his tie in front of the hallway mirror. I can feel anxiety wafting off him, and even without the ESP he once had, I'm sure he can feel mine too.

"I need you to tell me something," I say, skipping the hellos.

He looks at my reflection and continues to form a Windsor knot. "And what might that be?" he asks tersely.

"Did you leave the CIA by choice?"

Brian presses his lips together and yanks the cuffs of his shirt under his coat sleeve. "Yes, Kassandra. And to answer your next question: had I not quit, I would have been fired. I was broken by grief, no longer trusted anything or anyone, and was no longer useful to the Agency. But you already know all this."

I move to the stairs and sit, maintaining the mirrored eye contact. "Christopher Figg would have fired you?" I ask him.

He turns to face me. "He would have had to get rid of me, yes. So he privately advised me to take my leave instead."

As I search his eyes, puzzle pieces start coming together. *Get rid of me*: another euphemism for neutralize. Another euphemism for murder.

"He saved your life."

Brian nods. "That's correct."

"And that's why, when he wanted to run the kid camps with you here, you agreed. You owed him one. You literally owed him your life."

Brian turns back to the mirror, straightening his posture for a final once-over. "As I told you, the Agency has relationships with many of the world's best universities, so when Chris offered funding for a special joint project combining some of my research with his, I tried to view it in that context. To see it through a rose-colored lens, as opposed to seeing the cold truth: I was being manipulated." He looks at his watch and turns away. "Now, have I answered all your questions? Because unfortunately I need to head back to campus. The review board will shortly be deciding my fate."

He reaches for the doorknob. His hand lingers there for a moment before opening the door. Looking at my uncle now, I wonder if I'm being unfair. He's not the one who caused Dan's death, and from what evidence I have, it seems like he was a target too. Maybe keeping the lab open would, in fact, be the best revenge, a way to show the terrorists, whoever they are, that they haven't won.

"By the way," he asks quietly, his back still turned, "do you think any of the other HEARs know how this meeting turns out?"

I can hear the smile in his voice. I almost laugh. "I asked. Unfortunately I think we're all in a blind spot here." But I suddenly get an idea, and I'm about to suggest he call my dad to see if he has any thoughts on the matter, when a white-hot flash of pain cracks through my head. My insides heave and I clamp my hand over my lips to stop myself from vomiting on the rug.

That's when the doorbell rings.

Uncle Brian starts, spins toward me. "Were you expecting someone?"

I shake my head. It's all the response I can muster.

He moves to the side of the hall and peeks out the curtain. "Speak of the devil," he mutters, opening the door.

A man with longish white hair, rimless eyeglasses, and a burgundy silk handkerchief billowing out of his blazer's breast pocket stands on the welcome mat. "Brian!" Chris Figg says, holding his hands out expansively. He doesn't wait to be invited in. "It is a good day!" He beams as he crosses the threshold. Despite being as old as my uncle, his demeanor is more like a student's; the pride in his voice suggests he just aced another calculus test. "And hello, Kassandra." He sticks out his hand, then thinking better of it, pulls me into a hug. "How long has it been?"

I am trapped by the bear hug, unable to speak. It's so constricting, I wonder if he'll snap my ribs.

"Thirteen years," Brian replies. When Figg releases me, Brian pats him on the arm. "Chris, forgive me for being rude, but I need to leave to get to—"

Figg stops him with a shake of his head. "Brian, it's handled."

"Sorry, what?"

He smiles and a certain mischievousness animates his face. "I put in a call to Claire Shipman. She's acting head of the Internal Review Board. I told her that there's no need to put you through the wringer this afternoon when there's already a perfect solution for all of us."

Brian's eyebrows rise. "A solution?"

Figg seems to be enjoying both Brian's confusion and his own performance. He reaches forward and lays a gnarled hand on my great-uncle's shoulder. "I simply pointed out that they could easily make up your budget shortfall by funneling the money allocated for Graham Pinberg's lab to yours."

Uncle Brian takes a step back. His face registers a whirlwind of emotions: relief, remorse, and most of all shock. "That seems—"

"Like the only way to make the best out of a tragic situation? Like the best way to honor our friend's memory?" Figg interrupts. "I agree. You and I both know Graham would have insisted we all carry on. And now we can. I'll even be there to assist."

Brian nods automatically, but I can tell he's not present. His mind is racing, and I try to discern what he's thinking, what exactly he feels he owes this man who is once again his savior.

"But what about the fact that the university people don't like my uncle?" I blurt. "Was Pinberg's money really all it took to convince them to keep HEAR open?"

Figg smiles down at me then glances at Brian. "This one is almost too smart for her own good." There's an edge in his voice.

I sense danger at the edge, but I need to keep pushing. "And how are you going to be assisting here?"

"Well, Kass, as you so rightly noted, your great-uncle doesn't always get along with everyone." Figg slides his hands into his pockets, trying a more casual pose. "But I have a way with people and can be very convincing when I need to be. That's why I'm certain if we team up again, there's no end to what we can accomplish together. In fact, that's why I've decided to leave the Agency and work with Brian full-time once we hammer out some details."

Uncle Brian's eyes lock on Figg's. I wait for him to respond.

When he doesn't, I do it for him: "What details?"

"That, I'm afraid, is something your great-uncle and I are going to need to work out on our own," Figg says, eyes still on Brian. "You understand, I'm sure."

I do understand. I'm being told to leave. Which is fine, because if I stay a second longer, I just might puke on both of them.

CHAPTER TWENTY-FOUR

I stayed away from the house for the rest of the day, opting to wander the campus by myself. I wasn't in the mood to socialize. Not that I had to worry about speaking to anyone; the school grounds are like a ghost town now, deserted, quiet, and terrifying. The smell of the burned library still lingered in the air, and I watched a few of the remaining students load up their cars before getting out of town.

When I walked back to Uncle Brian's house later that night, I went directly to my room. I heard him puttering around on the third floor above me, and though I'm certain he heard me come in, he didn't welcome me home or make any attempt to say hello either.

A note was waiting for me on the kitchen table this morning: *Early meeting in town. See you all in the lab at 9:00.—BB*

WE'RE ALL SEATED BY the time Brian enters, and it occurs to me that this is the first time he's been with all of us together since the library bombing. I wonder if the others need my great-uncle to provide words of wisdom, or hear him promise everything's going to be okay, as much as I do. I glance at Pankaj, but his head is down, his bangs over his eyes, conveying the gloom we all feel.

Brian drops his coat on his chair and places his bag on his desk, then steps to the workstation at the front of the lab. "You would think that at my age I'd understand death, have some insight about tragedy," he begins. "But I'm sorry to say I don't. I still can't justify or make sense of it. I can't explain why some of us are taken, and some remain behind. Though we only had Dan with us for a short period of time, I think we all sensed what a bright and wonderful young man he was."

I hear Mara sniffling and pass her a pack of tissues from the plastic CVS bag that's become my de facto book bag since . . . the library.

"But we can't let the loss we feel paralyze us," Brian continues. "We need to stand against the forces of fear and let Dan's legacy be our lives." He pauses and looks at each one of us. "I believe we should pay tribute to Dan the same way we're paying tribute to my dear friend Graham, by carrying on with their work." His voice catches, and he steadies himself at the workstation. After a shaky breath, he goes on. "To be able to do this, we owe a debt of gratitude to my old friend and colleague Chris Figg who has conditionally agreed to save our lab. And in return for his help, we must help him."

My eyes meet Pankaj's.

Here we go, he says silently.

"How?" Alex asks.

"He has intelligence about another imminent attack, one targeting more of our best and brightest."

Alex used exactly the same phrase, "best and brightest," when he theorized why people would bomb Peabody Library. But that he was right doesn't give me any sense of security or confidence in our abilities; it just makes me even more uncomfortable.

Brian pauses, crossing his arms over his chest. "He believes you may be able to identify the terrorists involved."

I think of the memorial in the chapel planned for Erika and Dan tomorrow. People who've never met either of them will come and weep. After tragedies like this, you see these enormous outpourings of grief from the community. Strangers come to cry because they think, *It could have been me. It could have been my loved one.* And they feel connected by the shattered illusion of safety they once shared.

"And how are we supposed to do that?" Mara demands. "Identify these terrorists?"

"Remote viewing," Brian replies. "A version of one of the exercises we've done previously. I have no idea what the prompts are or what type of visions they may lead to." He heads to his desk and opens the large bottom drawer, removing a manila envelope. "But whatever the prompts inspire, I want you to tell me what you think or see or feel. Even if it seems to have nothing to do with terrorism as we tend to think of it. Understood?"

We nod in silence. Mourning is over, apparently.

"Now, we need to do this in a designated testing area. Come." Without another word, he leads us out of the lab. We follow him down to the basement. After we descend two flights in silence, he points to a door at the end of the hall. It's the same spot where Pankaj and I had our hushed conference, two lifetimes ago.

Alex clears his throat. "Professor Black, I had a thought," he says. "Given how urgent this situation is, maybe now would be a good time for us to try the booster you've been working on."

Brian doesn't answer. His gaze flickers over Alex's face, scrutinizing every detail.

"We all know what you're working on," Alex continues.

"What else do you know, Alex?" he asks.

After a moment, Alex shrugs. "The booster is designed to make ESP sharper for those people who have it. It also gives ESP to people who don't." He pauses. "Like you."

My uncle casts a sidelong glance at me, as if silently accusing me of sharing information that should have been our family's business alone. But I'm with Alex; this is hardly our family's business anymore. Three people are dead. More may die very soon.

"Professor Black, it *is* true that your drug could work on the wider population, isn't it?" Alex demands.

Brian turns back to the closed door at the end of the hall. "Yes," he admits.

"So if it's that powerful, why don't we all give it a shot?"

"Because I don't know if it's safe," Brian snaps. "The drug is still an x factor. I won't risk harming any one of you with it."

I shake my head, not caring that he sees. He's lying. At the very least, he's covering up, given how he's treated us to date. He'll deny me contact with my own father; he'll keep us on campus with terrorists at large; but he won't let us try out this drug that he's certain will work? Yet even as I lay out the conditions and contradictions in my mind, I get the logic: this isn't his decision. It's coming from Christopher Figg. Now that Brian has joined up with his old friend again, I wonder how much control my great-uncle really has . . . over not only his life, but ours.

THE ROOM IS EMPTY but for five soft brown leather chairs, lined up and facing the back wall. Directly across from each chair is a semirecessed light, its caged bulb partially protruding from the wall. It's like the set of a bizarro sixties game show.

"Please take your seats in this order," Brian says, "Mara, Pankaj, Kass, Alex."

"Restraints?" Mara says, wagging the straps on the sides of her seat.

"You need not concern yourselves with them," Brian says. "We won't be using them for this experiment."

Pankaj shoots me a look. *You caught that, right?*

For this *experiment,* I answer silently. *Yeah, I caught that.*

MARA DESCRIBES A COMMERCIAL landscape full of strip malls, fast-food places, and budget hotel chains. "Felt like what you see when you're driving on an Interstate in the heartland." In the distance she saw a car dealership's giant American flag waving in the wind. But what she heard was the sound of screaming, a small voice begging, "Stop!" She then saw the terrified face of a little girl. "And all of a sudden, there was this thundering crash," she says. "And the screaming ended . . . The little girl's screaming ended."

ALEX REPORTS SEEING SOMETHING similar, though his scene is more detailed: big American flag, McDonald's playground abutting a prefab hotel that was designed to look a chateau. "The girl was tortured before she was killed," he says. "And I heard the crash too. It was the sound of her skull smashing against a brightly colored slide."

PANKAJ REELS OFF A string of numbers: 6102429587. He describes his vision by saying it was like a computer overlay on his brain. He then gives a data dump, stating chains of numerals, all separated by dots, making them sound like geolocation coordinates.

I SEE NOTHING.

CHAPTER TWENTY-FIVE

After the experiment, Uncle Brian asks me to join him for lunch. His tone makes it clear that it's more an order than an invitation. I know he's worried that I was the only one who said I came up blank after hearing the prompts. Maybe he thinks that I was holding back. He doesn't know that I have reason to be worried myself: three had information to give him; one did not . . . and I *genuinely* didn't see anything. Maybe this is the moment when that partial vision I shared with Pankaj finally comes true. I'm the odd one out, and the other three are closing the circle without me.

Brian is pensive as we sit in a booth at the local pizza joint, our slices untouched. I know he's wondering if what the others gave will be enough to satisfy Figg. It seems hard to imagine how any of it could be considered useful. But since Uncle Brian has yet to ask me about the experiment, I decide to begin with my own question.

"Why do you trust him?"

Brian glances around the restaurant before answering. He leans in. "What do you mean precisely?"

I look around before replying too, but since I don't know what I'm looking for, I just start talking. "You know who I mean. I know you need money for the lab at this point, but you told me you left the CIA all those years ago because you stopped believing in the mission. Because you didn't like what they were doing. What makes you think 'the mission' or Chris Figg's motives are any different now?"

"People change, Kass."

"Do you mean him or you?"

He takes a bite to buy himself some time, then puts down his slice and wipes his mouth with his napkin. "Both, I suppose," he says after a while. "It's important to remember that the only thing that stays constant is our evolution. We all change mentally and physically. Our wants change; our needs change."

I push my pizza away, feeling vaguely ill. What is it that he needs? Is it the glory? Is he putting us all at risk just because he wants his ESP back? Is there yet another reason still unknown to me? I stare at my uncle, but I can't read his thoughts. They are locked behind those world-weary eyes, staring back at me.

WHEN WE RETURN TO the lab, the other three are already seated at their workstations. I want—I *need*—to check in with Pankaj, but he stares out the window and doesn't acknowledge me. When he finally turns, I smile at him. He immediately looks away, shifting his attention to the ground. I continue staring at him, but he won't glance back in my direction.

Something's off. I feel it the way you know something's wrong when a text goes unanswered for too long, or your calls keep going to voice mail.

Hey, are you okay?

Pankaj doesn't respond. I stare more intently, willing him to look at me, to explain what's wrong. He keeps his head down;

it's answer enough. He's not okay. Does the fact that the others had visions and I didn't mean they shared something that I *couldn't*? Has this altered what he thinks of me?

"We'll just have to wait and see," Brian says.

My head snaps in his direction, and I'm about to tell him to butt out when I realize he's not speaking to me. He's simply responding to a question Alex asked. But seeing the expression on my face, he says, "Yes, Kass?"

"No, I . . . Sorry, never mind."

Brian opens his mouth, but right then his cell phone rings on his desk. "I have to take this," he says with a glance at the caller ID. "We'll reconvene later this afternoon. See you back here at four o'clock."

Pankaj is first to leave the lab. He practically sprints out, making it clear he doesn't want company, so I hang back and wait for Uncle Brian to finish his call. But when he sees me lurking by the door alone, he motions that I too should leave.

Close the door behind you, he mouths.

Mara and Alex have disappeared too by this point, and by the time I get outside, I feel more depressed and alone than when I first arrived on campus. I start walking, not knowing where to go or what to do. Eventually I realize I'm heading in the direction of the boathouse where Pankaj and I shared our first vision.

That's where I find him.

He's sitting by himself on the dock, staring out over the lake. He doesn't turn as I approach, but he knows it's me. "I was wondering when you'd get here," he murmurs. Finally he turns and brushes that long black hair away from his amber eyes.

"Where are Mara and Alex?"

"Don't know and don't care," he replies.

Right. I sit down beside him on the uneven wooden planks. "Can you at least tell me if this is about that experiment? Is it because you saw something and I didn't? Because giving me the cold shoulder for that after everything else we've been through—"

"Kass, this isn't about you," he interrupts. "It's something else, I swear . . . I spoke to my mom."

"Your mom?" I repeat. Is this some kind of dodge? My mind races to put things together, but I can't make anything connect. "What does she have to do with any of this?"

"Mara kept mentioning my mother when she read my cards. She made it seem like my mom had some kind of knowledge, and that I *needed* to talk to her. Of course I didn't buy it at first—my mom and I don't have a good relationship—so I kept ignoring the advice to talk to her. But after I saw those pictures and you said Nisha *and I* had both been here before, I had to find out more. So before our testing session this morning, I called her."

"Okay . . . and?"

"The very first thing my mom says to me is, 'Have you seen Nisha?'" He gives a WTF shrug. "*Have I seen Nisha?* I'm like, Mom, I'm at Henley. She goes, 'Yeah, I know.'"

I shake my head, feeling like I've missed a step. "I don't understand."

"I didn't either," he replies. "I figured my sister just pulled another one of her disappearing routines—she does that, just leaves home with no warning, no note. But she always comes back eventually, so we've gotten used to it. That's why I couldn't understand why my mom would ask if Nisha were here, *at Henley* of all places." His eyes widen as he seems to be reliving the conversation. "She says, 'Because of the man who called for her. You know, the one with the ponytail who took you to Henley when you were kids—*Figgy*-something.'"

"But what does Figg want with your sister *now*?"

"Mom didn't know. And now my mind is racing; I start

thinking about the camp again, and I asked her how we got picked for it as kids. She goes, 'Pankaj, they never *picked* you. Nisha was the one they wanted. But I told them you were a package deal: you can't have my daughter unless you take my son." He turns from me and stares out over the lake.

I know what Pankaj is thinking: he doesn't belong. He never did. "But you have ESP," I whisper. "Of course you're supposed to be here with us."

He turns back to me. "Think about it, Kass. Think about our vision. I'm obviously not part of the group that matters. I never have been. I'm not one of the chosen three."

I see the pain on his face, and I want to tell him the "union of three" thing doesn't matter. But I'm not sure I believe that. "Of course you are. Think about *us*, about you and me." I take his hand.

He shakes his head; it's not enough for him.

"Then what about the experiment today? You were the one who rattled off all those numbers. Alex, Mara—they both saw something. I was the one who had nothing."

He pulls his hand from mine and looks me in the eyes. "I made it up."

"What?"

His lips turn in a sad smile. "I was so out of my head and screwed up after talking to my mom, I couldn't see *anything*. So I just started rattling off a bunch of numbers. Nisha's birthday, her cell phone number, zip code. Totally meaningless stuff."

I don't know how to respond, but I do know there's only one person who can explain it to us. "When we get back to the lab," I say, "we tell my uncle nothing else happens until we speak to Figg. Nothing else happens until we get answers."

CHAPTER TWENTY-SIX

It's three when Pankaj and I get back to the lab, and we find Brian sitting at his desk, writing notes on a legal pad.

"Uncle Brian?"

Startled, he jumps at the sound of my voice, then checks his watch. "What are you two doing back here so soon?"

"We need to speak to Figg," I say. "Do you know where we can find him?"

"No." He shakes his head. "But I believe he has some business to take care of just now. So why don't you come back at four?" He stands and walks over to us, making a "shoo!" gesture with his hand. "Four, like I said earlier." There's a look of concern on his face as he tries to move us to the door. "Go outside and enjoy the nice day!" He flashes an unconvincing smile.

Gee, I can't tell if he wants us to leave, I silently say to Pankaj.

He's being so subtle about it . . . Let's push him a little, see what we learn. Pankaj turns to Brian. "I think we should just wait here," he says out loud. "It's really important that we speak to Mr. Figg."

Brian shakes his head. "No, no, no. You'll see him later. Go on, get out of here, you kids," he replies, desperately trying to sound jokey. The tone doesn't work on us or Alex, who over-hears this as he strolls into the lab.

"Wow," Alex chuckles as he repositions the large gym bag he's carrying on his shoulder. "You don't have to be a psychic to see *someone* doesn't want you to stay here, huh?" Unlike Brian, Alex appears *genuinely* upbeat, as if he's somehow shaken off the sorrow consuming the rest of us. Whatever workout he's just done seems to have worked wonders on his mood. He takes a seat at one of the lab tables and drops the gym bag at his feet.

I watch my great-uncle, now literally wringing his hands. Though I don't know what's up, my goal is not to antagonize him. "Okay, guys, let's vamoose," I say, acquiescing to his wishes.

Pankaj shrugs then nods.

"You two go on ahead," Alex says. He spins on his stool. "I'm actually wanted here." He looks at Brian with expectant eyes. "Right, Professor?"

Brian glances at his watch again. "I, uh." He gives a hesitant shrug. "That's very possible."

That's very possible? That's *very* weird. I wonder if this has to do with the vision Alex had in the experiment earlier today. Maybe Pankaj and I are being excluded from . . . *whatever this is* because neither one of us saw anything.

"Where's Mara?" I ask. I look at Uncle Brian first. He shrugs, so my eyes go back to Alex.

"I don't think she got a written invitation like I did." He holds up his phone. From a distance, I can see texts have gone back and forth. "But it wasn't Professor Black who told me to come back here now. It was his old pal Chris Figg."

As if on cue, Figg walks into the lab.

Alex gives a jovial laugh. "Well, speak of the devil!"

Figg glances around the room. He turns when he hears

footsteps behind him. It's Mara. "You're all here." But he seems not only surprised to see us; he seems angry.

Brian's head shakes as if he's hoping to deflect the anger. "Chris," he says, "I promise you I told them to come back at four."

"He did," I confirm with a nod. "But now that we're all here, maybe you can answer some of our questions, Mr. Figg."

"Not now, Kassandra." Figg's eyes stay in motion, sharklike, as they survey the room. "In fact, I suggest you take your little friends out of here for a while."

"That's okay," I reply. "We'll wait."

"Point, Kass!" Alex laughs, clearly enjoying this. "Your move, Figg."

"Alex, why don't you just come with me?" Figg says. "We'll leave, so the rest of them can stay. Save us all a lot of trouble."

"That's okay," Alex says, his voice teasing. "I'm good here too."

"It's not a suggestion, son."

Alex shakes his head as he moves his bag from the floor to the table. "I'm not your son. And even if I were, I'd still disobey you. 'Cause that's kind of son I am." An eerily familiar grin crosses his face. In that moment, as I witness that grin—somehow boyish and somehow menacing—an intense feeling of déjà vu crashes over me. But it's not because of any ESP.

Faking a sneeze, I turn away, rattling the CVS bag looped around my wrist. Instead of rummaging for tissues, I rifle through the recently developed stack of photos. Mara catches the commotion, and in the charged stillness of the room, she strides toward me.

"I still have your tissues from earlier, Kass," she says. "Sorry about that. Here you go." She holds the package out to me as I come to the picture of the blue-lipped dead girl. Our hands collide just as Mara sees the picture.

She makes a barely audible gasp.

That's the little girl I saw screaming during the experiment, Mara says silently, her voice coming through clearly in my head. *She's the girl whose skull got smashed.*

I flip to the next picture, a close-up of the grinning little boy. *And he's the one who killed her.*

Even though she's speaking soundlessly, I hear her distress. I turn back to Alex. There's no doubt; I recognize that same grinning boy even though he's a decade older. One section of this puzzle has come together, at least. Now I understand Brian's urgency in getting rid of us. Figg's "business" is to come take Alex away. And our presence throws a wrench in the plan.

"You don't want to do anything you'll regret, Alex," Figg says.

"I'm not so worried about that, Mr. Figg. Regret's not one of my go-to emotions. Anger, yes." He stands and starts pacing. "Jealousy, of course. If I 'regret' anything, it's probably that I care too much, but it's not like I have any psychological or emotional hang-ups about it."

Pankaj laughs, not yet seeing what I do, not sensing the danger. "Dude," he muses, "the lady doth protest too much, methinks!"

"You're right, Desai." Alex nods with appreciation. "I don't know why I'm even bothering to justify myself to this clown. Especially when I know he would have done the same thing had he been so wronged."

Pankaj's smile drops. "Uh, what?"

"How were you wronged, Alex?" I ask. I wonder what a little girl could have done that would have upset him so much.

"She broke up with me." He looks baffled that I hadn't already assumed this was what he meant. "*I told you Erika broke up with me. And we were in love.*" He shakes his head as if still struggling to believe the rejection is real.

My mind races; I can't figure out how Erika relates to the girl he killed. And forget the fact that Erika's now dead too—that she dumped him seems to be what Alex is fixating on. *That's* what seems to be upsetting him most.

"I mean, it was love at first sight," he continues, "incredibly deep and intense, and it just grabbed both of us by the throat."

I recall that last conversation with Erika at the library. She also used the word "intense," but she used it to describe Alex's behavior . . . and his intensity was one of the reasons she broke up with him.

Alex approaches Brian, his palm out. "You know what that's like, don't you, Professor?"

Brian's mouth drops open, but he hesitates before answering.

"Of *course* you do," Alex replies for him. "That's how you got on this whole kick of yours to begin with. You're also trying to regain lost love."

Brian shakes his head. "No, Alex, that's not why I—"

"Don't be coy. Maybe you're not trying to get your girlfriend back specifically since she's been gone for so long." He rolls his eyes as if *that* would be crazy. "But you're trying to get the feeling back—and what *the feeling of being in love* does to you. You know, what it *gives* you." Alex smiles as Brian takes a step back. "You see? We're not so different after all."

"That's not true," Brian manages. But I can see that he's been affected by Alex's words.

"Okay, Alex, you've made your point," Figg says. "It's time for us to go."

"No, I don't see that happening. Remember, I'm really smart, Mr. Figg, and I don't want to be the puppet of an idiot puppeteer anymore." Alex moves his arms like a marionette then grabs his gym bag. "So I'm cutting my ties with you, and I'm leaving here. By myself. And you and I are going to say goodbye forever."

"Bravo!" Figg says loudly. *"Bra-vo!"* he repeats, even louder the second time.

Bravo?

It's only as two men in dark suits storm into the lab that it becomes clear "bravo" isn't a compliment. It's a code word. Now flanked by two fierce-looking men whose jackets bulge with what no doubt are concealed weapons, Figg faces Alex. "Drop the bag, Alex. It's over."

"You don't get to end this," Alex replies.

In a flash, Alex pulls a large knife from the bag's front pocket, and in a few quick steps, he's seized my great-uncle in a choke-hold. I am momentarily paralyzed, as if not truly present, as if watching in a vision, while Alex's knife waves perilously close to Brian's carotid artery. But this is no vision. This is happening, here and now.

Brian gasps for breath. His eyes are wide behind his glasses. His limp arms dangle in front of him.

Before thinking twice, I run at them, but just as instinctively, one of the CIA suits runs at *me*, tripping me. I land on my palms with a smack. All at once, there's a very painful bone digging into the small of my back. It's his knee, pinning me to the floor.

"Get off!" I rasp.

"Alex," Figg whispers, trying to sound composed, "now let's not do anything rash. You know you don't want to hurt Professor Black."

"Do I?" he asks. "Do I know that? Because I thought the fact that I hurt people was one of the things you liked best about me. In fact, should we tell them who suggested I get that merit badge in knife skills? Wink, wink."

Figg's expression is blank, a perfect poker face. From my very uncomfortable position at shoe level, I can see that Pankaj and

Mara are frozen in fear as they stare at Brian, who's turning red in Alex's hold.

"Listen to me, Alex," Figg says evenly. "You've always been an incredibly talented young man, and your abilities can still be of great use to the country."

Alex snorts. "Figg, I know how you work. You'll burn me just like you burned the good professor. You should thank me! I'm just doing the work that you'd eventually do yourself anyway."

My eyes move to Figg. The old CIA deputy director takes a step back, blinking. Whether or not Alex's accusation is true, no one in this room doubts it could be, not even the man whose knee is currently bruising my kidneys. I flash back to what Uncle Brian said about rattlesnakes, seeing for the first time both Alex and Figg for what they truly are. Still, in this moment it's impossible to determine which of the two is the more poisonous.

"Alex," Mara says, "Kass and I know you killed that little girl. But Mr. Figg and the professor knew it too. They've known about it for a long time. So think about it," she pleads. "It must not have bothered them. Obviously they must not have cared, so . . . don't do this. There's no need to do this."

"Mara," Alex says, mimicking her tone, "you *obviously* don't know *everything.*"

The only thing that's clear to me now is that Alex will kill my great-uncle.

Out of the corner of my eye, I see Pankaj edging toward them.

"Come on, man," Pankaj says. "Let the professor go. He's old and he never meant you any harm. You need a hostage; take me instead of him."

Alex laughs. "Uh, no offense, Pankaj, but he's the one of value here. He's the one with the ESP booster. You're just a delinquent."

Pankaj shakes his head, looks somehow disappointed. "Alex,

the booster's not ready yet. He'd be using it on himself if it were. You're smart. You have to know that. So the professor can't help you now, and he doesn't have ESP. But *I* do. And if you and I team up, what could stop us?"

I feel a twinge of unease as I watch Pankaj getting closer to Alex. I know he must be doing this to help out my uncle, but there's something dangerously convincing in his performance . . .

Alex pauses for a moment, loosening his grip on Brian's neck. "You are reasonably intelligent yourself, Pankaj," he says. "And I have been impressed by the way you've conned Kass this summer."

Conned?

"She hated you at the beginning. Now you have her wrapped around your finger."

"I only wanted to prove to myself that I could make her fall for me," Pankaj says. "But like you said, it was just a good con." He gives a dismissive laugh.

The words hit me like a kick to the gut; the laugh feels like a grenade.

"Anyway, it's not like her family would ever let the two of us be together." Pankaj shakes his head. "They'd destroy me before letting me be with their daughter."

"That's actually true," Mara quickly adds. "The cards have always said that. That's why I told you to stay away from him, Kass."

This is one comment too many. I struggle to break free and get up, but it's hopeless. I'm trapped, forced to endure this torture.

Pankaj doesn't look at me as he walks past, moving closer to Alex. "Come on, man. Let's do this. Let's go."

"I have always liked you, Desai, and it would be nice to have a partner in crime." Alex smiles sadly at the room. "So here's how this is going to work: Desai, you approach the door. Get down on your belly when you reach it."

Pankaj follows his orders, sliding his legs into the hallway and keeping the top half of his body in the lab.

"Good," Alex says. "Now braid your hands together behind your back."

Once Pankaj's hands are behind him, Alex picks up his bag and starts walking Brian out, using him as his human shield. When he gets to the doorjamb, Alex slowly bends down. In one fluid motion, he violently releases Brian and grabs hold of Pankaj's clasped hands.

As Brian crashes to the ground, Alex stays focused on securing Pankaj's hands. But what he ignores are Pankaj's legs. They spin into Alex's ankles, knocking him off balance. Pankaj wriggles away as another body, leaping in from the hallway, hurtles itself on top of Alex.

I watch Pankaj struggle to stand, his hand holding his bleeding midsection where the wound from the bombing has reopened. Still on the ground myself, I can't see the face of the person now holding Alex. But as I look across the floor, I recognize him from his shoes: Flip-Flops. From his waistband, the man-boy I'd assumed to be no more than a drunken college student pulls out an industrial-size garbage bag tie. He wraps it around Alex's wrists and yanks it closed.

Pankaj helps Brian to his feet. "Professor, are you okay?"

Brian closes his eyes. "I will be."

Nobody bothers to ask this question of me. But that's okay. I doubt I would have given the same answer.

CHAPTER TWENTY-SEVEN

Mara sits between Pankaj and me at one of the picnic tables in the lobby of the Merion Building. Uncle Brian and Chris Figg are on the other side. It feels like we're in some sort of bubble within a bubble. The people who casually walk by have no idea what we've just been through. They couldn't begin to understand. How could we possibly explain it?

After Alex was hauled off, Uncle Brian, still shaken and rubbing his bruised neck, suggested we too leave the lab. "We can all probably use a cold drink and some refreshments," he said as he shepherded us out. "We'll make Mr. Figg pay for it," he added with a meaningful glance in Figg's direction.

But I don't want a drink. What I really want is time alone to process what just happened . . . and what was said. Still, what I most want is for Figg *to pay*, so I went with them.

Here, at this ridiculous indoor picnic table, as I sit next to my "allies," I can feel the distrust and disgust boiling on our side of the table. We all still want and need answers, but none of us seems ready yet to speak to Figg or to one another. I look at Mara and Pankaj and shake my head. With allies like these . . .

Fine, I'll start.

Both of their heads turn in my direction. Message (obviously) received.

"So while you were running Camp Dodona, you were also training an army of violent children. You needed them to do your dirty work; is that right, Mr. Figg?"

He takes a sip of his drink and sets the can down before answering. "We want to be careful not to stigmatize by calling those children violent, per se, Kass. We use the acronym CU, for callous-unemotional."

Even after all that happened this afternoon, the old spook's still trying to spin the story.

What a dick, Mara says silently.

"You're a dick, Figg," Pankaj says out loud. "We're all thinking it."

I nod. "And I'm curious, Uncle Brian: Did any of those *CU*s have ESP?"

"No," Brian replies. "The CU children did not possess any extrasensory perception as far as I'm aware. But, truth be told, there's a very fine line between psychopath and telepath neurologically speaking."

Glancing at Mara and Pankaj, I realize *that* was information I could probably have done without.

"And for your information, callous-unemotional people excel at certain tasks that those with a conscience frequently find difficult to accomplish," Figg says. "They require very little convincing to become snipers, for example. And though *you* may consider this dirty work, it's work that's necessary to the security of our country." The man is unbowed; he's argued this point of view many times before.

I can't even look at Figg. I'm so angry I might spit on him. So I refocus on my uncle and try to make sense of this. "Didn't you personally invite Alex to be part of the group here this summer? Or did he force you?"

Brian's nod of admission is more like a pathetic shake of the head. "I invited him myself, under no orders from Chris. I was under the misimpression that he had talent for some reason."

I recall the research I did on my fellow HEARs. The pages of Google results attesting to Alex's abilities scroll through my mind . . .

They were all lies.

"Your friend created a false history for him," I say. "He planted stories for you to find so you'd invite him into the program."

When Figg rolls his eyes suggesting he can't believe it took me this long to figure that out, Mara takes my hand and squeezes it hard. *Cool it*, she tells me, sensing I might jump across the table to throttle him. *You want some ginger?*

No. But thank you.

Pankaj sits up, wincing in pain and clasping his open wound. "So if you had Alex so well trained, what happened?"

As Figg looks at us, he knows he must concede at least this one point. "It's the problem with psychopaths: they're unpredictable. That can cause *issues* from time to time."

"But you'd been watching him the whole summer, hadn't you?" Mara asks, hugging her knees to her chest.

"Of course," he replies. "You don't take your eye off someone like Alex, even when you're using him as an asset. *Especially* when you're using him as an asset."

"So he wasn't just being paranoid when he said someone was following him."

"No, he was not." Figg shakes his head. "And still he did what he did."

My head tilts in confusion. *Did what he did?* I'm fairly certain he's not referring to our recent hostage-taking situation. "What do you mean?"

"Pinberg," Pankaj mutters.

This is the first thing Pankaj has said to me directly since . . . the lab.

"You're wrong," I reply curtly, holding myself back from telling him *all* that he's wrong about. "Alex didn't kill Pinberg. He couldn't have. He didn't have the time to get to that mall."

"Alex was not responsible for Graham's death, no," Figg says. "But he *did* plant the bomb in the library that killed his ex-girlfriend and your friend, Dan."

That's what Alex was rambling about in the lab. He bombed that library because Erika broke his heart. I react to these words like a windshield struck by a baseball bat; I absorb the blow and shatter. Tears blur my vision, and I feel Mara grab my arm. When she takes Pankaj's on the other side, everything whites out.

That's when the three of us have a simultaneous vision of the past. We watch as Alex calmly walks into the library to plant the bomb. He sees Erika working behind the desk in the Special Collections Room, and he stares at her for a while as he keeps himself hidden from view. When she turns her back to look through a filing drawer, he darts toward the information desk and leaves a book bag full of explosives in front of it, less than ten feet from where she stands.

The Peabody Library bombing had nothing to do with the US Army Research Institute archive or Uncle Brian. Alex perpetrated the crime because he was angry at Erika for dumping him and he wanted revenge. Dan was simply collateral damage. Dan ran to the library either to stop Alex or to warn us, or both, and he paid for his empathy with his life.

"Brian will be the first to tell you," Figg says, "love can make you reckless, make you do crazy things."

Despite myself, I steal a glance at Pankaj.

I couldn't risk Alex hurting you, he tells me. *That's why I said those things in the lab.*

But I am so broken and exhausted I don't know what to think or how I feel about anything anymore. I don't respond.

You have to believe that that's not how I really feel. I am in love with you, Kass.

When our eyes connect, I feel the truth. I take a deep breath, and I'm finally able to breathe again.

"The good news," Figg continues, "is that we can all keep an eye on one another as we continue to work together."

The three of us let out a shocked roar of laughter.

"I'm quite serious," Figg says. "I've made arrangements so that you will all be able to attend Henley tuition-free next year."

"Not a chance in hell," I reply. "Why on earth would we stay here?"

"Because you have nowhere else to go, Kass," he says matter-of-factly. "None of you do."

"I'll go anywhere else. *Anywhere* is better than here." Mara shakes her head. "We're not safe here."

"You're not safe *anywhere*, my dear." Figg utters this as a promise. Then he extends his arms as if he's the ringleader of an exotic circus. "So what do you say?"

What do we say? Pankaj asks us silently.

I can tell he doesn't yet know the answer himself.

What can we say? We're trapped, Mara reasons.

But we're not powerless, I reply. *We have each other. We determine the future from here on out.*

EPILOGUE

When I jolt awake, my heart feels like it's trying to beat its way out of my chest. My eyes scan the room searching for what's on fire.

This has been happening a lot lately.

But the feeling I have this morning seems like more than just the PTSD I've been experiencing since the library bombing. The panic attacks escalated when I went home to pack my belongings for the new school year, and they've been even worse since I returned to Henley earlier this week. Though fall term doesn't start for a few more days, I was hoping if I came back to campus early, I could ease my way in. But this morning, the alarm is more acute than ever; it feels like something truly terrible hangs in the air.

When my phone vibrates moments later, I fumble to grab it, and when I hit the touchscreen, a male silhouette avatar with the word "Dad" beneath it lights up.

"Hi, Dad," I croak.

"Oh, Kass, I'm sorry. Did I wake you?"

"No. I was . . . Don't worry about it." I look at the alarm clock.

It's 7:30 A.M. On a Saturday. If he's trying to get back into my good graces, this is not the best tack. "What's wrong?"

"Nothing's—" He pauses. Obviously *something's* wrong. "Actually," he says, recalculating, "I think it's better if we discuss this in person."

"Fine. I'll be home for Thanksgiving. We can talk then."

"I'm here," he says.

"Here?" My eyes search the unfamiliar dorm room; I'm still close enough to sleep to feel discombobulated by his statement.

"I'm in town. I'm staying at the Beckwith Inn."

"Not with Uncle Brian?"

"No." He stops there, not choosing to give an explanation for the strange accommodations. "Why don't you meet me at the hotel for breakfast?"

Ugh. "Today?"

"Let's say eight thirty."

Ugggggghhhh. "I might be a little la—"

"Kassie."

Ugggghhhh! "Fine," I repeat, though this time my tone indicates it's anything but. "I'll see you at eight thirty, Dad." I put down the phone and crash back on the pillow, yanking the sheet over my head.

"Hey!" Pankaj mumbles, grabbing me by the waist and pulling me toward him. "And good morning." He kisses the back of my head.

"I doubt it."

Pankaj flips me over to face him and cracks open one eye. "That doesn't sound good." He gives me a sleepy grin. His hair is rumpled, and a dark shadow of stubble rings his face.

There's nothing I want to do more than spend the day in Pankaj's bed with his arms wrapped around me. "Promise me you'll stay here, just like this until I get back."

He looks at the clock and winces. "That will not be a problem."
I kiss him again then get out of bed.

IT'S RUMORED THAT GEORGE Washington slept at the Beckwith
Inn, and with its wooden ceiling beams, stacked stone panel walls,
and early American folk art decor, you can see why a founding
father would feel at home here. My own father, dressed in his
casual Brooks Brothers attire, looks fairly comfortable himself as
he sits in an oxblood-red leather wing chair near the large fireplace in the lobby. He glances up from the paper he's reading as
soon as I walk in the door and stands as I approach.

"Hi, Dad."

"Kass, you look . . ." He eyeballs me before saying anything
more. "Well."

"Thanks." I have no idea what he truly sees when he looks at
me anymore. Our relationship has gone from frosty to heated
in the last few weeks, neither of us pleased by recent revelations.

"Have a seat." He points to the other wing chair as he sits
down. "Do you want coffee?"

I shake my head. "I'm going to go back to bed when I leave." I
think about Pankaj waiting for me in his room, and I try to focus
on this happy thought. "So . . . what brings me to the Beckwith
Inn so early on a Saturday morning?"

A look of disappointment crosses Dad's face as he continues
to scrutinize me. He knows. "Kass, before you left home, we
came to an agreement," he says severely.

"No, Dad." I'm not going to allow it. I refuse to let him bully
me. "You came to an agreement. By yourself. However, since I
disagree with your thinking, I decided to ignore your advice."

"Kass, I wasn't giving you advice," he replies, carefully enun-
ciating every word. "Nor was I making a request. I told you very
specifically you were not to date that boy."

I stand, shaking my head at him. "Okay, bye, Dad. Tell Mom I say hello." I begin walking away, but my father catches me by the arm.

"Do you think I get some sort of a kick out of this, Kass? Do you think I told you not to date Pankaj because it's a power trip for me? I'm trying to protect you," he says in a stern whisper, close to my ear. "Who do you think killed Graham Pinberg?"

My eyes widen. Pankaj didn't kill Graham Pinberg. I am entirely certain of this. I know it. And yet my knees still buckle at the implication. My father's hand on my arm is the only thing that keeps me from crumpling.

"Sit down." He guides me back to the chair.

I should regain my composure before I say anything. "Are you suggesting Pankaj killed Graham Pinberg? Because that's—"

"No," Dad replies, shaking his head. "But I need you to listen to me very carefully, Kassandra. I had a vision when I was in China with your mother—it was hazy and only partially formed, so I didn't understand what it meant at first. That happens occasionally. It was only when you mentioned Pankaj that pieces started coming together. That's why I forbid you from seeing him."

"Well, that's stupid," I say resentfully. "He hasn't done anything wrong."

"I know that now." Dad pauses and looks out across the lobby before refocusing on me. "But the vision sharpened for me last night, and that's why I came here this morning: Pankaj hasn't done anything wrong yet, but he will. And intentionally or unintentionally, his actions will put you in grave danger."

"Why would you even say that?" I throw my hands up, exasperated in the way only a parent can make you. "He's done nothing but help me through this crap, and you just said yourself Pankaj had nothing to do with Pinberg's murder."

"No," my father says, "but his sister did. On Chris Figg's orders."

My mouth opens to respond, but I don't know what to say.

Dad seems satisfied by this; my nonresponse is exactly what he wanted. "You need to stay away from them, Kassie. Trust me when I tell you this is a dangerous family."

In my father's cold stare, I find the words to answer. "Do you mean their family or ours, Dad?"

AS I WALK BACK to Pankaj's room, I think about how to break the news. *How do you tell someone his sister's a killer?* Unfortunately, despite everything else, I don't doubt that my father is right about Nisha. I'm still not sure what to say when I reach Pankaj's dorm room, so I just take a deep breath before knocking on his door.

"It's open," Pankaj calls out.

Though the world was already sent spinning for me this morning, it's *still* early on a Saturday morning, and as promised, Pankaj is still exactly where I left him an hour ago. He holds the sheet out, beckoning me to join him underneath. I slip off my shoes and climb into bed.

"How'd it go with your dad?" he asks, spooning me.

"And here I thought having Mara return to campus today as my roommate was going to be the worst part of my day."

"*That* good, huh?" he says with a smile.

I can't tell him. I can't tell him yet.

"The past few days have been really nice," I say instead.

"Yeah, they have." Pankaj puts his arms around me and kisses me. The sheet tangles between us as we clutch at one another until suddenly he stops. Like an animal who's picked up a scent, Pankaj bolts upright. His head turns to the side, and his nose lifts to search the air.

There's a knock at the door a moment later. His eyes widen as the doorknob twists and the still-unlocked door swings open.

Though I've never before seen the girl who barges into the room, I instantly recognize her. She cocks one of her dark, full eyebrows and lets her giant duffle bag drop to the ground. Then she flicks her head, tossing her long black hair behind her, and the smell of her pomegranate shampoo fills the small room. "Oh brother!" she says with a throaty laugh. "What have we here?"

"Nisha." Pankaj scrambles out of bed.

"You must be Kass!" She maneuvers around Pankaj and extends her arms to me as if she expects an embrace. "I've heard so much about you."

"Yeah," I reply, uneasily, "likewise."

Nisha slowly spins, taking in the room. "Wow, I still can't believe I'm here—I'm so lucky." She smiles. "And we are all going to have such fun together!"

"What?" Pankaj and I say simultaneously.

"You mean you guys don't know? Why, I could just kill that Mr. Figg! I guess I'll just have to do the honors myself." She shakes her head, and there's a sparkle in her obsidian eyes. "Since your friend Alex got busted for all those *terrible* crimes, he's obviously out of the program for a while. So Figgy asked me to come. I'm taking Alex's spot and joining you as the newest HEAR."

"No," Pankaj replies, taking my hand and moving me away from his sister.

"Oh yes, Brother," Nisha says with a familiar smile. "And I don't know about you, but I can hardly wait to see what happens next!"